T0070047

The Radiant Dawn

J. Eifie Nichols

authorHOUSE®

AuthorHouse™
1663 Liberty Drive
Bloomington, IN 47403
www.authorhouse.com
Phone: 1 (800) 839-8640

© 2016 J. Eifie Nichols. All rights reserved.

No part of this book may be reproduced, stored in a retrieval system, or transmitted by any means without the written permission of the author.

Published by AuthorHouse 02/22/2016

ISBN: 978-1-5049-8083-8 (sc)
ISBN: 978-1-5049-8084-5 (e)

Print information available on the last page.

Any people depicted in stock imagery provided by Thinkstock are models, and such images are being used for illustrative purposes only. Certain stock imagery © Thinkstock.

This book is printed on acid-free paper.

Because of the dynamic nature of the Internet, any web addresses or links contained in this book may have changed since publication and may no longer be valid. The views expressed in this work are solely those of the author and do not necessarily reflect the views of the publisher, and the publisher hereby disclaims any responsibility for them.

Prologue

The Ancient Rites

Inca burial ground, Peru
2024
11:56 PM

A couple stood at the ancient temple to a god whose last worshiper died many years ago. The temple, with a nearby burial ground, was built to honor Supay, the Inca god of death. When Pizarro came to Peru under the Spanish flag, he and his men smashed the stone altar and sacked the temple, condemning it as idolatry. The temple sat idle ever since, with one obvious exception. It was now occupied by an altar made of human flesh, inscribed with the sign of the demon lord Tyadrig – three claw marks overlaid with an empty ring.

Nearby was a moldy tome. It lay open to a page that could be read.

And on this day, the Thirty-First of May, in the year 1994, we, the War Council of the Unholy Trinity, placed the Sacred Altar of Tyadrig on the site of Supay's temple. Built from the flesh of the worshipers of Jehovah, it will prove to our Lord that we are true. For it is here, in the land of the ancient dead, where Tyadrig will rise and claim this world. Our Lord favors his agents, sparing us the suffering He will bring upon the rest of the world. We will summon Him forth from this very spot, and from here, He will slay mankind and drag his souls to the Abyss, where He will torment them for all eternity. But we, the agents of His arrival, will be spared death. He will make us immortal, and grant us the honor of helping Him torture the souls of man.

But we will not stop here. From Earth we will move outward and onward, using the reach of our Lord. Alien worshipers will aid us in our quest to conquer and torture the universe. They will summon the other Brothers to their worlds, creating the Trinity once more. Once, Tyadrig the Empty, Krovon the Fiery, and Aarix the Toxic were gods, worshiped by many. But Jehovah ended this through the words of his three prophets, Moses, Jesus, and Mohammed.

The spread of the Religions of the Book extinguished the worshipers of the Brothers, but we have returned with a vengeance. We will slay the followers of the Prophets with the power of our Lord. We will force Jehovah to the defense of his followers, and when he comes, we will defeat him and subdue him for the Brothers to torture for all eternity. Jehovah will finally pay for his crimes.

Now, thirty years later, Aaron and Stacie stood ready to accomplish what the worshipers had planned. The original worshipers had gathered in great numbers at this site to witness the ritual. That had been their downfall, drawing riot police to counter them. Tonight, Aaron and Stacie Murphy sneaked up here alone for the ritual, eluding the notice of any authorities.

Aaron wore black metal armor adorned with skulls. His blonde hair was cropped close, his striking blue eyes glistening in the moonlight. He carried a blade adorned with a skull on the hilt, made of the same black metal as his armor and bearing an edge sharp enough to slice through iron. His six foot four, broad-chested frame was impressive and gave this death knight a fearsome appearance.

Stacie's black spellcaster's robe was adorned with runes of death. Although shorter than her husband, she was exceptionally fit and appeared rather formidable. On her back she wore a staff with a shrunken skull headpiece. Her eyes, so dark brown they appeared black, showed no glow or reflection from the bright moonlight. Her irises and pupils simply appeared as dark voids against the white. A leather pouch hung at her side, branded with a symbol of an eye with swords crossed behind it.

"Stacie! What are we waiting for?" Aaron impatiently asked.

"We have to wait until midnight, or the ritual won't work. Be patient, Aaron. It's almost time."

The couple paced back and forth, constantly checking their watches and the moon. Aaron drew his blade and swiped a few times at the air, occasionally pointing his blade at the throat of an imaginary foe. He glanced at his wife, then returned to his fictitious enemy, viciously picking him up by the collar and slamming him into the ground.

"It's time," Stacie said as the clock struck midnight.

She lit a single white candle and walked to the east of the altar. "Air, may your swiftness bless our strikes and spells, such that they may land with renewed fury! Howl as the moon shines, to deny our foes sleep! Slow down their march, so we may overtake them!" After her prayer, Stacie placed the candle on the palm of a bony hand protruding from the ground at that spot, and the hand began to glow a deathly purple-black.

Walking to the west of the altar, Stacie lit a red candle. "Fire, blaze forth from our weapons and our hands! Ignite the flesh of our foes! Destroy anything that resists us or stands in our way! Carry our fury with you!" She then placed the candle on the palm of another eerie hand and it too began to glow ominously.

A blue candle was placed at the South corner where another bony hand protruded. "Water, grant us the clarity to win the strategic battle, and muddy our enemies' vision. Let us pour over them like an unstoppable tide, wearing away at everything they hold dear! Chill our enemies as they try to rest, and freeze them to their cores!"

She lit a fourth candle, this one green, and carried it to the altar's north. "Earth, imbue us with your resilience and strength, and parch our enemies! Crumble beneath their feet whilst you hold ours firm! Your strength will be ours in battle, ours and not theirs!" As it received the green candle, the fourth hand, like the others, began to glow.

At the center of the elemental circle, Stacie placed a candle as black as pitch. The flame leapt as she called upon the darkest element. "Death, come to us! We are your harbingers, the extension of your will! Grant us the power to bring those in your realm back into ours, and we will repay you a thousand fold! With the force you lend us, this entire world will belong to you!"

"Power of the Great Dark Beyond!" Aaron roared. "Let us become the royalty of Death, so we may spread chaos and destruction across the land! Let us reap horror and darkness, and bring to an end the greatness of man! Let us usher in a new age of suffering!"

Aaron planted the blade of his sword into the fleshy altar, to the left of the candle. Stacie drove the base of her staff to the candle's right. Dark power began to flow through the altar, quickly enveloping the weapons and then Aaron and Stacie. The power snuffed out their life, replacing it with death's animation. It removed any trace of a soul either one had, replacing it with a void. They were bound together in spirit closer than they had ever been before.

"And now, let us consume the altar in the process, hereby sealing us and us alone as the harbingers of death!" Stacie called out, raising her hands and calling on dark fire. The fire leapt to life, rapidly burning away the flesh of the altar. Dark energy swirled around them as the altar burned, releasing all of its power. Aaron and Stacie reached out, absorbing it as it escaped from the burning altar. The altar would never be used by another, for its power now fully belonged to them.

A warped demonic face, surrounded in purple-black glow like that of the hands, appeared on the back wall.

"My warrior, you will be the instrument of death here. Lead your army against the pathetic mortals, wipe them clean from this earth, so that I may have a suitable world to come to. Blight the land and destroy the life here, so that I may have a suitable world from which to rule!"

"And my warlock, raise the dead that he creates in my image. Snuff their souls out and replace them with my power. Build for me a mighty army, an army of the dead powerful enough to bring Jehovah's gates tumbling down around him!"

"Yes, master! The Blade of Death is yours to command!" Aaron cried out. "Yes, master! The Spire of Suffering is yours to command!" Stacie called out after.

"Do not fail me!" the demonic face shouted as it faded back into nothingness.

Husband and wife walked out of the stone ritual chamber to the vast Inca burial ground nearby. Stacie raised her staff and spoke to the earth.

"Rise, ancient bones of the Incas! You will be my first of many! Rise, and serve the royal family of death!"

In all corners of the ancient burial ground, bony hands began to protrude from the earth, followed by the arms and eventually skulls, torsos, legs and feet. Stacie kept her staff raised high as the skeletons rose from the ground and turned to face her.

"This is only the beginning," Stacie said to Aaron as the field of undead continued to grow.

"The bones remaining here are few, and won't be enough to conquer the world." Aaron replied. "But there are cemeteries all over the world, full of dead for us to raise. It will be with those bones that we take the world by force."

"Here's our plan." Stacie stated. "We will travel the world finding those who want to watch the world burn, those who call for power to overthrow their oppressors, and those who call for power to rule as tyrants. We will show them our power. They will join us, and through them we will raise the dead from cemeteries everywhere. Once the world is in crisis, fighting our undead, we will poison water supplies to destroy their ability to fight back. The mighty militaries of the world won't stand a chance when their personnel can't reach the bases."

"I like it," he replied.

Chapter 1

The Mountain Retreat

Light's Bulwark Fortress, West Virginia
One year later

Several groups of refugees had gathered in a forested area north of US Route 60 in Kanawha County. These groups had assembled by chance over the past couple of days, using the time to exchange intelligence about the undead. They talked about numbers of undead, the strange zombies mounted on undead bears, and a monstrous creature of unknown creation. Just then a scout came back into camp.

"There's some huge fortress south of here!" the scout shouted as he ran into the campsite. "What ya thinkin'?" one of the refugees asked. "Should we try to get in?"

"Might as well." one from another group said. "Let's go."

The crowd of survivors struggled up the dirt road that led from the base of the mountain to the fortress and were stopped by a large moat. A bridge was drawn up on the other side in front of a massive set of gates. The gates were shut, but a bell was hung on a post on their side of the moat. One refugee started ringing it to draw the attention of anyone inside. Others picked up rocks and dirt clods and flung them at and over the high walls, hoping to alert any occupants that they were there.

They watched anxiously as the drawbridge lowered and the gates were opened. The survivors raced in across the drawbridge, some with pointed weapons, branches or hunting knives at the ready, many looking back to watch for undead. Others surged forward haphazardly, fighting

1

to get into the courtyard and behind the protective walls of the fortress. Once inside, they looked up to see a man on a balcony controlling a large lever that closed the gates and lifted the drawbridge back up. Next to him stood a girl. Looking down they watched the refugees entering the compound. Though a pair of automatic rifles lay propped against the wall, neither held a weapon.

The girl seemed unassuming, about five foot five, stocky build, with blonde hair left loose to curl about the collar of her green jacket. Over her jeans, the green of her jacket intensified the green of her eyes that, even at that distance, seemed to reflect the bright sunlight.

The male was nearly six feet tall, lean and muscled. Draped in a long navy overcoat, he looked like a formidable fighter. His eyes were also green but colder than his partner's – jaded and dark, the eyes of a warrior, constantly watching his enemy. His hair, nearly as long as hers, was light brown in color. His strength and speed were apparent and though he looked like a leader, it was the girl who addressed the crowd.

"Attention, refugees. I am Dawn Cahill, and this is my apocalypse fortress." Gesturing to the man at her side she introduced him as Julius Adams.

"In one short year, the warlocks and their undead army took this world. The world's people numbered seven billion before the war. Now, the enemy numbers seven billion, and our numbers dwindle every day. But NEVER will the undead army penetrate our walls."

The refugees below looked anxiously around the compound. Almost everyone in the crowd, save for a few, seemed panic stricken. One of those who wasn't was a man in Army camo, with graying hair and a beard. Another was a short, thin man wearing wire-frame glasses, who quickly looked over the fortress and determined it was safe. Dawn paused and looked at Julius. He nodded to her, and she continued.

"This place can protect us and supply us for a hundred years. Look to our towers! The barrels of our heavy weapons shine in the midday sun! Look to our walls! They stand, six feet thick, seventy feet high, and constructed of solid brick! Look to our moat! Thirty feet deep, lined with blades at the bottom to shred their remains beyond repair!"

By this point, Dawn was getting caught up in the energy of her own speech. Every word she spoke incresed in volume and enthusiasm.

"Tunnels deep beneath the earth carry enough supplies to last our natural lifetimes! This place is built from hope and forged in spirit!

We can stand and we can fight! Humanity will not end with us! We will build upon the world's ashes, reforging civilization in the wake of Aaron's destruction!"

The ragged crowd was moved by her words. "Maybe we can win," one said to another. "Look at this place, it's got to be the greatest fortress ever built!" another said.

"There's no way the undead will get in here!" a third replied.

"It's working." Dawn whispered to Julius. "They actually believe it. They actually think we can win."

"We can win," he replied. "They can't penetrate our walls."

Dawn then directed Julius to oversee the opening of the supplies and ready them for the forklifts. Thousands of skids full of bullets, bombs, and every supply imaginable were stored in the tunnels underneath Light's Bulwark Fortress. As Julius left her side, Dawn turned to the job of organizing the newcomers.

With the people gathered around her, Dawn began to ask if any of them had special skills. They needed pilots. The helicopter parked on the landing pad would be capable of venturing out into undead-held lands to retrieve any supplies she could salvage, and could even be used to drop explosives and burning fuel onto undead forces. Sadly for the defenders, there were no trained pilots among their ranks. The closest was a dark-haired girl with multiple tattoos on her arms, who identified herself as Nadia Dragovich. She was a mechanic for the LifeFlight helicopters, and had practiced using the flight simulators when no pilots were using them.

"Can I ask why it matters that I know about helicopters?" Nadia asked.

"Look over there." Dawn pointed towards the Soviet helicopter sitting on the pad. "Wow, that's a military grade helicopter. How did you even get that?"

"Um... the internet?"

"Oh..." Nadia replied, still in slight disbelief.

Next, Dawn asked for forklift operators. The fortress had forklifts for moving the skids of supplies. Julius knew how to operate a forklift, but additional operators were needed. Two of the survivors knew how to operate a forklift, one from a steel mill and another from a chemical plant.

Then she called for veterans. Military veterans would already know how to properly care for the weapons and explosives, and would be able to train others to do the same. Ten of the survivors were ex-military, and eight of them had served in Afghanistan or Iraq. One, named Jim, had been an Army Master Sergeant, and served in operations Desert Storm, Desert Fox, Enduring Freedom, Iraqi Freedom, and Kurdish Shield.

Most of the survivors were miners, mill workers, or students from the nearby engineering university. Many knew how to handle a firearm, as most people in West Virginia do. Many were also physically strong, capable of lifting heavy loads, running faster and farther than the norm, or staying on their feet longer. It seemed fortunate to have so many physically capable people in their midst, but these were truly survivors. There were no infants or children, no elderly, no disabled among them. All of those weaker members of society had already been killed by the advancing tide of undead. Only the fittest had escaped.

Dawn tasked the veterans with training people on the various defensive weapons in Light's Bulwark's arsenal and sent the forklift drivers down to Julius in the tunnels so he could get skids moving. Others she put to work unloading skids of ammo and cooking food. Though the stockpiled food at Light's Bulwark would sustain the defenders, it was all preserved rather than fresh. Canned vegetables and fruits, salted and cured meats, and dry milk, along with thousands and thousands of stockpiled MREs, made up the reserves of Light's Bulwark. Some of it might initially be unsavory to the defenders, though quickly they would grow used to it. It could provide sustenance, which has always been the most important factor in a war.

The glasses-wearing man in the crowd approached Dawn as the survivors filed into the building.

"How did this place even get here?" he asked.

"I inherited it from my dad. Roger Cahill, from Cahill Energy."

"Isn't he the one who was always on the news for being obsessed with the apocalypse?"

"Yeah, that's probably why he had this place built."

"They called him crazy on the news. Turns out he was crazy like a fox."

"Agreed. Oh, I noticed, you seemed to figure this place out immediately. How?"

"I'm an engineering student from the university. And we can't be the last humans still alive. I'm sure there's holdouts elsewhere, and there's probably ships at sea too. You wouldn't happen to have broadcasting equipment, would you?"

"Yeah, we've got broadcast equipment... what are you planning?"

"I'm gonna start broadcasting. It might tell the undead where we're at, but if there's American sailors still alive, they have to know we're here. The highway's plenty straight to land a fighter jet on ever since the rebuild. Is there any way up here from there?"

"Yeah. We've got a lift that goes there, the food storages, and the water plant. There's other stuff down there too, like the gas harvesting machines and the forge."

"The Navy can land aircraft on this highway. We'll be able to get reinforcements in. The undead won't secure the lower level since they can't get in that way."

"Get on that broadcast equipment then. It's on the roof of the main keep, under the ledge off the anti-air tower. And call me Dawn."

"Rick. Rick Sylvan."

Chapter 2

Preparing for Battle

Light's Bulwark Fortress, West Virginia
10 AM, a few days after

Dawn awoke to find many of the others already at work and Rick fiddling with the broadcasting equipment.

"Status report." Dawn called out to her various leaders.

Jim, one of the ex-Army survivors, reported in. "Training is going as planned. I don't want to waste much ammo in training, but everyone we've trained seems able to fire their assigned weapons. I'm assigning guard posts and shifts, and putting at least two veterans on each shift."

Dave, an engineering student, reported in. "I've been going over the engineering of this fortress and found something really odd. That statue you have in the courtyard? It's giving off power somehow. I'm still working on how to harness it. I've never seen anything like it. I'm gonna get some other engineers to look at it."

Julius answered as well. "My forklift crews are moving supplies from the back of the storerooms up front so we can use them. All waste metal is getting stored near the forge so we can flush the moat at a moment's notice."

Rick reported in his status. "I've almost got this equipment configured. It should be up in about another hour, and then I'll be able to find out who's still out there and if the American subs have launched their nukes. Intel is vital here. I'm gonna see if I can use the equipment to get an up-link to the American intelligence satellites, that way we know what we're actually up against."

"Excellent job guys." Dawn replied. "I'm gonna check out that statue as well. The Vanderbilt I bought it from said it was an ancient Greek artifact. I don't normally believe in magic, but if it's emitting power there's got to be something up with it. Dave, trace the wires of this place and make sure we aren't powering it or magnetizing it somehow."

"Consider it done."

Dawn went down into the courtyard and started examining the statue. It was a statue of a female warrior, depicted wearing sturdy metal plates over much of her body and carrying a hoplon, the iconic shield of Spartan warriors. On the shield there was an inscription in Greek. When she bought the statue, she thought it beautiful, but never could read the inscription on the shield.

Μέσα μου ο ζουν σε

Dawn stared at it for some time. She converted the letters of the Greek alphabet to the English one, but still the words seemed to be gibberish. Eventually she just copied down the inscription and climbed up to the roof where Rick was working on the communications equipment.

"Rick, how's the up link going?"

"I'm patched in to radio already. Any survivors within a fifty mile radius with a radio on know where we're at. As long as we've got guards on shift we'll be able to let any of the holdouts into the fortress. Just make sure the guards can open the gates."

"And the Navy?"

"Still haven't managed to get a satellite up-link yet. So I can't reach them."

"Hey, you're smart. Can you read Greek by any chance?"

"I can," a female voice said from inside a large crate that was tipped on its side.

A tall, strong woman with brown hair emerged from the crate, carrying a length of cable and an antenna. "Laina. Laina Rémy. And you're Dawn?"

"Yeah. And you are...?"

"Rick's girlfriend. I'm helping him fix the comms equipment. I don't know much about electrical but I do speak Greek. I'm a history major, specifically studying ancient Greece."

"Can you translate this? I copied it off the statue in the courtyard. It's emitting some kind of power but the engineers can't figure out how or why."

"Let's see now... it's some sort of motto or creed. 'Through me the Solari live on'."

"What's that mean? What's a Solari?"

"I remember something about that from my Ancient Greece class. The Solari were Athenian female warriors who worshiped Apollo, the god of the sun. The Roman general Sulla and his men killed the last high priestess and stole a statue of a Solari warrior when he sacked Athens. There was a poem about that statue. Apparently it was a holy artifact to the Solari. I know this, I had to memorize it for my nineteenth century American history class."

"At the world's darkest hour
When the dead walk the land
The Icy Queen and Shadowed King
Will threaten every hand
Redemption comes only from one
When the sun is shining bright
Her light will guide us forward
Into the deep dark night
The rays of the sun will fly from her hands
Her touch will heal the weak
From her castle, she will guide
The strong, the skilled, the meek
Her blade will seek the Shadowed King
Her mate will slay the Queen
Until the dead will rise again
There the Dawn will be"

"I have engineers taking a look at it now. They're trying to trace the power and everything in the fortress. Maybe they need to know what you know. Come with me."

Dawn and Laina left the rooftop and made their way down to the courtyard, where the engineers were still examining the statue. A male and a female engineer came up from the freight elevator to the basement. They shouted at Dave, who was still standing near the statue with Laina.

"Dave!" the male yelled to get his attention.

"We haven't found anything downstairs," the female engineer reported. "No wires feed into it, and the strongest power readings aren't down there either. The readings we got from the shield are still higher."

"The shield!" Nadia called out. "Can we take that shield off? The Solari used these shields because they reflect sunlight. If we take the shield off and give it to Dawn, it would satisfy the prophecy too."

"Prophecy?" one of the engineers asked.

Laina read the poem again to the engineers.

"And here the dawn will be?" Do you remember, that poem. When it was written, did Dawn have a capital letter?"

"Yeah, the Greek word in the original was 'Avgí', with a capital alpha. I always wondered why it had a capital alpha."

"Because it's not the sunrise. It's our host."

"You don't seriously believe this, do you?"

"Well, if we're wrong, we haven't lost anything." Laina chimed in. "And you realize the odds against us, right? Scattered across the world there are nearly seven billion undead. We have three hundred defenders. Once Aaron and Stacie know we're here, they'll throw everything at us. They have very powerful magic, we've seen it. They've raised undead. Anything is possible."

"Maybe. Let's get a cutting torch and take that shield off the warrior's arm. We can fasten an arm strap and a handle back on it so Dawn can use it. Problem is, we still don't know how to activate it."

"You said it was a shield of Apollo, yes?" Dave asked.

"Yeah, everything Solari's based on Apollo."

"So I'm thinking there's a specific prayer somewhere to activate it."

Nadia chimed in immediately. "Laina, that's your department, isn't it? There's a library in the compound. Go see if there's anything on it."

Chapter 3

First Contact

Light's Bulwark Fortress, West Virginia
Midday, the next day

An excited call came out over the intercom. "Patched in! Satellite up-link active!"

Rick finally had the communications equipment patched into a satellite up-link. Now, his voice could reach anywhere in the world – including the various floating fortresses on the open ocean, where zombies could not reach.

"We did it. We can reach out to the world's navies. Not just the Americans either, the British, Russians, and Chinese all have ships at sea. We don't know how long they can stay at sea though. Those sailors need food eventually. And I can't speak Russian or Chinese. See if anyone here can. The university has international students, and international students often speak several languages, not just two. I'll call out to the Americans and British and see if I can get anything."

"I'll use the intercom, if we have any, they'll come up here."

Dawn called out over the intercom immediately. "Any survivors who can speak Chinese or Russian, please report to the rooftop. Anyone who can speak Chinese or Russian, please report to the rooftop."

"This is Light's Bulwark Fortress broadcasting." Rick called out over the radio. "Any survivors who can hear this message, we have a human-controlled land base still operational. Repeat, we have an operational human-controlled land base."

There was no answer. Rick sent his broadcast again, and still he heard static in return. He sat at the communications panel for several minutes, hearing nothing but white noise over the satellite link. He only started getting a response when he stood to go to the bathroom.

"This is the USS Abraham Lincoln. We received your broadcast, Light's Bulwark. Convert to secure up-link code US-44-AHA."

Rick ran back to the comms array, just in time to receive two more messages.

"This is the USS Theodore Roosevelt. We received your broadcast, Light's Bulwark. What's going on out there?"

"This is the HMS Queen Elizabeth. We can read you loud and clear, Light's Bulwark. Stand by."

"Someone did receive our message, but they want us to convert to a secure up-link that we don't know how to do. What should I do?" Rick asked Dawn.

"Broadcast back to them on whichever frequency they picked us up on that we're civilians and don't know what that means," she replied.

"USS Abraham Lincoln, this is Light's Bulwark Fortress. We are a civilian-owned position and do not know American secure up-link codes."

"Light's Bulwark, this is USS Abraham Lincoln, stand by for instructions."

"USS Theodore Roosevelt, this is Light's Bulwark Fortress. USS Abraham Lincoln is requesting to convert to US-44-AHA secure broadcasting. Stand by to receive us."

"HMS Queen Elizabeth, this is Light's Bulwark Fortress. Radio USS Abraham Lincoln to receive instructions on US-44-AHA secure broadcasting."

"Light's Bulwark, this is USS Abraham Lincoln. Broadcast your location on US-AHA channel 44. Your equipment cannot decrypt signals on that channel without us dropping in a communications technician."

Rick switched the broadcast unit to broadcast over US-44-AHA only.

"USS Abraham Lincoln, this is Light's Bulwark Fortress. Our location is at 38° 12'56" N 81°23'28" W. It's a giant brick fortress, your pilots should be able to see it from the air at altitude. We have a helipad to land helicopters on inside the walls, and there's a highway that can be used to land fixed-wing aircraft."

A broadcast came across on an unsecured frequency.

"Light's Bulwark Fortress, this is USS Abraham Lincoln. USS Dwight D. Eisenhower is offshore outside of its home port. They have been contacted to approve you for US-44-AHA secure broadcasting. Stand by."

"Light's Bulwark Fortress, this is USS Dwight D. Eisenhower. We are preparing a communications technician for delivery by CH-47F Chinook. ETA 140 minutes."

"Naval Chinook inbound, ETA 140 minutes. Naval Chinook inbound, ETA 140 minutes." Rick announced over the intercom, and then looked over at Dawn. "Let's hope the enemy didn't pick up our location we sent out over the secure frequency."

"Now, let's get the base ready to receive the naval personnel."

Dawn took the intercom mic and broadcast to the fortress. "Engineering, make sure the road level doors are operational and that the lights are bright enough to direct helicopters."

Engineering personnel, scattered throughout the castle, all reported to the 1F lift gates. Rick, the de-facto leader simply based on his constant contact with Dawn, called his engineers into the lift. The lift was the size of a full scale living room. The sixteen exposed cables were each a thickness comparable to a baseball. The inspection certificate taped to the side of the control panel claimed the elevator was rated to carry twenty tons. Its steel floor was clearly not designed for comfort or elegance, but purely for moving large amounts of material or entire platoons of soldiers at once. With just Rick and four others on board, the room-sized elevator was incredibly open and vacant. Rick set the lift in motion to B3F, and it started with a sharp jerk. The elevator was jumpy, more like the high capacity freight elevator it was than common office elevators.

The third basement level was little more than an entry level from the road. Electric lights powered by the generator on the fourth basement floor lit a hallway from the lift to the immense vault doors. On the inside, a lever operated the doors and their locking mechanism. Rick pulled the lever to its open position, and the doors slowly separated as their hydraulic motors strained against their great weight. On the right side door, metal bars a foot in diameter could be seen protruding. On the left side, holes perfectly dimensioned for the metal bars opened up. Each door was sixteen inches thick of titanium alloy steel, completely impervious to all damage save for a direct hit by a nuclear warhead.

The engineers worked quickly, watched over by gunners on the rear ramparts. They were in the middle of the Route 60 corridor, only approachable on their flanks. As they worked on the lights near the entrance there, they had a sheer drop-off to their backs and the fortress to their faces, leaving them only vulnerable on the left and right sides. The two-lane highway occupied the entire width of the ledge the engineers worked from, allowing a limited fighting front. The heavy GAU-9 Gatling guns mounted on the rear ramparts were now facing down, one to a side, covering the engineers on the flanks. These weapons were capable of laying down five thousand rounds a minute, able to shred any attack force that moved down the open highway easily.

The engineers powered on a string of red lights along the stretch of highway. Clearly intended to mark for aircraft, these lights were bright, but they were colored red as to not strip the pilots of their night vision. All lights went up except for one. The repair on that light took mere minutes, simply re-insulating a section of wire that was bare and short-circuiting against another. The engineers quickly retreated back inside the fortress, sealing the door behind them and taking the vastly powerful lift back upstairs to the above ground level.

"Lights are up, Dawn. The choppers and planes will be able to land there now. Those red lights will be bright enough to see from a ways out. Problem is, they're a beacon to the cavaliers too. Dave's gonna shut them off as to not attract hostiles. We'll only bring them up when there's incoming air traffic."

"Excellent."

"Chinook Alpha-Echo-One to Light's Bulwark Fortress. ETA two minutes. Repeat, ETA two minutes. Over."

"All hands be ready! Get those lights on! Stand by to open the lower doors! Man the Gatling!" Dawn announced over the fortress's intercom.

The red lights, which had just been turned off, came right back on. A survivor stood near the control panel for the heavy vault door on the lower level. Gunners returned to their seats at the Gatling emplacements.

"Chinook Alpha-Echo-One to Light's Bulwark Fortress. ETA one minute. Where ya want us to land? Over."

"Chinook Alpha-Echo-One, this is Light's Bulwark Fortress. Set down on the lighted highway. Over."

The gray Navy helicopter came in over the highway and hovered with its nose facing the fortress. It slowly reduced power, causing the helicopter to descend and touch its stabilizers to the black top. The engine took a minute or so to power completely down and stop spinning the rotor blades. Four Navy personnel emerged, two soldiers in battle dress wielding assault rifles and two engineers, each carrying tools and equipment as well as an automatic pistol. They were followed by a Navy officer in dress blues, with the name "C. White" on her name plate and captain's bars on her shoulders.

The gate operator opened the vault door for the Navy staff, and a lift operator rode up with them. The two operators escorted the Navy personnel all the way to the main rooftop where Dawn awaited. Dawn saluted them as they came up the steps, and they saluted in turn.

"Captain, this is our commander," one of the Light's Bulwark staff said as he motioned towards Dawn.

"Dawn Cahill, commander of Light's Bulwark Fortress. And you?"

"Captain Carrie White, US Navy. I will be your liaison. You will retain command of this fortress, I will simply operate the secure frequency equipment. These are Sergeants Brady, Fabian, Heinermann, and Windsor. Commander, where is the broadcast equipment?"

"Over here. This is Rick Sylvan, my chief engineer. He will work with your engineers to get it patched in at the secure frequency."

While Sergeants Brady and Heinermann went off with Jim to look at the heavy weapon emplacements, Sergeants Fabian and Windsor walked over to Rick and placed their toolboxes down. They immediately got to work. As Rick showed on the schematics where things were, Fabian and Windsor attached other components into various points on the communications rig. The job took about an hour and required a few components to be rewired, but they were able to bring the Light's Bulwark rig up to spec for the secure frequency being used by the US ships. Captain Carrie White sent a test message over the secure frequency.

"USS Abraham Lincoln, this is Captain White, broadcasting from Light's Bulwark Fortress. We believe we are patched in to the secure frequency as per US-44-Alpha-Hotel-Alpha. Respond on this frequency to confirm."

"Light's Bulwark Fortress, this is USS Abraham Lincoln. You are broadcasting on US-44-AHA. If you received this message, you are properly patched in."

"Mission accomplished. We're oscar-mike," Captain White replied. "Commander, get my weapons men back up here. We're moving out."

"On it," Dawn answered. She then broadcast over the fortress's intercom system. "All Naval personnel, report to the communications mainframe. All Naval personnel, report to the communications mainframe."

After a few minutes, Sergeants Brady and Heinermann came up the steps onto the roof of the fortress.

"Commander... this fortress is amazing!" Sgt. Brady said. "How did this place even get here?"

"I don't know exactly. I inherited it. No idea what my bio dad was doing when he built the place. I only found out he was my dad shortly before he died."

"We're trying to track the living, but we don't have the instruments to do it. Only other living we know of besides us and now you guys is the Swiss. Somehow the dead didn't get out of the ground there."

"Nice to know we're not alone." Dawn replied. "So it's us, you, and the Swiss against the world. Better odds than I thought."

"After this long, we didn't think anyone was still out there. We only heard contact from the Swiss a few days ago. We needed a resupply, bad. Good thing they're still alive."

"Brady, we have to move!" Captain White called at her sergeant.

"On my way, Captain."

The five Naval personnel left down the stairs of the main keep and were escorted to the lift by a pair of survivors. The Navy helicopter still sat on the highway where it was parked. All entered the helicopter, the survivors locked the heavy doors behind the Navy, and the bird took to the skies, back to the USS Abraham Lincoln.

Chapter 4

First Battle of Light's Bulwark

Light's Bulwark Fortress, West Virginia
A couple days later

Jim and Dawn stood on the rooftop with Rick, who was still fiddling with the communications equipment. Jim was asking Rick about all sorts of things, technical details of the computers and comms array. Though Rick answered in full detail, Jim didn't fully understand. Dawn understood slightly more, but not the full extent of Rick's knowledge. Suddenly, sirens started to blare from the array. Rick, who had crawled under the array to change a wiring configuration, quickly got back up and away from one of the sirens. He grabbed the microphone and broadcast over the intercom.

"Alert! Alert! Enemy scouts detected, one thousand yards out. Repeat, enemy scouts detected, one thousand yards."

"I got him." Jim announced as he lifted a rifle. Through the scope of his rifle, he could see two wandering zombies, seemingly used as scouts. He aimed through his scope, focusing the scout's head, and fired one shot. Then he aimed at the other scout and fired a second shot. The ex-Marine sniper's shots found their marks, easily felling the creatures.

"Two zeds down."

"Hopefully the scouts didn't detect anything before they went down. Out here, they probably won't expect a major base. It's the middle of West Virginia, they'll think some hick with a rifle shot a couple scouts."

"Some hick with a rifle DID shoot a couple scouts." Dawn immediately replied.

"Hey now. Just cause I'm from West Virginia don't mean I'm a hick," Jim replied with a clear Southern accent.

"Alert! Alert! More hostiles inbound, one thousand yards! They're coming from the forest!" Rick called out.

Dawn hit the intercom and immediately broadcast to all the survivors. "All hands to battle stations! All hands to battle stations! Blast those hostiles!"

From their perch on the main keep's rooftop, Dawn and Jim could see the entire battlefield. The walls crawled with gunners and supports as the gunners unloaded into the swarms of zombies now emerging from the trees. Light's Bulwark had been detected, and now everyone knew it. Undead of all levels of decomposition started to emerge from the woods surrounding the fortress. The mindless ranged from slightly decomposing, recently-dead bodies to grotesque monstrosities of flesh and bone, all the way to fully clean skeletons. Some very recently dead human warriors even rode on undead beasts. Wolves, bears, goats and horses, all undead, were scattered through the ranks of the enemy, and these undead cavaliers seemed to steer the ghouls and skeletons towards the walls. Many of the cavaliers carried lances that seemed to glow deathly purple. As the cavaliers pointed the lances, the mindless moved in an organized formation toward the fortress.

On the left flank, a girl swiveled a railgun on a pivot point as a bulky man loaded a steel shell the size of a football into its breech. "Fire!" she shouted as she pulled the trigger. Her shell slammed into an undead cavalier mounted on a zombified black bear with enough force to blow it apart. Bone shards at high speed struck nearby infantry, taking out additional enemies. A couple of riflemen leveled their rifles at other cavaliers and opened fire. The next gun emplacement was a machine gun nest, with two men operating. One continuously fed belted ammunition into the weapon while the other suppressed the oncoming zombies. The zombies on the flank fell row by row as the gunner swept his field of fire left and right.

"Get that drawbridge secured!" Dawn shouted over the intercom. Workers placed ladders on opposite sides of the drawbridge and carried a large chain up. They fastened the chain across the opening and in front of the bridge chains, as an additional layer of protection. The drawbridge, with enough force, could be pulled down, and even though the enemy currently had no way to pull it down, Dawn wanted to be sure they didn't bring one in the future. Other workers climbed the towers to where the drawbridge winches sit, to apply steel beams into the cogs of the winches to prevent the drawbridge from being pulled down by anything short of the Hulk.

In the center of the wall, four gas-powered flamethrowers were positioned near ground level. A woman fired up one, using a camera on the other side of the wall in conjunction with a targeting monitor. The cavaliers tried to halt the undead advance against the flames, but they too found themselves under heavy fire. As a cavalier fell, the mindless under his dominion were released from his command. Mindless with no nearby cavalier to guide them simply shambled towards the fortress's red brick walls and were burned up. Each of the other flamethrowers was quickly started by other survivors, and with concentrated effort, the undead fell here too, in an arc away from the drawbridge. The fallen undead continued to burn even after they were brought down, spreading the fire to still active undead beyond the range of the flamethrowers. The fire continued to spread as the flamethrower operators kept the heat on even after the zombies were out of range of their jet. Burning zombies walked towards the fortress, fell into the dry moat, and burned up many feet below the ground.

On the far right flank, an automatic twenty-millimeter cannon emplacement was raining high-explosive rounds down onto the hapless zombies. Explosions ripped up the ground, sending bits of dirt, rock, flesh and bone flying back ten feet or more. Here, too, riflemen picked off the cavaliers, and by killing the cavaliers in an area it seemed to remove any semblance of command of the mindless undead. The great number of misses among the untrained riflemen seemed to make no difference with the amount of lead going downrange. Another railgun operator couple selectively dropped railgun shells into the mass of oncoming undead. The railgun shells created craters on impact and buried themselves in the dirt, blasting earth outward into the oncoming attack force.

As Dawn watched the battle unfold, she noticed that her riflemen were naturally drawn to target the mounted cavaliers instead of the rank and file mindless. She also noticed a pattern as cavaliers fell. The mindless immediately near the cavalier that fell would stop attacking with the group, falling into a natural instinct to attack the nearest enemy. Her eyes lit up as she made the connection, and she immediately grabbed the intercom microphone.

"Shoot the cavaliers! Command goes through them! Take them out and the other zombies will just charge our walls!" Dawn called out, and every man and woman with a rifle took aim at the beast riders. In very short order, all of the cavaliers had fallen, and as each cavalier fell, more undead started to simply shamble towards the walls, making them easy prey for the machine gunners and flamethrowers.

"What the hell is THAT thing?" one of the gunners in the center of the wall called out over the intercom. "It's... it's disgusting!" A twelve-foot tall mess of flesh, guts and bone was coming towards the wall. The riflemen's shots were clearly hitting, but seemed to do no damage to it. "We... we're not doing any damage! We can't kill it! AAAAAHHHH!"

Dawn's voice echoed across the compound. "It's some sort of flesh golem! Hit it with something high-explosive!"

The left flank railgun operator pivoted her weapon around towards the front of the fortress. "Formation center, hit the deck!" she called out as her strong companion loaded another railgun shell. The riflemen on the outer wall dove on the floor for cover. With a sonic boom, the shell left the barrel of the gun at nearly four times the speed of sound and hit the flesh golem. The golem's fleshy body rippled as the powerful round passed through its center of mass, blowing off the head and extremities and turning the entire torso of the monstrous golem to a mess of charred bits and blood.

"Yeah! Direct hit!" she yelled. "Flesh golem down!"

One last undead, wearing spellcaster robes, stood off in the distance channeling a spell. Eerie howls started to pierce the air as the sky began to darken.

"One left." Dawn said calmly as she lifted an anti-materials rifle onto the wall of the main keep roof. "I got it." Dawn braced the bipod of the weapon over the castle's wall, aimed, and fired. The twenty-five millimeter shell burst from the rifle's barrel with a tremendous boom. The necromancer stood no chance against the anti-materials rifle. She scored a hit on his shoulder, separating the arm from the body and driving fragments of shattered shoulder and metal deep into his body. The necromancer died instantly as shards of his own collarbone were driven through his brain by the force of the blow.

"All clear. No more hostiles on radar." the radar operator called out over the intercom. "Any casualties?"

"No friendly casualties. All forces accounted for."

Dawn hung up the intercom receiver. "So, think we've got a chance yet?" she asked Jim, the doubtful ex-Army man she had tasked with training the survivors to shoot.

"Lady, we're still outnumbered a hundred million to one. We dropped about eight thousand today. It's just a drop in the bucket. Let's take on a billion at a time from here. If we still win, then we can survive to the end."

"Julius, get the spray tank up to the courtyard." Dawn announced over the intercom.

A few minutes later, the freight elevator opened into the courtyard. Julius was driving a forklift carrying a large metal tank with a pump fitted to it. Many of the fighters, now gathering nearby, exchanged quizzical looks. Dawn quickly answered them.

"This tank has a pump that allows us to extract gasoline from the underground tanks of the gas stations. The gas remains in those tanks and is untouched by the undead. We plan to use it to destroy the dead zombies after battles by spreading and igniting it. This prevents hostiles from recovering parts and making more of those flesh golem things we saw today."

Jim gasped at a random thought. "Those flesh golem things. They can probably build bigger ones. If they get one of them up to the drawbridge, they might be able to pull it down. If they pull our bridge down, we'll get overrun in no time."

"We can amp those flamethrowers up. All I have to do is change the gear ratio on the gas pump and replace the lines, and those things can triple in range." Rick chimed in.

"Then do it. If you need parts, ask Julius. If we don't have something you need, tell me and I'll use the Helix to retrieve it." Dawn answered. "And by the way, I've got charges set at the hinges of the drawbridge. I hit the switch and the entire bridge drops into the moat. Nobody's getting in that way."

"All over it."

"Nadia, you're my co-pilot. We're gonna go out and get some gas."

The Helix chopper, formerly a Soviet naval helicopter, sat on the helicopter pad inside the walls of the fortress. Dawn and Nadia climbed inside the crew cabin, and Dawn started the pre-flight checklist. Julius pulled the forklift carrying the tank alongside the Helix. The tank, an oblong tank measuring two and a half cubic meters inside, was designed to refuel Soviet military vehicles. It was intended to be airlifted by a Helix to refuel special operations vehicles. Dawn had a sprayer nozzle fitted onto its safety drain when she bought the tank from the Russians. A thick hose emerged from its main nozzle and was currently wrapped around the body of the tank.

"Pre-flight checklist finished. Starting main rotors. All clear!" Dawn yelled. The heavy coaxial rotor of the Helix started to spin, blowing the grass around the helicopter pad flat. Dawn lifted the helicopter off the ground a few feet and held it stable.

"Julius!" she yelled. "Attach the tank's hooks to the loops on the underside!"

Julius lifted the two hooks, one in each hand, trailing the chains behind. He affixed one and then the other to the loops on the body of the helicopter. After pulling on the chains to make sure they were secure, Julius moved out of the way and gave the all clear sign. Dawn increased the power to the rotor, pulling the helicopter from a hover into a climb. The helicopter pulled the chains taut, then lifted and carried the gas tank away from its position on the forklift skid.

"So where are we gonna get gas from?" Nadia asked Dawn.

"There's a town across the river from here. It's got a BP 7-11, there's three huge underground tanks of gas there. We're gonna pull six sixty-six gallons exactly out of it, that's how much our airlift tank holds."

"And how are we gonna get the nozzle into the tank?"

"You're gonna have to climb down the ladder on the side of the helicopter, unhook the nozzle and plug it into the gas tank, then latch the nozzle in place. Once that's done, hold the end of the rope on it and climb back up. When we're full, you pull the rope and it'll unlatch the nozzle."

"Okay, so I go down the ladder, plug the nozzle in, take the rope back up, and pull it when we're full?"

"Exactly."

The Kanawha River looked just the same as it did before the war. This part was too far upriver for most barges to come. The chemical plants, coal mines, and steel mills were farther downriver, closer to the city of Charleston. Just by the river and the surrounding banks, one could not even determine there had been a war. The river flowed fairly smoothly from east to west, as it has done for hundreds of millenia.

The town of Montgomery told a story of two very separate populations. The students of the university there had disappeared shortly before the zombies reached them. Many of Light's Bulwark's defenders formerly attended here. The university side of the railroad tracks that bisected the town was mostly untouched. There was some damage to non-university buildings from bullets and close-quarters combat, but beyond that there was nothing to show of the war's horrific aftermath. On the other side of the tracks, nearer to the river, most of the buildings were damaged or destroyed. Indentations in the dirt the size of skillets led every which way through the town. Impact damage tore down most of the buildings here. Several of the brick and stone buildings on this side of town still stood, including the city building, fire department, and one of the fraternity houses. The 7-Eleven Dawn intended to steal gas from had not been touched during the battle.

"I guess the survivors kited the zombies around the 7-Eleven. Normally I'd call that a good idea. Gasoline's highly flammable, I really wouldn't want to shoot near this stuff." Nadia mentioned to Dawn.

"I don't know. Maybe they'd have wanted to draw them into the area and blow the whole place sky high. Anyway, it helped us out that it's still intact."

"Nadia, throw the ladder down." Dawn commanded as she moved the helicopter into position near the 7-Eleven's gas pumps. Nadia did as she was told, unraveling the ladder and dropping it out of the helicopter's sliding door.

"Go! Go! Go!" Dawn shouted, and Nadia climbed down the ladder, unfastening the hose from the tank on the way down. The hose fell to the ground with the distinct sound of metal on rock. She found the opening for the gas tanks, the same ones the trucks formerly used to fill the tanks with gasoline for use in automobiles. She opened the cap, placed the nozzle, and forced the locking mechanism into place.

"All locked! Start pumping!" Nadia shouted up to Dawn as she drew the rope up to the chopper. Nadia climbed up the ladder, rope still in hand, all the way into the chopper's cargo bay from where she came. Dawn intently watched a dial as the pump on the tank extracted the highly flammable liquid from the underground tanks. The dial, labeled in gallons and ranging from 0 to 666, slowly moved from left to right. This pump was about ten times faster than standard gas pumps, designed for military applications rather than civilian gas pumping.

It took nearly ten minutes of hovering to fill the tank. Throughout the maneuver, Dawn had to constantly make adjustments to keep the unstable lifting helicopter in place. As soon as the dial hit the full marker, Dawn called out, "Pull the rope!" Nadia pulled the rope, unlocking the latch and freeing the nozzle from the ground. Gasoline dripped from the end of the nozzle onto the ground around the tank as the hose lifted from the tank. Dawn quickly amped power up on the rotors, pulling the Helix into the sky. The Helix lifted the filled tank into the air with little difficulty, carrying it over the Kanawha, the road, Light's Bulwark, and the battlefield.

"Dispersing fuel." Dawn radioed back to Light's Bulwark. She pulled a couple of levers, opening the spray valve on the tank. Gasoline sprayed from the tank, coating the broken corpses that littered the ground in a layer of flammable liquid. It took far longer to empty the tank than it did to fill it. The precision involved in dispersal of the fuel, along with the lower flow rate needed to spread the fuel over the entire battlefield, dragged this mission out to fifty minutes, compared to the ten it took to fill the tank.

"We're coming in." Dawn radioed. "Get ready to detach."

Dawn flew the Helix over the castle walls, lining the once again empty fuel tank up with the forklift skid. She slightly lowered the power on the chopper's rotors, easily placing the fuel tank on the skid. Dawn struggled to keep the Helix hovering in place as she yelled at Julius.

"Unhook me!" she shouted at him. Julius ducked under the helicopter and reached up, lifting both hooks out of their eyelets and dropping them on the skid. He ran out from underneath the chopper, turned back to Dawn, and gave the all clear sign. Dawn sat the helicopter down on the landing pad next to the tank. With a signal, the flamethrower operator fired up one of the flamethrowers for a split second, igniting the hundreds of gallons of gasoline spread across the thousands of square meters outside the fortress. Black smoke started to rise into the air outside the fortress, thick enough to block line of sight going north from the fortress. The walls kept the smoke out of the main part of the fortress, along with a friendly wind that seemed to carry the smoke east.

"We have won the day." Dawn said to the survivors. "But we're far from winning the war."

Chapter 5

The Strongest Union

Dawn's Chamber, Light's Bulwark Fortress
The night after the battle

Dawn lay on her ornate four-poster bed in her battle clothes. Her white blouse had turned a shade of gray from exposure to gunpowder, soot, and ash. Her blue Levi's smelled slightly of burnt sulfur. Her brown boots sat on the floor, carrying some dust that made them appear grayer than normal. Out her window, she could still see the fire raging. The fire had spread beyond its original intent and was now burning some of the wooded areas beyond the field of battle. Her castle was still untouched.

Dawn's room, the master bedroom of the fortress residence, was the most ornate section of the castle, along with the entry hall. The four-poster bed Dawn lay on was hand-crafted and hand-carved by one of the greatest American craftsmen from before the war. Dawn's family crest, a swift eagle perched on a branch with its wings slightly limp, was carved into the foot-board and headboard, painted in silver against the dark wood finish of the bed. The bed was made with sky blue bedclothes, the comforter also bearing the Cahill silver eagle.

The Persian rug on Dawn's floor, a hand-woven floral pattern, would have cost Dawn over thirteen thousand US dollars before the war. The walls were painted with the highest grade paint, in intricate patterns clearly done by hand. The solid wood crown molding and baseboards, just like the bed, were hand-carved, perfectly fit in with miter cuts. Dawn's closet was stocked primarily with jeans and blouses from Sears, in stark contrast to the opulence of the rest of her room.

Julius entered the room coming from the master bathroom. Dawn continued to lie on her bed, completely oblivious to his presence. Her jade eyes glistened with tears.

"Dawn? Are you okay?" he asked her.

The gates within her broke open at his words, unleashing a flood of sorrow.

"I can't... I can't do it..." Dawn sobbed.

"You can't do it? What are you talking about?"

"Everything... I have to put on this all-knowing perfect leader thing... I can't do it..."

Dawn buried her face in her pillow. Julius closed the distance quickly and wrapped his arms around her.

"You're doing amazing. Better than anyone could have hoped for. Look how everyone rallies around you. You lead with kindness, grace, and strength. You have no need to doubt yourself. I don't doubt you, Rick doesn't doubt you, Jim doesn't doubt you, and none of the troops doubt you. When you gave that speech to the survivors when they came in, you moved them to tears. You gave them hope, something that nobody else anywhere in the world has. Because of you, Light's Bulwark can actually stand."

"But..." Dawn sobbed. "But I have to do everything right... if I mess up, they'll judge me..."

"Every leader messes up, Dawn. General Eisenhower, one of America's greatest military heroes, doubted himself even after D-Day. He always thought to himself about the tactics he used and thought he made the wrong decision. He always wondered if more Allied lives could have been saved by doing something different. He thought about more bombing of the Atlantic Wall. He thought about letting the Russians push farther into Germany before making the assault. He thought about letting the strategic bombing of Germany do more damage to their war effort first. He thought about pulling more forces from the Pacific and fighting a defensive war there to win faster in Europe. He thought about special forces, Naval involvement, Chinese forces, Commonwealth forces. He made mistakes with the odds in his favor, but still nobody judged him."

"But... what if I lead them wrong and we lose?"

"Then we die. But still nobody will judge you. Even if there is some life after death, nobody will judge you. You will stand before St. Peter or whoever it is that guards the gates of paradise, and he will open them for you. He will call out to the angels to play a hymn of bravery for you, the commander who stood and fought, with only three hundred, against the entire might of the zombie horde."

"And the prophecy? What's all that about? It's predicting me to 'let the rays of the sun fly from my hands' and 'heal the weak with my touch'. I don't know how to do that! I'm not a wizard, I'm not a Solari, I'm not a priestess, I'm just a recent billionaire. I'm just the bastard child of a CEO with the whore he hired! I'm not special! I'm not a 'chosen one'! I'm –"

He cut her off. "My chosen one, prophecy or not."

The emotion within Dawn boiled over. She broke into uncontrollable sobbing, burying her face in Julius' shirt.

Julius pressed his lips against Dawn's and pulled her into a kiss. The surprise kiss stunned Dawn for a split second, but then she melted into it. His kiss was soft and strong at the same time. She held him there, wrapping him in a tight embrace. She pushed all her doubts away as he rolled with her onto their sides. She placed her hand against his back under his shirt, gripping at his lean body. He pressed himself against her, pinning her to the bed.

"I..."

"Shhh." he whispered. "Just kiss me."

Kissing Julius lifted Dawn's heart clear of the sorrow that gripped at her. As she lay there holding him, the worries of how she would fight the undead lifted. All thoughts of the undead left her as he ran his lips along her neck. She focused only on him, the warmth of his embrace, the softness of his kiss, the strength of his body pressed against hers. With his soothing touch surrounding her, she found sleep easily.

She found herself at the front of a group of warriors dressed in Greek battle gear from the time of the Athenian Empire. Surrounding her were warriors, male and female, intermixed in battle formation. The males bore the emblem of Athens on their shields, while the females had the emblem of Apollo. Dawn's body was different. She, too, was dressed as an ancient warrior, with four angelic wings protruding from her back. All of the warriors, male and female, looked to her for guidance. The Roman legions amassed further away. Roman ballista bolts hammered the city walls. Athenian ballistae rained bolts back down on the Romans. Beside her, a warrior dressed in an armored drape stood, wielding a two-handed crescent blade nearly the length of his body. The sigils of Artemis and Boreas gleamed in the sun, their magic empowering the blade and the wind reaver who wielded it.

"Charge!" Dawn shouted, and the hoplites and Solari formed their shield wall and pushed forward towards the Roman lines. The Romans held their shield wall strong against the Greek charge, triggering a legionnaire on hoplite close-quarters fight. The single wind reaver fared much better against the legionnaires, his well-crafted crescent blade ripping apart the shields and armor the warriors relied so heavily on. His quick moves made it difficult for the Romans to get effective hits on him, and his drape deflected the glancing blows they were able to land. The Roman general standing opposite Dawn commanded his legionnaires to form a constrictive wall around the mobile wind reaver.

Dawn's wings lifted her into the sky, her shield shining bright in the midday sun. Light collected at the center point of her shield, concentrating into a ranged blast that leveled the flank of a legion. Legionnaires charged at Dawn, frantically trying to stop what they saw as the most destructive weapon the Greeks had. She took to the skies, bringing her dark blade down into the raised shield of a legionnaire. The shield shattered beneath the strike, allowing her blade to penetrate his arm and face. She moved and stabbed at another legionnaire, breaking his shield and easily slaying him. The shields of the legionnaires were completely useless against her, shattering like glass under the weight of her blade thrusts. Her radiant shield and the barrier it created made her impervious to the gladius strikes of the Roman soldiers.

On the other side, her wind reaver was shredding legionnaire after legionnaire with ease. His crescent blade seemed absolutely unstoppable as he cleaved through any soldier who engaged him. The Roman legionnaires ordered to fight him were starting to drop their shields and flee, but the gesture was futile. The wind reaver cut down fleeing soldiers as easily as he cut down fighting ones. Suddenly, the ballistae fired a volley of bolts at their own legion – the one the wind reaver was ripping apart. Several bolts hit their mark, piercing the wind reaver's drape, hands, and heart. The terrible momentum of the projectiles carried the wind reaver back, pinning his lifeless body to the walls of the city.

Dawn turned away from her fallen wind reaver and continued to shred the soldiers from the sky. She dive bombed legions holding back her hoplite phalanxes and Solari warriors, often forcing the Romans to raise their shields to the sky and open themselves to spear thrusts and sword blows. The hoplites and Solari were starting to gain ground on the legions, a result the Roman general was clearly unhappy about. So far, his only victory was the defeat of the wind reaver.

Ballistae fired a volley at Dawn, a tactical move she saw coming but couldn't dodge. She raised her shield, blocking the shots, but their momentum knocked her back. Her wings lost their lift, and the power of the shots carried her over the wall and into the side of a building beyond.

Upon impact, Dawn awoke and sat bolt upright in bed, gasping for air. She looked around, seeing the familiar silhouettes of her furniture from her room at Light's Bulwark. She saw Julius, still asleep, lying beside her. Realizing that her experience was merely a dream, she cuddled up against Julius and fell back asleep.

Chapter 6

Death's Conquest

Flame Point Fortress
That same day

"What the hell is going on in West Virginia?" Aaron asked Stacie.
"What do you mean?"
"About fifty cavaliers in the same area went down."
Her eyes narrowed. "Holdouts?"
"No way. With that many cavaliers there had to be about eight thousand mindless. If they took out all those cavaliers, they had to have taken out the mindless too. And holdouts can't take out eight thousand mindless. There should have been a flesh golem in the area too. The weapons the holdouts have can't damage flesh golems. They've got to have some serious numbers and major firepower if they're still alive."
"I can call on a demon's eye to get sight on them, to see what we're up against."
Stacie walked across the throne room to a large glass window. The window was blocked on the other side by a solid metal wall, but Stacie could still project the demon's eye sight onto it. She pointed to the place on the map where the undead were taken down and started to channel magic.
"Tya vikzon rathiel eiyos, qapith adali gavetol!"
A floating eyeball appeared in front of Stacie, then quickly dove into the map near where Stacie was designating. A panoramic view appeared on the window. The demon's eye was revealing an area being ravaged

by a great fire. The smoke was so thick that the demon's eye couldn't see very far through it. The base of the flame, on the edge where the demon's eye could see, was burning off an invisible layer over the flesh rather than consuming the flesh itself.

"I found the eight thousand undead. They're burning. The entire forest is burning. But there has to be some kind of accelerant, fire doesn't usually burn this way without one."

"Accelerant? What the hell's an accelerant?"

"Liquid fuel. Someone or something poured out a lot of liquid fuel here. Something like gasoline or lighter fluid. Probably whoever killed the undead started the fire too. But I can't find any trace of humans, the smoke from the fire's too thick. I can't see very--"

Suddenly, the window reverted from being a display for the demon's eye back into a window with a wall behind it.

"What the hell? I can't sense my demon's eye!"

"How come?"

"Someone shot the damn thing down!"

"Shot it down." Aaron stated in disbelief. "We've tested those things, it would take an anti-aircraft missile to shoot one down."

"I know that, you idiot. Someone has anti-aircraft missiles, but I can't see them through all the fire and smoke. Get your forces from all over the southern US diverted to that area. They can hunt down holdouts later. We've got to find wherever these people with missiles are and take them out. Our lord won't appreciate all his work going to waste."

"I don't get why he can't just come here anyway. I mean, we own the entire world. It's got to be a suitable place for him already."

"He already told us that the summoning spell doesn't work if there are still living intelligent beings on the planet. Their mental capacity must mess with the magic somehow. We've got to wipe them all out before we can summon him. In the meantime, I'll work on crafting a spell that seeks the signatures of intelligence. Other than the West Virginia situation, what do we have still?"

"The same as usual. Killed a couple more living, lost a few more undead to holdouts in remote places. Still can't do anything about the ships at sea, but they can't dock to get supplies so they'll starve to death eventually anyway. And there's still that pesky monastery in the

Himalayas. Can't get anyone up there cause of the terrain. Can you get a demon's eye up there yet?"

"No, I already told you. The demon's eyes can't get to above twenty thousand feet, they freeze."

"Well, there's no way they have enough supplies to last very long. We'll just put our forces around there and starve them out. I'm gonna send all of my forces in Europe over to West Virginia too. It'll take them a couple months to get across the Atlantic though. Hopefully we won't need them."

The undead tracking display behind Aaron, a map of the entire world displaying the location of his cavaliers, lit up as Aaron tapped into his mental link with them. They still struggled in the Himalayas, trying to access the monastery. Though the forces outside the monastery outnumbered its defenders ten thousand to one, the monastery's position atop a peak made it all but inaccessible. The monks, through their strength, could make the climb, but the undead could not climb high enough to reach it. The monks had stores of food, but soon they would run out and starve.

Before the war, the monks of Cloud Peak Monastery were known for their extreme martial prowess. Each monk was worth a hundred fighters in melee combat. Their intense training high in the Himalayas made their bodies as strong as steel, able to shrug off most physical attacks. Their extreme health had honed their internal organs as well. They did not age the same way as normal humans, and their livers and immune systems were more resilient to poisons and disease. The steep climbs and narrow passes that accessed the monastery made it nearly a perfect defensive structure. The hundred or so monks that lived at the monastery could hold their monastery against any ground forces, simply because of the climbs and passes. They could defend the rock faces from the top, knocking off any who tried to climb them. They could stand in the passes, laying waste to any force dumb enough to charge them.

The Chinese Army had made a tunnel into the monastery grounds through the mountain when they attempted to assert their authority, over a decade before the war. The monks were able to hold it by moving a large boulder over the tunnel entrance. Now, after the defeat of the People's Army, the monks were using this tunnel to raid the abandoned cities below and their stores of food. Unless Aaron found out how they were doing this, they would be able to hold out for a couple more years until the now-abandoned cities ran out of food. Since Stacie's demon's eyes could not reach this high up, they were safe – for now.

Aaron turned his attention to his cavaliers in Africa. Here, his conquest was easy and absolute. The warring factions here gave death's royals a new option – appear to be friends of one of the warlords. The warlord, when shown the power of their magic, allied with them. Stacie snuffed the life from him, turning him into an undead general. Though Aaron and Stacie still had dominion over him, he had control of all the cavaliers in his area. Those who would willingly submit to their rule were also turned into intelligent undead, and they came to be Aaron's commanders. The undead marched across the open lands here swiftly, decimating all opposition. None of the warlords wanted to align with each other. They could not put up a united front, and so each pocket of resistance was overrun and annihilated. And with every warlord who fell, more forces were added to Aaron's army. Stacie raised the fallen as undead fighters, allowing the undead army to swell with every victory. There were still some US Special Forces living off the land here, sent on a mission before the war to do only Jehovah knows what. Occasionally, undead would be taken down a handful at a time, by these elite warriors. No cavaliers had been taken down here for a while. Stacie, for the most part, hadn't sent a demon's eye up over Africa for a long time.

"Africa seems completely won. We haven't had any cavaliers downed in a long time. I don't think there's any survivors here. Moving on. Europe."

Aaron focused on the forces in Europe. The nation of Switzerland still held on. Decades before the war, a cult leader, known only as Zarakeil, convinced people that he could make them into gods. To do this, he told his followers to place sigils of the god Ankou, the Celtic god of death, on as many graves as they could. As he gained followers, his reach expanded, eventually encompassing the whole of Switzerland. His plan was foiled when INTERPOL arrested him on charges of human trafficking, and the cult fell apart without Zarakeil's leadership. The sigils of Ankou still line most of the graves in Switzerland. It was these sigils, containing the magic of a Celtic deity, that blocked the demonic magic used by Stacie to raise the dead.

With no dead rising from the ground in Switzerland, the only way to take Switzerland would be to storm it with the quickly amassing army of undead at their command. The mountain passes, the only way into the nation, were heavily guarded. Every Swiss man already owned an assault rifle before the war. Famine hit hard here due to the war. 90% of the Swiss population had died in the famine and had subsequently been cannibalized by the remaining defenders. The drastically reduced population could be fed by hunters, supply runners, and farmers, allowing their remaining people to become self-sufficient. It seemed Switzerland could only fall when the iron mines in their nation stopped producing, allowing their defenders to exhaust their ammunition supplies.

The rest of Europe had not been so fortunate. Most of Europe is flat land, easily traversed by the undead. The low countries were easily overrun. France, Spain and Italy were quickly overrun as well. Eastern Europe stood even less chance than Western Europe. With no real powerhouses in terms of military, the former Soviet Bloc nations fell like dominoes before the advancing tide of undead. Russia fell too, due to the lack of effectiveness of their natural defense. While Napoleon and Hitler fought into Russia and eventually succumbed to the cold, Aaron's undead army were completely impervious to it. Undead do not feel cold, nor do they need food or sleep. They overwhelmed the Russian defenders simply by constant pressure through the bitter cold.

"Stacie, get a demon's eye over Switzerland. Maybe some new holes have opened up in their defenses."

"Aaron, nothing's changed there except maybe their ammo count. We'll win that when they run out of ammo. And they have anti-air, they shoot the wards down as soon as they spawn."

"Grrrr... South America."

South America was where it all began. The first army was risen here, from the ancient bones of the Incas. The South American governments had no hope of a strong armed response to the undead. Most of the governments here were owned by the drug cartels, who seemed to not care about the undead until it was too late. The undead here also did not need to climb the treacherous Andes Mountains. Since they came down from the Andes, they already owned the mountains before they moved on anything else. For a while, holdouts managed to kill undead occasionally. But, high in the Andes with no way to find food, the holdouts there starved to death, leaving South America completely clean.

"Excellent. Nobody left. Stacie, do you have any kind of spell that tells me if an area's clean?"

"Not yet. I'm working on it. When I've got a working spell, I'll use it."

"Finally. Australia."

Australia, with its land being mostly comprised of flat desert, was quite easy to take. About twelve years before the war, the Australian government had outlawed most types of firearms. Without their firearms, the Australian citizens were defenseless against the rampaging undead. Troop movements were easy to conceal in the desert sands, and since undead do not need water, sleep, or food, the undead army was able to win here too. Still, however, holdouts in the deserts of Australia plagued Aaron with hit-and-run attacks on undead forces. Deserts, unlike cold highlands, do have plants and animals that holdouts can eat.

"What the hell can we do here? We can't find them in the sand. They're always on the move, and their tracks are covered by sand drifts." Aaron said, frustrated.

"I'm working on that too. I've almost got a life sense spell ready that I can imbue your cavaliers with. They'll be able to detect life out to about a mile in all directions. Even if it doesn't help catch the living, it'll let the undead hunt down all the food supply and destroy it, and then the living will die of starvation. Which begs the question, why didn't you destroy the food as your armies marched?"

"Don't demons need to eat?"

"I have no idea. And we can't exactly ask our lord either. We can't contact him again until we're ready to summon him."

"So we leave the food until we summon him. Once we summon him, then we ask. If the demons don't need it, then we destroy it. If they do, then we leave it."

"The Swiss are growing their food within their own borders, so we can't starve them out. The Australian desert holdouts are getting their food off the land, and I'd bet the West Virginians are too."

"So I'll send the order to the troops in both Australia and the US to kill all the food."

"Fine. But if this goes horribly awry, you're to blame."

Aaron tapped into the link with his general in Australia. Formerly a worshiper of Satan, Roger Wellington eagerly embraced Aaron and Stacie when they showed themselves as the commanders of death. Stacie gave Roger the power of intelligence when she took his life and revived him as an undead, so that he could lead the undead on their conquest of Australia. He remained there with the undead forces that were now tracking the remaining living.

"Yes, master?"

"Destroy the food. Burn the plants. Hunt the beasts. Take away whatever means the holdouts have of living off the land. The holdouts can run and hide, but the plants can't. Take out the plants, and the animals and humans will die of starvation. Then, when we find the bodies, we can raise them as mindless. Go! Now!"

"The hard part of the battle is won. Tracking the last remnants of humanity will take time, but it will be easy. At least once we overrun the damned West Virginians it will be."

"What about those ancient blades you wanted to find?"

"Let's see. Falkenskold!"

"Yes master?"

The soulless form of a tall Norwegian barbarian appeared on the display. Olaf Falkenskold was a worshiper of chaos when the undead leader came to Norway. Falkenskold, like Wellington, embraced his command, believing Aaron to be the herald of the end times. His body still possessed all of its muscle, giving his six foot five frame an extremely imposing appearance. His black metal armor was dull and unfinished, stark against his ashen skin. The glow of death's magic shined in his eyes.

"How goes the hunt for Ondesverd?"

"The blade still eludes us, master. The mindless have been digging through the snow since we claimed the land, but have uncovered little. We have uncovered Viking tablets describing the blade though. It details a battle between avatars of the brothers, Thor and Loki. Loki's champion wielded the blade Ondesverd, while Thor's champion wielded a blade called Maktdrikker. In the legend, Maktdrikker was destroyed, but Thor's champion still managed to win and banish the avatar of Loki. It says the champion of Loki was put to rest somewhere on Inner Vikna, so I've deployed the bulk of the mindless there to search."

"Excellent. Keep me posted."

Aaron then tapped into his mental link again, this time focusing on Kgosi. Kgosi was the first African warlord to embrace him and his conquest.

"Kgosi, how goes the hunt for Damupanga?"

"It goes futilely." Kgosi replied. The African bush warrior was one of those that embraced Aaron on his arrival. Aaron and Stacie's command of magic greatly impressed the warrior, driving him to worship them as gods. Kgosi's lean, six foot eight frame, even turned undead, was still quite imposing, though not to the degree of the muscled, armored barbarian of the north. Unlike his Scandinavian counterpart, Kgosi wore next to nothing, merely a loincloth made from the hide of a gazelle.

"Da mindless here comb da jungle, da savannah, da desert, all to no avail. We killed all da voodoo priests when we attacked, so we can't get nuttin from dem. We can't learn da lore, so it be just a blind search. It could take centuries to find it. Send me some necros to take da secrets from dere bones."

"The only necro capable of anything like that is Stacie, and she has to develop a spell for it first. Keep looking, Kgosi. Just keep looking." Aaron replied to his field marshal. "Stacie!" he snapped as he shut the communication link off. "Another spell you need to create, one to withdraw information from the dead."

"I'll get to it when I get to it, Aaron. If you haven't noticed, we have forever. We aren't on a timetable."

Chapter 7

Survivors

Light's Bulwark Fortress
A week later

"Rick, get the Helix prepped. Julius, get the electromagnet up here. We're going out retrieving supplies." Dawn said to her chief engineer.

"Um... why do you need the electromagnet? What are you going after?"

"Did anyone notice anything about the shells we were using?"

"Yeah, they weren't quite as heavy as they should have been." Jim chimed in.

"That's cause they're steel, not lead. That's why I need the magnet. We're going out over the battlefield now that the fires are out, and we're retrieving our shells for recycling. All Light's Bulwark shells are steel so we can pick them up with the magnet. Nadia, you're going with me. I need you to operate the magnet while I fly the Helix."

Rick checked many of the Helix's systems and fueled the helicopter up. Julius pulled the forklift carrying the electromagnet into the courtyard and set it down. Dawn started running the pre-flight checklist. The Soviet-built Helix required less maintenance than its American counterpart, making it perfect for such a task. In under thirty minutes, the Helix was prepped, fueled up, and hooked to the electromagnet by a hook twice as heavy as the ones used to lift the fuel tank.

The Helix's engines came to life with a roar. The twin rotors spun up in opposite directions, blowing the grass in the courtyard flat in all directions. The powerful helicopter lifted into the air as the ground crew scattered, pulling the large magnet with it. Dawn guided the helicopter upwards and over the wall.

Dawn flew the helicopter out over the now charred field. Rain that had fallen since soaked the ash, turning it to a disgusting black goop. All of the flesh from the undead had burned off in the fire, leaving only bones and metal behind. Dawn brought the helicopter down, keeping the magnet only a couple of feet off the ground as she made each pass. Nadia powered the magnet on as Dawn came in for the first pass. Metal fragments leapt from the ground and clung to the magnet, ranging in size from tiny shards to football-sized railgun shells that were fully intact. With each subsequent pass, more metal shards came up to meet the magnet. The magnetized metal already attached to the magnet served as a conduit of magnetic force, allowing the metal to be layered on the magnet. After several passes, Dawn returned the Helix to the base.

Situated on one of the towers was an opening that fed all the way down to the basement where the forge was located. This chute, made of aluminum, had an opening large enough to fit household furniture. Its sides were raised five feet off the floor of the tower as to prevent people from falling inside. Dawn brought the magnet over the chute's opening and slowly lowered the helicopter.

"Now." Dawn said to Nadia, who shut off the power to the electromagnet. The magnet's power, derived from the electricity that Nadia had just shut off, disappeared instantaneously. Hundreds of pounds of metal dropped in a clump from the magnet into the chute with a series of loud clanging sounds. When the cargo weight reading reached zero, Dawn pulled the Helix back up and piloted it back over the walls of Light's Bulwark and into the battlefield once more.

Dawn swept this pass out in a wide arc, claiming the far reaches of the expended metal. The magnet once again picked up metal fragments of all sizes and sources. Out here, a large number of the shards picked up were machine gun bullets that had missed or penetrated their intended targets. This was also the range of the railgun shell that decimated the flesh golem. Dawn moved the Helix out specifically to pick up the fragments of this shell from when it hit a stone after passing through the monstrosity it made contact with.

"Light's Bulwark Fortress to Helix One," a radio call came out.

"This is Helix One," Nadia replied to the radio call.

"We've got good news and unknown news. Good news is Rick and the others got the radar beefed up. We can see for about a hundred miles now instead of a thousand yards. Turned out there was a short circuit somewhere. Unknown news is we're picking up ten human-sized moving points on radar now. They're out in the trees. I'm sending you the coordinates. Go check it out."

A location came up on the Helix's global positioning device. The still-active space based GPS systems transmitted a location far beyond the battlefield, about twenty miles out.

"Nadia, we're gonna drop our load and our magnet first. If they're friendly, we'll want to pick them up and bring them back, and if we've got the magnet we can't do that. Relay that to the base."

"Light's Bulwark Fortress, this is Helix One. We're coming back to drop our metal. Get Julius at the pad to detach the magnet. Once we've dropped the magnet we'll go after the unknowns. Over."

Dawn pulled the helicopter into a banked turn to face towards the fortress once again. She completed the drop maneuver again, flying the helicopter over the chute and ordering Nadia to power down the magnet. Much less metal fell this time, as Dawn's second pass was not yet complete. As the weight gauge read zero once again, Dawn flew the heavy lifting chopper down to the pad and sat the magnet back on the skid it came up on. Julius, who stood waiting on Dawn to return, unlatched the hook that held the magnet to the helicopter, placed it back with the magnet, and got clear.

"Clear!" he yelled, and Dawn pulled the Helix up to altitude. Now unburdened, the Helix could fly far faster than with the heavy cargo. It took the chopper about eight minutes in straight line flight towards the unknown radar points. A quick flyover revealed the radar points to be humans, dressed in camouflage and carrying rifles. One lifted a blaze orange flag from a pouch and waved it at Dawn's helicopter. Dawn put a spotlight into a clearing as Nadia grabbed the chopper's microphone.

"Human survivors, go to the clearing we spotlighted. We'll pick you up there."

The hunters followed Dawn's beam to the forest clearing. Nadia kept the beam centered on the clearing as Dawn flew towards it and set the Helix down on the grassy field. Nadia climbed out of the helicopter's co-pilot seat to open the side doors for the survivors.

"Who'n the hell are you?" one of them shouted at Nadia. Another raised his rifle at her.

"Red, hold your fire. They're living," the leader of the holdouts said to his deputy. "Who goes there?"

Nadia replied to his question. "We are the defenders of Light's Bulwark Fortress, a stronghold of human power. We want you to come with us to our fortress. You'll be safe there."

The leader of the holdouts looked to his deputy. "What'cha thinkin', Red?"

"Imma thinkin' they ain't no better 'an us out here. I reckon that's their fort 'at burnt down a couple suns ago."

"Well, I reckon we should go with 'em," one of the girls in the group said. "That wadn't their fort 'at burnt down. 'At was gas burnin', ya could tell by the smell."

"Ya got food?" the leader asked Nadia.

"Enough to feed three hundred people till they die of old age," she replied.

"How's about water?"

"We've got our own treatment facility that's still up and running. We couldn't ever run out of water."

"Ammo?"

"Enough to keep an entire army stocked for years."

"I want in. What'cha say, guys?"

"How ya plan to hold the place? What's stoppin' the zombies from runnin' through ya?"

"We've got – you know what, how about we show you and then you can decide? If you want to stay, you can stay, if you want to leave and take your chances out there, we'll bring you back here and drop you off again."

"I can live with 'at." Red said in agreement.

"That settles it. We're in."

The survivors, formerly farmers and hunters from before the war, filed into the Helix's cargo hold. The group carried a mixed group of weapons, from 30-06 hunting rifles to 12-gauge shotguns. They were, as far as anyone could tell, run-of-the-mill backwoods West Virginians, lacking in education but skilled at survival. Many of them wore camouflage, with coverings made from animal hides. The hides were extremely warm, good at keeping them from freezing to death in the cold nights.

The Helix lifted back off the ground with all passengers in tow. The bright sunlight gave full visibility from the air to all aboard. The scorched plain where the undead charged Light's Bulwark stood out, black against the green lands beyond. The burn zone was a plain of ash, cracked and broken bones, and mud. The bones had been damaged in the fire, cracked by the intense heat. Their marrow had since burned up and their moisture boiled away, leaving blackened, dried-up bones behind. The imposing fortress wall stood off in the distance, forming a barrier to the burnt plain.

As the team approached Light's Bulwark Fortress, the holdouts were awestruck. The sun caught the gleaming metal barrels of the array of defensive weapons atop the ramparts of the fortress. Life at the fortress continued. Many of the defenders were milling around outside on the beautiful summer day. Some played cards atop the ramparts. Others cleaned weapons, stocked ammunition, or ate. Even from the air, it was clear that the outer walls of the fortress towered over the moat below. The walls appeared as solid as ever, their brick surface lined perfectly with mortar in the gaps between bricks. The scorched earth beyond the walls of the fortress gave a clear indication as to where the fire burned at. From this angle, Light's Bulwark truly looked like the castle it was modeled after, only equipped for modern war instead of the medieval battles castles were originally designed for.

"Well I'll be a monkey's uncle! Look at 'at place!" Red shouted as he looked down on the fortress.

"How'd we not know 'is was here?" another asked.

"'At must of been where the gunshots came from!"

"That's right." Nadia replied. "We took out about eight thousand undead when they charged us, then we set the fire to destroy the bodies."

"Let me tell you about this place." Dawn started. "Those walls are pretty much impervious to anything the undead can throw at us. We've got the power to flush the moat of anything that lands in it. We've got guns, anti-air capability, and way more supplies than you could ever imagine. This place can't fall, there's not even a chance."

As the Helix moved in towards the pad, Julius and the others moved in to prep it. The others, the ones not on the prep team, stopped what they were doing as the helicopter approached. Word had made it around the fortress that living had been detected outside. Everyone, from gunners to engineers to laborers, wanted to see who had managed to survive out in the open for so long. Many came down into the courtyard. Others stayed atop the ramparts where they were working, but watched as the former Soviet vehicle approached.

Dawn brought the Helix up over the walls, clearing the heads of the onlooking defenders by a few feet. She slowly reduced rotor power, allowing gravity to pull the helicopter from its height. It descended at a low rate of speed, controlled with precision from the panel in front of Dawn. The large landing skids of her helicopter hovered over the pad, slowly lowering as Dawn made minute adjustments constantly. Now just six inches off the ground, Dawn cut power to the main rotors, causing the Helix to drop the remaining few inches and come to rest on the pad.   Nadia ordered all inside to wait until the rotor blades stopped spinning to exit the helicopter.

Dawn and Nadia exited the helicopter, followed by the ten holdouts. The place erupted into cheer as they filed from the helicopter. The entire defense force of Light's Bulwark now stood, either in the courtyard or on the ramparts, celebrating the arrival of the new defenders.

"What in tarnation?!" Red asked.

"They're cheering for you guys. It's not exactly a common occurrence for Light's Bulwark to bolster its forces, considering there's not really anyone still alive out there." Nadia replied.

"Okay team, let's get these guys up to speed." Dawn said to the leaders, now clustered around the helipad.

"This is Jim." Dawn said while motioning towards Jim. "He's in charge of training."

"This is Nadia." Dawn said, pointing towards her co-pilot. "She's my co-pilot."

"Rick." she said, pointing to the man currently working on the Helix. "Chief engineer."

"Laina, chief historian." Dawn said. "You'll see why she's important later."

"Hey!" Laina called out on mention of her name. "That's not fair!" Dawn ignored her plea for attention.

"And this is Julius. He's the chief of supply distribution." Dawn said as she pointed at the forklift Julius was currently using to move a skid of ammunition crates towards the eastern ramparts. Julius did not acknowledge, as the sound of the forklift drowned out Dawn's words.

"Follow me." Dawn said to the rednecks as she moved towards the fortress's main entrance.

The foyer of the fortress was as ornate as they come. A chandelier hung from the ceiling out over the first floor, sparkling with glowing blue crystals in place of bulbs. A silver-trimmed azure carpet ran from the front door up the stairs to the mezzanine. The stairs themselves were lined with a sturdy oak railing, hand-carved the entire way up. The white marble floor glistened in the blue light of the chandelier. The silver handles, hinges and accents reflected the blue light back through the room. All of the benches, crown molding, and baseboards were hand carved out of solid oak. The silver Cahill eagle sat at the base of the stairs at a point where the carpet formed a circle before ascending the staircase, directly under the crystal chandelier.

The West Virginian wilderness survivors' jaws dropped at the magnificence of the fortress's interior.

Dawn led them into a great hall off the entry hall. This hall had five long marble tables, one across the back wall and the other four stretching longways nearly the rest of the room's immense length. Each had a silver-trimmed blue tablecloth, again bearing the Cahill silver eagle. The polished stone tile floor reflected the blue light of yet another crystal chandelier. The rednecks' muddy boots tracked across the floor, leaving footprints wherever they stepped. Before the war, Dawn would have never allowed them to track mud through her sanctum.

"How'd you even get this place?" one of them asked.

"I kinda inherited it before the war." Dawn answered him.

"Dawn, you're needed on the rooftop. We're picking up something bouncing off the satellite."

Dawn pressed one of the intercom buttons on the wall. "On my way."

Dawn ran off out of the great hall up the stairs, taking them two at a time. The bewildered rednecks, with no idea as to what to do, followed her. The main rooftop, lower than the towers but still high enough to see over the walls, required Dawn to climb from the first floor through the mezzanine up to what would have been the fourth floor. Each staircase she climbed was designed similarly to the first one, carpeted with the azure and argent of her coat of arms.

Engineer Dave sat at the communications point awaiting her. "Dawn, we're picking up communications from the Swiss. Apparently the Navy was right about them, they're alive and well somehow."

Dawn immediately grabbed the microphone. "Swiss defenders, are you there? Can you read me?"

"I read you, loud and clear. Who are you?" an accented voice answered, French from what Dawn could determine.

"This is Dawn Cahill of Light's Bulwark Fortress, United States."

"United States? Isn't that place an undead-held wasteland now?"

"Most of it is, yes. But my private fortress in backwoods West Virginia held. We've got three hundred and twelve defending it. We're sitting on a natural gas site, and we're using it to power the fortress. It's like a miniature city with a vast stockpile of food underground."

"And it's just the fortress you guys are trying to hold?"

"Yeah. We've got some heavy weapons lining the ramparts. Machine guns, railguns, the whole nine yards. How did you guys manage to hold your entire country?"

"Mountain passes. We just built walls across the passes. The zombies are beating on our walls, but they can't do any damage. We've got plenty of water from melting the snow, so we can flush them away from our walls after we kill a bunch."

"Nicely done. Any estimates on how much damage you've done?"

"About half a billion mindless so far, plus a lot of cavaliers. But it seems like after we wipe out a bunch of mindless, a few days later an army of flesh golems comes after us. Those things are way stronger than the mindless. They can damage stone walls. Every time they attack, we have to repair our walls, and it takes a lot of firepower concentrated in one pass to cover our engineers while they repair the walls."

"How many defenders do you guys have?"

"About seven ninety thousand. We lost a lot in the initial defense month when we were erecting the walls for the first time, about three mil then. Once we had the walls up, the zombies didn't kill many more, but famine started to hit. The population we've got now is sustainable, but just. The general ordered all the weak and unskilled killed off when the famine hit, and ordered them eaten. Pretty much everyone left now is a warrior, engineer, or resource gatherer."

"You guys ate them?"

"General Mannheim doesn't care about customs. He cares about survival, and he drills it into us. Whatever we have to do to live, we do."

"Luckily Light's Bulwark doesn't have to resort to cannibalism. We've got enough food supplies to last us."

"Good for you then... what the hell? All units, shoot down those flying eyes!"

"Flying eyes?"

"There's these demon eye things watching us from the air. Haven't you guys encountered them yet?"

"Someone said they shot down something in the smoke, but we don't know what it was yet. It could've been one."

"I think they're used to spy on us. I don't think they can attack, we haven't seen them shoot at us yet."

"We'll kill 'em off as we see 'em then. Light's Bulwark out."

Chapter 8

The Solari High Priestess

Light's Bulwark Fortress
A day later

"Dawn, you're needed on the rooftop. The engineers made a major breakthrough."

"On my way."

As Dawn approached the communications array on the rooftop, she could see rather quickly the changes that had been made. There was additional computer equipment from the networking room moved up to the rooftop. A bunch of it was linked into both the Light's Bulwark network and the communications system.

"Rick, what the hell are you doing?"

"I've hacked into some of the satellites orbiting the planet. One of them actually has life-sensing equipment aboard for detecting life on alien worlds. I've turned it to face Earth, and here's what I've found."

Rick brought up a display of the world on a monitor. It showed the world, with concentrations at Switzerland, Light's Bulwark Fortress, Cloud Peak Monastery, and a half dozen points in the open ocean. It also showed scattered dots throughout the United States, Australia, Canada, Siberia, and Africa.

"This is what we have. All the living humans in the world. I've reprogrammed the sensor to only pick up human life forms. The undead don't get picked up, they don't have a life signature. Looks like the only strongholds of human power left are here, Switzerland, and someplace in what looks to be Nepal, or maybe Tibetan China. They've probably only got a few dozen defenders though, I think they're only alive because the undead can't scale the mountains."

"This is good. We need to track the holdouts down and bring them back to Light's Bulwark. Out there, they can just be turned into mindless and then turned against us. In here, they can't be made part of the enemy army. Now if we can just find places to refuel the Helix..."

"I've got an idea. We can probably land it on the carriers. They can refuel it, and they can also move the carriers and battleships up and down the coast. Some of the ships can even go on the rivers. We'll be able to have a mobile base from which we can fly. And I think we need to abandon the carriers and bring the Navy people here anyway. I'm gonna contact the Navy people to see what kind of supplies they have left afloat. If they're anywhere close to being out, they'll fly out here. And they've got more choppers and pilots to help us recover supplies or start fires too."

"Good idea. Let's make it happen."

Rick flipped the communications point's channel over to the US-44-AHA secure frequency.

"USS Abraham Lincoln, this is Light's Bulwark Fortress. Are you there?" Dawn asked through the radio microphone.

"Light's Bulwark, this is Lincoln. We read you." the radio operator replied.

"What's your food supply look like right now?

"We've got plenty of food, we're getting some help from the Swiss. Our fuel's looking low though. They can't help us with that since they don't have gas either."

"We can. We've got this refinery that combines molecules from natural gas to make gasoline.

"Can you? We'll bring you a gas tank over to fill with gas."

"Make sure your bring a nozzle so we can fit the pump to it. I don't think our Soviet nozzle fits your American equipment."

"Consider it done."

"You guys need any help?"

"Any chance you can spare a flight prep crew? It'll make our jobs way easier trying to fly out."

"Sure thing. We'll send you the flight crew with the gas tank. Send the pilot back with the gas tank and keep the prep crew."

As Dawn closed communications with the Navy officers, Dave came charging up the stairs two at a time. Laina was behind him, panting and wheezing as she tried to keep pace with the much thinner man.

"Dawn! Dawn! We think we figured out the shield! You already had a book in your own library on the topic!" Dave said in an excited, hyper, overly loud tone.

"What do you mean?"

"There was a book about the myths of the Solari in your library. You probably forgot you had it. It even talks about your statue." Dave opened the book, which he had brought here from the fortress library, to the proper page.

"I'd bet my dad bought the book before he died, cause I didn't stock the library with anything." Dawn replied as Dave searched through the book.

On the page, a picture of Dawn's statue, complete with inscription, sat, with a paragraph. Dave began to read from the book, a part written originally on a Greek scroll by a Solari high priestess.

"We Solari cannot expect our order to last forever. The Romans are coming. They are many more in number than we Athenians, and they possess weapons the likes of which our walls cannot protect us from. This statue is our last effort to protect the world from evil. One worthy of our order will find this statue, imbued with our power, and she will take on our strength. With it, she shall guide the world from darkness into a new dawn. – High Priestess Amynta."

"It has another prophecy in it too, on the next page." Dave turned the page and read aloud again.

"Aphrodite's strength has turned, replaced by the realm of Styx;

Former allies part under no uncertain terms;

One, the Dawn of a new world, the other, the sadist of his own prison;

But together once more, they will be rejoined;

On the fields of battle, against the world's greatest foe;

His blade and her shield will guide the path to survival."

Laina added some knowledge of Greek history to the myths. "Amynta was the last high priestess of the Solari order. She died sometime around 88 BC, when the Roman general Sulla crushed the Athenian rebellion. Her Solari warriors reinforced the rebels as Sulla's men charged in, causing heavy losses to the Roman forces, but in the end Sulla's vastly superior numbers were too much for Amynta's warriors. Amynta was captured as a prisoner of war and claimed by Sulla himself, but she refused to pleasure him. Sulla was outraged, so much so that he had her crucified. All of the rest of the Solari either died in the battle or fled afterward. Sulla took the statue from Athens and sold it in Rome. It was supposedly sold many times between then and when Dawn bought it."

"The prophecy." Dawn replied. "Let's see if we can decipher it. Aphrodite is the god of beauty, yes?"

"Yes." Laina answered. "She also holds dominion over the realms of love, lust, and fertility. So Aphrodite's strength could be any of those."

"What about Styx? What does Styx do?"

"Styx is the goddess of hate, which leads me to believe Aphrodite's strength is love."

"One, the Dawn of a new world. I feel like, based on these prophecies, that's me somehow. The other prophecy called me that too, assuming it's about me. Was it capitalized in the original Greek?"

"Yes, that one had a capital alpha too, just like the other book."

"But... the sadist of his own prison? No idea who or what that could be."

"But together once more, they will be joined, on the fields of battle, against the world's greatest foe. Whoever or whatever the sadist is, he and you will be on the same side, or his power will be with you, or something like that. I think it's his power, because it mentions 'his blade and her shield'. Your shield is clearly the Solari Aegis. I think 'his blade' is a metaphorical blade, meaning some kind of power."

"But when does love turn to hate?"

"I have no idea."

"We found something else. It's another poem, but I don't think it's a prophecy. Listen. Oddly enough, it rhymes in English, but not in the ancient Greek."

"Under daylight we will stand, triumphant, bright and tall
Under our relentless strikes, the enemy will surely fall
Break their ranks, break their hearts, break their armor too
Solari strike and Solari live, for that is what we do
Outnumbered and outflanked, we will always stand up strong
They might think they can beat us, but they are sorely wrong
Solari light will always win, the sun can never die
Wings of angels carry us, let the Priestess fly!"

"I don't know what it –" Laina started, but Dawn interrupted her. "I do. Follow me!" Dawn said as she dashed down the stairs, sliding on her hands down the rails. Laina chased, nowhere near fast enough to keep pace with the much more agile Dawn. Dawn reached the foyer, where the shield from the statue now sat. The engineers had disconnected it from the statue with their tools, placing it in the foyer for easy access. Dawn grabbed the shield and strapped it to her arm with the strap that the engineers had installed.

"Let me see!" Dawn said as she snatched the book from Laina, reading the poem while holding her shield in battle position.

"Under daylight we will stand, triumphant, bright and tall
Under our relentless strikes, the enemy will surely fall
Break their ranks, break their hearts, break their armor too
Solari strike and Solari live, for that is what we do
Outnumbered and outflanked, we will always stand up strong
They might think they can beat us, but they are sorely wrong
Solari light will always win, the sun can never die
Wings of angels carry us, let the Priestess fly!"

The inscription on the shield began to glow brilliant yellow. Dawn raced back up the flights of stairs back to the main rooftop as the glow enveloped the shield and then her. Though Dawn was normally fast, as the light began to wash over her, her speed increased threefold. She moved faster than even the fastest humans now as she climbed the stairs. As she reached the rooftop, Laina lagging far behind now, the glow had fully enveloped her. The light emanating from Dawn caught the eyes of some of the defenders, who were mingling in the courtyard below. They all turned to look up at her.

"I've got it! I've got it! The shield works! The Solari Aegis works!" Dawn shouted to the still-staring crowd. The light was now forming two pairs of wings behind Dawn, one high and stretching out over twenty-five feet in span, the other low and close to Dawn's body, reaching only knee height and shoulder width. The glow faded, leaving Dawn with distinct white angelic wings. Her blue top was not ripped, indicating that the wings had magically attached rather than grown from Dawn's back.

Dawn attempted to flap her wings to take to the air. The powerful wings lifted her into the sky, allowing her to hover over her command station. The defenders watched on in awe at Dawn's transformation. She changed before their eyes, from a mortal leader that directed men into battle into a radiant valkyrie capable of nobody knew what. The Solari Aegis glowed bright like the sun in the middle of the night. A ghostly image of a woman appeared in front of Dawn, bearing the same warrior angel appearance as Dawn had just taken, but clad in traditional Greek warrior battle gear.

"At long last," the spirit said, audible to the entire complex. By this point, all the remaining defenders had come outside to see what was going on. "At long last, the Solari have been reborn, as per the prophecy we had written so long ago. The next High Priestess has finally arrived, and she is just as magnificent as we imagined she would be. What is your name, High Priestess?"

"D-Dawn Ca-Cahill," Dawn stuttered as she stared in awe of the magnificent creature before her.

"High Priestess Dawn Cahill. I know not what Cahill means, but Dawn is a name befitting of a Solari High Priestess. Dawn, the time that the sun rises over the horizon, giving new light to the world. You, too, will give new light to a very dark world. It has been over two thousand years since my reign as High Priestess. I am Amynta, the last High Priestess of the Solari.

I imbued the statue with Apollo's light, but it would take a special person to wield it. When Sulla executed me, command over the statue passed to a girl that was born on that day somewhere in the world. Those girls never grew to realize their power. They likely lived somewhere outside of Greece. They could have been Phoenician, or Persian, or Roman, or one of the tribal peoples that lived to our north. So when that girl died, the power passed on to another, born on the day the last wielder died. That is how the power to activate the shield passed to you. Over the three millenia since the statue's creation, potential High Priestesses have taken their place in the tree of Apollo by taking their first breath as the former wielder takes her last. I have slept for three thousand years within the statue, waiting for a wielder and the statue to cross paths. This is the third time it has happened, but neither of the other two realized their power."

"The statue's crossed with a wielder twice before? And nobody's claimed it?"

"Yes. I could feel the presence of the wielder twice. I could track the passage of time from within the statue, but little else. One was two hundred years ago, and the other was nearly a thousand. Many wielders could have been poor girls, born far away from the statue."

"I think I've seen the statue before, now that I think of it." Laina added in. "I remember seeing art featuring it. I think it was the courtyard of the Vanderbilt manor."

Amynta looked around the courtyard at the Light's Bulwark refugees now watching from all over the compound.

"High Priestess, I see no warriors. I only see commoners. Do you not have warriors?"

"Those commoners you see are my warriors."

"I have never seen warriors look like your warriors. Where are their armor? Their weapons?"

"The armor of my warriors? The walls of my fortress are our armor. And our weapons? Look at those metal devices atop my towers. Those are the weapons of my warriors, along with these." Dawn lifted her sniper rifle and showed it to the spiritual Solari. "They're called rifles, and they're incredibly powerful. They shoot a small piece of metal at over twenty-eight hundred feet per second."

Laina, at Amynta's obvious dismay, quickly converted the modern units into ancient Greek units. "Rifles shoot a piece of metal weighing forty-seven obols a distance of five stadia in the time it takes to do this." Laina snapped her fingers, indicating one second. "They're kind of like a bow, except way more powerful. The ones on the towers are even stronger, hurling the equivalent of shot-put balls faster than your voice. All the weapons here are dependent on the principle that hurling a mass extremely fast does a lot of damage when it hits. Some shoot big masses, some shoot lots of little masses, but they all have one thing in common – they all shoot mass very fast."

"The Romans used a weapon that did that. They called it a ballista. It shot a heavy metal bolt fast enough that it could pierce anything except the stone city walls. Gates, armored men, buildings, statues, even Solari shields couldn't hold against their power."

"Exactly. Our siege weapons are just like ballistas, except way more powerful. That one over there, called a railgun, could punch clean through the walls of this fortress if aimed at them."

"Listen to me, young High Priestess. Your weapons might be exceptionally strong, but no Solari High Priestess can stand without her blade. Not just any blade will do for a Solari High Priestess. Each Priestess has their own blade. Some wielded weapons other than a sword. High Priestess Pherenike, the second High Priestess, was known for her use of a spear in place of her sword. A couple used an axe-like weapon called a thanaeko. But none ever used a javelin or a bow or any form of ranged weapon. Find it, forge it, whatever you need to do, but get yourself a melee weapon."

"Will do, High Priestess Amynta."

"And stop calling me High Priestess. You're the High Priestess now, not me. I am simply Amynta."

Chapter 9

The Second Battle

Light's Bulwark Fortress, West Virginia
A few days later, 2 AM

The fortress and its occupants slept soundly. The sounds of crickets could be heard around the mostly silent building, with the occasional hoot of an owl. There were only a few people awake in the fortress, and all of them were in the radar room. The night shift had only a radar contingent, just enough to awaken everyone if the compound fell under attack at night.

Points began to appear on radar as they emerged from the trees. The fire had burned a large amount of trees and grass, taking the tree line back a significant distance. The fortress radar now had better ground coverage, able to pick single units out all the way to the treeline two miles away. More points appeared around the edges, eventually forming a half circle around the fortress from the upper side.

"Hit the lights," one of the radar crew members said to another. "Something's out there, we need to see what it is."

One of the radar crew crossed the room and flipped the spotlights on. The lights expanded the vision of the radar crew, allowing them to see robed spellcasters at the treeline opening portals. Mindless swarmed from the forests beyond, where they couldn't be detected on radar through the trees, past the necromancers and towards Light's Bulwark. Cavaliers rode through the portals, commanding the mindless into a battle formation. Some of the disgusting flesh constructs emerged from the portals behind the cavaliers, followed by mindless in great numbers.

"We're under attack!" one of the observers yelled. "Sound the alarm!"

A klaxon sounded through every intercom speaker in the fortress. The sleeping refugees leapt from their sleeping bags and bedrolls as they woke suddenly. A handful realized that the klaxon was an attack warning, and that the fortress was under attack. Most of these were either military veterans, who had been on real bases while they were under attack, but some were former Call of Duty players who recognized the siren from their game. Most, however, were confused, having never been around any sort of raid siren.

"What the hell?!" one asked another.

"I don't know! What's that noise?"

For a few panicked seconds, the refugees looked around, unsure of what to do. Then, the voice of one of the radar operators came over the intercom, accompanied by the still-sounding klaxon.

"We're under attack! All hands to battle stations!"

In their room, Dawn and Julius awoke from their beds at the sound of the horn. Julius, like the others, did not realize that it was the zombie attack warning.

"What the hell, is the building on fire?!" Julius asked Dawn as she ran for her shoes.

"We're under attack!" she shouted back at him. "Get your rifle!"

Having both slept in their day clothes, they were mostly ready. Dawn and Julius put their boots on. Dawn grabbed the Solari Aegis off her nightstand. Julius threw his coat over his clothes and grabbed his rifle. Both raced out the door of their room and up the stairs to the rooftop. From the roof, they could see the entire battlefield. Strange creatures were starting to exit the portals. These creatures looked much like the gargoyle statues that graced certain old buildings, made from stone but animated by magic. Machine gunners were starting to turn their fire on these stone enemies, and though their attacks chipped away at the stone, they were mostly ineffective. Occasionally a bullet would hit near where the wings connected to their bodies, cracking and separating the wing and sending the creature plummeting to the earth below.

Julius turned his rifle on a cavalier and fired. Gunners started reaching their positions at Light's Bulwark's heavy weapons. As the heavy weapons came online, mindless started to fall in droves. The railguns and cannons were turned on the flesh golems, unable to be damaged by other means. Dawn held her shield in battle position, reciting the ancient oath of the Solari.

"Under daylight we will stand, triumphant, bright and tall
Under our relentless strikes, the enemy will surely fall
Break their ranks, break their hearts, break their armor too
Solari strike and Solari live, for that is what we do
Outnumbered and outflanked, we will always stand up strong
They might think they can beat us, but they are sorely wrong
Solari light will always win, the sun can never die
Wings of angels carry us, let the Priestess fly!"

Dawn's wings returned to her back, extending out to their previous dimensions. The Solari Aegis glowed brilliant yellow as she flapped the wings. Light poured through her, radiating intense heat, but to her it felt comfortable, like a day on the beach. Her body glowed yellow as her feet lifted off the ground. She felt stronger and faster from the shield's light.

"Going up! Julius, command the defense of the fortress! Let's see what Solari magic can do!"

Dawn's brilliant wings carried her into the air, charging straight for one of the flying stone beasts. The heavy shield, which she struggled to wield before, was now light to her as she soared through the air with it. She held the shield out in front of her as she charged the stone demon, swinging it in a sweeping arc as she flew past it. The Solari Aegis made contact with the gargoyle, shattering the spell that kept it aloft and sending it plummeting to the earth below. The statue crashed into the undead lines on the ground, killing several mindless and damaging others.

"Danielle, take out those flesh golems!" Julius called out. The girl who operated the railgun in the last battle was operating it once more. She turned the heavy siege weapon as her assistant loaded a shell into its breech. "Clear!" she shouted as she fired the weapon. The football-sized shell slammed into the farthest left flesh golem, blasting a hole through its torso and midsection. The shell's energy rippled the woven flesh as the golem fell, its animated heart disintegrated from the impact. The man loaded another shell into the breech with urgency as Danielle swiveled the weapon around to face another golem.

"Get those flamethrowers operational!" Julius shouted at Rick. The chief engineer was rushing around on the ground level to bring the cameras up for the flamethrowers, as the intense heat from the fire had warped internal components. The new cameras were having technical difficulties that Rick rushed to fix. The flamethrower operators stood, awaiting his orders to use their weapons. "Flamers, get on your guns! Ignore the cameras, just fire blind!" Julius ordered, and the flamethrower gunners took their chairs as Rick worked to get the cameras fixed.

Dawn's Solari-powered wings were proving to be a major edge in the battle. She found herself far more nimble than the flying gargoyles, allowing her to pass behind or alongside one and knock it out of commission. Dawn found herself endlessly repeating this process as the gargoyles tried desperately to move into position to assault her or the castle. Gunners on the castle ramparts were doing a good job of repelling the gargoyles, their constant attacks chipping away at the stone that made them up.

On the right flank, the machine gunners and riflemen were not having so much luck. Five flesh golems made it to the moat. Though they could not cross it, the golems were able to hammer at the walls of the fortress. The machine guns, unlike the heavy railgun, could not damage the flesh golems. Their magic repaired the holes as they were blasted. They were now too near the castle to fire the large cannon atop the upper ramparts facing down towards the wall without risk to the building's structural integrity. Jim, who was now on the right side of the lower ramparts, grabbed the intercom microphone.

"Dawn, we've got a situation! Five flesh golems on the east wall, we can't hit them with the cannon because they're too close! Do something!" Jim broadcast over the intercom system.

Dawn banked into a sweeping turn as she sent one of the stone gargoyles into a tailspin towards the ground. She came in, flying low, straight at the flesh golems lining the moat. Dawn performed a quick aileron roll as she came in, slamming one of the golems in the head with her Solari Aegis. The impact of the shield knocked the golem forward, causing it to lose its balance and fall into the moat. The other golems lashed at her, to no effect as the angular motion of her aileron roll deflected most of the impact force.

A rift in the sky beyond where Dawn fought the golems opened, revealing a floating eyeball. Dawn quickly turned to charge it, her four angelic wings carrying her through the air at dangerous speeds. The eye started moving left when Dawn charged it, though the ungainly sight ward was no match for Dawn's aerial agility. Dawn slammed shield-first into the eye at over a hundred miles per hour, her shield letting off a blast of light right as she struck the eye's retina. The blinded eye burst apart as Dawn passed through it. By this point, she was far beyond the main battlefield and flying fast in the opposite direction. She turned straight up and spun around, rolling back over to return to the battle. Her surprise Immelmann maneuver caught the enemy necromancers completely off-guard. Instead, they expected her to perform another wide sweeping turn and approach the golems from the side.

Now behind the golems, Dawn raised her shield again as the battle raged on around her. She came in low and fast, soaring over the mindless and momentarily drawing their attention before she flew far out of reach. The golems, still trying to attack the wall, completely failed to notice as Dawn came in behind them and pulled straight upright, using the full power of her wings to cause a pressure wave. The pressure wave's power pushed all the remaining golems forward slightly, enough to cause them to topple over and fall headlong into the moat.

The battle raged on around her, as Light's Bulwark's defenders fought furiously to keep their weapons loaded and firing fast enough to cut down the undead. Fires raged outside the fortress, the burning flesh of undead slain by the flamethrowers igniting the fallen undead that were slain otherwise, and even the still-moving undead that marched across the flames.

"There's no end to these things!" one of the defenders exclaimed.

"Necromancers, at the edge of sight! They're summoning more undead!" another shouted.

Julius picked up Dawn's sniper rifle, leveling it at one of the necromancers. The rifle's crack was lost in the sounds of chaos all around, but its effect wasn't. The necromancer dropped from the shot, his head blown into an unrecognizable state. Immediately a gap started to form in the undead lines as the portal he held open collapsed on itself. Dawn took to the skies once more, lighting a trail through the stone sentinels that still polluted the skies on a direct path to the necromancers on the left flank. Julius turned his rifle to the right flank, leveling it at the farthest right necromancer and firing. He, like his brother, dropped immediately, his portal collapsing on itself and preventing more undead from joining the battle.

"Take those necromancers out!" Julius called out over the intercom. "If we kill the necromancers, the portals collapse and the undead stop coming!"

The sky by this time was beginning to brighten. The sun wasn't peeking over the horizon yet, but light from it filtered into the lower atmosphere. The Solari emblem on the shield glowed brightly in the new light. Dawn continued through the wide arc set by the necromancers, dipping and rolling to dodge the shadow bolts they were now targeting her with. One hit her shield and ricocheted, hitting the ground at the necromancer's feet and blowing a chunk of earth free. The necromancer dodged backward, but was unable to dodge Dawn's diving strike. She came in at waist height, flying straight at him in level flight. Though her shield was too far left to hit him, she caught him in her opposite hand and dragged him skyward. He struggled to get off a spell against the extreme conditions as he was being carried, but never got the chance. Dawn expertly performed a split-S maneuver, pulling her into a screaming dive straight for the ground. She released the necromancer and leveled off, allowing him to slam into the ground at terminal velocity.

By the time Dawn's second necromancer made contact with the ground, Julius and the other riflemen had eliminated most of the necromancers on the right side of the fortress. The tide of undead advancing against the fortress had slowed, and the defenders on the right side were nearing the end of the first necromancer's forces. Still, the defenders fought a hard battle to keep them away from the fortress walls. Dawn was completely unaware now of the greater battle for the fortress as she flew out towards another necromancer's portal.

The mighty roar of the heavy artillery piece atop the east high tower shook the battlefield as it loosed an explosive round into the oncoming enemies towards the front. The shell hit and exploded, sending red-hot shards of sharp metal in every direction. The riflemen on the right flank, with the approaching numbers dwindling, started moving towards the center to reinforce them. The kill line started to move backwards slowly as the center got reinforced.

As Dawn approached, a stone gargoyle closed in on her. Not wanting to have it on her tail when she dive bombed the necromancer,

Dawn pulled into an inside loop to circle behind the gargoyle. Unable to perform the maneuver, the gargoyle continued straight as Dawn fell in behind it. Dawn closed behind it and struck it down with the Solari Aegis, returning to the necromancer as soon as the gargoyle was slain. In the time it took her to slay the gargoyle, another Light's Bulwark defender was able to shoot the necromancer.

With the last of the necromancers dead, and all the portals closed, the endless flood of undead pouring towards the fortress had ended. The remaining undead, those who had passed through the portals but had not died yet, would still need to die. The defending riflemen reinforced the center, shredding rank after rank of mindless. Still, thousands of mindless remained.

Dawn hovered over the center of the approaching enemy and held her arms out. Light shot from every pore in her body in a prismatic attack. The radiant beams fired in rapid succession, searing the mindless on contact. The angles rapidly shifted from each beam, killing new undead with every change of angle. Under the combined fire of the prism, machine guns, and riflemen, the thousands of undead remaining were obliterated.

"Any known casualties on our side?" Dawn asked over the intercom, her Solari light now fading.

"None." a voice replied. "No casualties on our side. Your east flank might have taken some damage though."

"We'll start fixing it in the morning. Dave, Rick, you guys will have to use the suspension cables to work on it."

"Gotcha, Dawn. You need to figure out everything you can about the Solari and your shield and the magic. You've just proven it's a valuable weapon. Now we need to figure out how to really use it. The prophecy says you'll be able to smite the undead and heal people."

"Well, didn't I just smite undead? I'm halfway there." Dawn said, laughing.

Chapter 10

Loki's Ancient Blade

Flame Point Fortress
That Same Time

"Cavaliers are going down in West Virginia again, Stacie. There's another battle going on, and there's a few hundred cavaliers in the area this time. Get a demon's eye up so we can see what's going on."

She selected the place on the map where her demon's eye needed to be spawned, a site where one of the cavaliers was slain, right outside Light's Bulwark Fortress. Focusing everything she had, she channeled her demonic power onto the spot, summoning a flying sight ward nearly ten feet in radius.

The spell went off as planned. The nether rift opened on the site and the eye emerged, displaying its frontal vision on the back display. Stacie could see everything now. A colossal fortress, armed to the teeth, laying waste to rank after rank of mindless. Their cannons and railguns ripped apart the great flesh golems, the creatures Aaron and Stacie believed would devastate the remainder of the living. Riflemen lined the walls, felling cavalier after cavalier with well-placed shots. The machine gunners filled the air with lead, each shot chipping away at the stone gargoyles. And among them, a four-winged angel flew, taking gargoyle after gargoyle down with light-blessed shield slams.

"No!" Aaron shouted as he grabbed a stone and threw it at the display.

Aaron and Stacie continued to watch the display, focusing on the airborne angel. She dived in, guarding her flank from the flesh golems at the walls. With a roll of her wings and a strike from her shield, she sent one of the golems toppling headfirst into the dry moat and onto the blades below.

"Rift stable." Stacie reported. The summoning spell had finally stabilized. The eye was now fully operational, showing all three hundred and sixty degrees of vision from ceiling to ground. They could see the angel make a quick turn away from the castle and scale her flight angle upward.

"What the hell is she--" Aaron started, but was cut off by Stacie.

"Evasive maneuvers!" Stacie shouted at the display, calling on her magic to move the eye out of the way. She quickly found that steering the ward was like piloting a zeppelin. The slow, bloated ward was no match for Dawn's blistering speed. Just before Dawn made contact with the eye, she pulled her shield in front of her and charged it up. A burst of blinding light shot through the eye and the display into the command room of Flame Point Fortress, hitting the back wall over Aaron and Stacie's heads. The blast cut a hole through the demonic metal of the fortress, leaving a panoramic opening behind. The metal not touched by the light held firm and prevented a collapse, but it was clear immediately that this was a bad strategy.

"I'm not summoning any more of those things, Aaron. This time that angel punched a hole in the fortress. Next time that blast could hit us, and there's no way we'll survive it. We need a better vision source. I'm gonna do some major magic craft. I need to downsize the eyes so I can embed them in constructs... oh no. Had that angel realized the error I made, she'd have flown through the eye uncharged. If the light can blast us through the eye, she can probably go through it too and come through the display. That was almost the end of our reign."

"I'm bringing the plague cannons in. Only problem is, all the necros are down in the entire East Coast. The nearest necros I have are all the way out in Montana. Mindless can't drive, only the necromancers can. When I had one necro warp the others in, I made a blunder. I left three dozen plague cannons in Braxton County, and now I can't get them to Kanawha. Stacie, more magic craft for you. I need to be able to drive all of them from here. Otherwise I'm gonna run out of necros and the cannons will be useless."

"I've already got several projects running, and you keep taking my necros and techs away and sending them to the front lines--"

An alarm sounded in the command hall for a process a level down, in the magic lab. Stacie cut herself off and immediately ran through the door. One of the two helix ramps led her down the spire to the next level down, the lab floor, where many of Stacie's magical projects was underway. One of the devices she was using, a magical matrix analyzer, had printed a reading of the high altitude Himalayan terrain. Above twenty thousand feet, the cold temperatures and thin air froze the demon's eyes Stacie used to scry on her enemies. Thus, Cloud Peak Monastery, atop one of the highest mountains in the world, was immune to any scrying. This troubled Stacie and Aaron, who wished to eliminate the monastery to further their summoning of the demon lord Tyadrig.

Stacie grabbed the paper from the reader. It showed remnants of magic from shaman long ago who practiced elemental magic here. The magical signatures of these spells showed that they called on the element of fire to protect their people from the bitter cold. By accounting for the time involved, Stacie could re-create the original signatures, giving her a spell pattern she could easily cast. The flame ward the shamans used on their people could be used to ward her demon's eyes against freezing. Excited, she raced back to the command chamber with her findings.

"Aaron! I got it! I can cold-proof the demon's eyes!"

"Cold-proof them... why would you... Cloud Peak!" Aaron suddenly exclaimed. "We can figure out how they have food, then we can put a stop to it! We'll break one of the three remaining strongholds without even needing Ondesverd and Damupanga! Do it! I'm gonna check on the blades!"

Aaron again called on Olaf Falkenskold, the Norse barbarian leading his forces in the area. Most of the mindless were in this area, digging through snow to find a mythical blade. Olaf led the effort as a field marshal, keeping the monumental task going all day and all night, every day, since victory in the theater was claimed.

"Falkenskold!" Aaron bellowed through his mind link. "Progress update!"

"More intelligence came up. It details the blade being laid to rest in Loki's Cave, but there's no maps of caves around. It makes finding the place far easier though, since digging to find a cave is far easier than digging to find a sword. I'm directing the mindless specifically to places where caves are known to exist. I'm gonna need some necros to--"

"Commander!" a voice said from Falkenskold's end. It was an undead cavalier, another form of intelligent undead, mounted on a zombified grizzly bear. "We've found something! A cave buried in the snow! They're digging it out now! Come!"

"My lord, send one of those wards out here. You can watch the discovery of Ondesverd yourself!"

Stacie summoned another demon's eye to Olaf's side as he mounted up on a powerful undead horse. The cavalier's bear lead the way, Olaf and the demon's eye in hot pursuit.

They trekked across what seemed like miles of endless snow before reaching the cave. It had been buried by an avalanche in one of the coldest parts of Scandinavia long ago, protecting the cave and its contents from discovery for hundreds of years, since this part of the world never warmed above freezing. Undead laborers were inside the dark cave, still digging the snow out in an organized chain. Stacie stopped her sight ward at the entrance of the cave.

"The demon's eye won't fit in there." Aaron pointed out.

"Aaron, you're an idiot. Surely he's got at least one necro with him." Stacie answered.

"I've got one, why?" Olaf replied.

"Warp me in." Stacie ordered as she grabbed Aaron's hand.

A necromancer, one of Olaf's overseers at the dig site, focused his energy through his hands. A ball of corrupted energy began to form between them. He stepped back from it, muttering an incantation in Demonic. Green light projected onto the snow, forming the image of Stacie and Aaron. The same green light enveloped the real Stacie and Aaron, back at Flame Point Fortress. The light faded at Flame Point as the light at the dig site intensified, and eventually the light faded fully at the fortress. Stacie and Aaron appeared in the green light at the dig site.

"Let's go." Aaron commanded.

Olaf made a gesture to the cavalier who guided them to the cave, ordering him to wait outside. Stacie took point, holding her hand out and shining a light from it to see by. The trio walked deeper into the cave, branching into the left tunnel. The snow had been cleared out here, allowing free passage. The cave twisted and wound in a wide helix downward, eventually reaching what looked to be a tomb. Stone burial fixtures sat in recessed holes in the walls, with words written within in an ancient language. At the far end of the tomb, an ornate burial fixture rested. Olaf rushed to the ornate fixture and kneeled to the plaque on the side. It, too, had an inscription in Old Norse. Olaf began to translate.

"Here lies Gunther Sigurdsson. His prowess in combat knew no bounds. Surely Loki chose him as his avatar because of this. He fought valiantly, though he was ultimately defeated by Njall Vollundsen, Avatar of Thor. Though he fought for Loki, he died bravely in battle, and Valhalla will welcome him with open arms."

"Loki chose him as his avatar?" Aaron repeated. Surely this would mean that Ondesverd was buried with him.

"That's what it says. I didn't even think that myth was real." Olaf replied.

Aaron walked triumphantly over to the tomb and pulled the stone cover. It didn't budge.

"Olaf, pull the other side," he commanded. The massive barbarian did as ordered, and between the two of them, the heavy stone moved towards them, revealing the frozen, preserved body of Gunther Sigurdsson, his hands clasped around a shining sword. Aaron reached down and seized the blade by its hilt, prying it from the hands of the dead warrior. As he held the blade, its power awoke. The ancient magic of the Norse people flowed through Aaron, reacting to the demonic magic he already carried. The voice of his dark lord could be heard echoing through the cave.

"My champion, you have uncovered an instrument of my dominance! The ancient blade of the Norse god of death is now yours to wield! With this blade, slay the angels that stand against me and bring me their wings!"

"Tyadrig!" Aaron and Stacie shouted out in unison. But there was no response – the demon lord had already returned to his own realm.

"No matter. We have what we came for."

Aaron slid the blade under his belt, then pulled a small stone from a pocket. The stone was polished and engraved with a single rune, one that could roughly be translated to "home" from the ancient heiroglyphics. He traced the rune with his finger, and the stone began to glow. Stacie did the same.

"Olaf, gather your forces and await further orders. I'm going to deploy you to a battle zone soon."

"Of course, my lord."

The runic stones' glow slowly enveloped Aaron and Stacie, pulling them through the realm of magic back to their fortress.

"One down." Aaron said as they made it back. "One to go."

Chapter 11

Weapons of Science and Magic

Dawn's Chamber, Light's Bulwark Fortress
After the battle

A small amount of light peeked into the room from outside. Though the days were getting shorter, and the windows of the room faced towards the north, some sunlight could still enter the room and illuminate parts of it. Dawn sat on her bed with her back to the headboard, still wearing her battle clothes. The Solari Aegis lay on the nightstand on the left of the bed. The expression on Dawn's face was one of worry.

"How are we gonna hold out..." Dawn muttered to herself as Julius removed his heavy coat. "That was still less than a million undead that attacked us, and there's billions left. If they throw everything at us at once, we'll never survive..."

"Dawn." Julius replied as he untied his armored boots. "You've got the answer right beside you. That prismatic attack you just did. Did you see what it did, how fast it shredded their rank and file?"

"No, using that attack blinded me for the duration. I wasn't sure what was doing what damage."

"You did almost all of it, and the next source after you was the already-burning fires set by the flamethrowers. Maintain that prism long enough for us to snipe the necromancers warping enemies in, and any force they have can't get here."

"What about the golems that got to the walls?"

71

"We now know about the weakness on the right flank. We can bring something else to bear there. I bet your anti-materials rifle can damage the golems, and I'm sure Red's strong enough to fire the thing, maybe even without the bipod. On top of that, they still can't jump the moat, so a hole in the walls doesn't help them. They'll get a few cavaliers in, and with the riflemen trained on the hole, they won't get far."

"We'll still get overrun. The moat won't keep them out forever. Eventually they'll fill it up, and there isn't much we can do to stop it."

"And when they start falling in the moat, I'll hit the flush levers in the basement. That moat's gonna turn into a raging river and wash them all off the back of the cliff. They'll all fall apart when they hit the road, and that's just the ones that didn't fall apart when they hit the steel bottom of the moat."

Julius wrapped Dawn in his arms. "You know more than anyone what the defenses of this place are capable of. You're also forgetting a major weapon in our arsenal, the Helix."

"What can I do to undead with the Helix? And if I'm flying the Helix, I can't do your prismatic thing either."

"Can't Nadia fly the Helix?"

"Okay, so Nadia flies the Helix. They've got what, four thousand shots before they're done? So they turn that machine gun on the enemy, spend all their shots, then what? They're useless up there."

"False. I wasn't thinking of the minigun at all. I was thinking more of the fuel tank we used to burn the slain undead. What happens if we spray them with it while they're alive?"

"The flamethrower fires are gonna catch, and everything is gonna burn."

"Exactly. We just douse anything we don't like in gasoline. There's plenty of it in all the tanks at all the gas stations. Nobody had power to get it back out. Plus the refinery downstairs makes more every day out of the oil we're pumping out of the ground. And Rick said he could amp the flamethrowers up. That's gonna bring the burn line farther out, and keep everything back."

Dawn relaxed at the mention of Rick and the flamethrowers. "Rick really is brilliant, isn't he? Guy can make anything work. Maybe he can build us something that'll solve the problem."

"Then we'll talk to him after we've gotten some rest. They blew their load in that last attack. They've got nothing around to hit us with for a long time."

Julius held Dawn as her tired body relaxed and dozed off. He too dozed off, but it was a fitful sleep fraught with nightmares of Light's Bulwark falling and Dawn dying to the undead. He awoke with a start, finding himself back in their room at Light's Bulwark. Dawn still slept beside him, undisturbed. He laid back down, but sleep would not return. He still worried about what Dawn had said, about how this battle, though it took all night and pressed the defenders to their limits, was only against less than a thousandth of the enemy's total force.

He got out of bed and crept across the room to where he had removed his boots and his coat. He put both back on and left the room, going down the stairs to the courtyard. He took the freight lift to the basement level, where Rick and the other engineers had been given a workshop area. Inside, Dave and Jason stood over a table looking at a drawing of a conical device. They did not notice Julius enter.

"We have to put a couple refractive balls in." Jason said, pointing to something on the drawing. "It's the only way that's gonna work."

"How are we gonna give Dawn a place to stand then?" Dave asked. "If we put balls at the focus points, then she won't be able to get in."

"What are you doing?" Julius asked.

"Oh, hey Julius." Dave replied. "We think we can make something amazing if we can get the details right."

"That prismatic attack Dawn did in the battle?" Jason mentioned. "We think we can harness it and turn it into a sort of laser. This device we're working out the details of basically focuses all that omnidirectional light into a single beam pointing out the top. We're not sure how we're gonna aim it yet, but once Rick gets up he can probably figure something out. Maybe we'll build a turret or something."

"And you need refractive balls... what, at the focus points of the mirrors?"

"Yeah. But right now, the mirrors focus exactly where Dawn needs to stand." Jason replied.

"What would happen if you changed the angles of this row of mirrors?" Julius suggested. "These are the ones focusing where Dawn needs to stand, so if you angle them up, they'll focus downward. Does that help?"

"They'll still hit Dawn though." Jason answered.

"But if we did that, we could build a mirror ring around where her feet would go." Dave figured. "She could step over it to stand where she needs to, and it would reflect the beams into the ground. Those mirrors are focused on the lens, so the light will go in the right direction eventually."

"Julius, you aren't an engineer, are you?" Jason asked.

"I was a civil major for a couple years. Took some of the initial engineering classes and some of the math." Julius replied. "I couldn't pass the bridges class. I just can't seem to get some of the math, so I changed my major. Dropped out the next year and started working down at Eagle driving a forklift."

"Oh." Jason said. "Well, that still explains how you saw that. You've probably had about two thirds of what Dave and I have. We're only juniors, we haven't had senior mechanical classes yet. Emily's a junior too. Rick's the only senior among us."

"Rick's only a senior in engineering school?"

"Yeah, what did you think he was?"

"A grad student maybe?"

"That place doesn't have grad school. They do a three plus two program with Morgantown, but that's it. Rick's just smart as hell. I don't know how he does it. Em and I studied like four hours a night, did all the homework and went to class every day and we still made C's. Rick doesn't even show up for class half the time, never does the homework and still had straight A's. I swear he's a legit genius."

"Wow. In that case you guys didn't even need me. I'll go back upstairs and leave you guys to this. Good luck, I really hope you can get that thing working."

"Thanks. And thanks for the help."

Julius took the freight elevator up to the courtyard and climbed the stairs to the second floor. The library was on this floor, taking up the entire western wing of the floor. Laina sat in an oversize chair reading an old tome titled "Heroes of the North". She never looked up from her book as Julius entered, only acknowledging his presence when he spoke.

"Laina? What are you doing?"

"Oh, hey Julius. I couldn't sleep. I'm too wound from the battle, so I came in here to read. Hey, check this out. There's a passage in here you need to see."

"What's it about?"

"It's about an ancient battle, but the part about the blades is what I wanted to show you. Looks like this battle took place in Scandinavia. You're familiar with Norse mythology, right?"

"A little. Like, I know a few of the gods. Mostly what they've touched on in the Marvel universe."

Laina laughed at the Marvel comment. "So you know about Thor and Loki then."

"Yeah. They're brothers, and Thor's the good one and Loki's the evil one. And they hate each other."

"Well, I guess they decided to see who's followers were stronger. Each brother was to choose a champion, and those champions would fight to the death. My guess is Loki thought he could trick his brother into a battle he couldn't win, since Thor's superior strength didn't mean anything here since he wasn't the one fighting."

"Yeah, that sounds like Loki. I like this, keep going."

"Loki chose a warrior called Gunther Sigurdsson. He was considered by his tribe to be a peerless warrior, and he wielded a sword Loki blessed himself. It was called Ondesverd, translated from the Norse as "the sword of the dead". Sigurdsson was supposedly able to rally his troops to fight through grievous injuries and slay their enemies, even injuries that should have crippled them. Thor thought long and hard about who he would choose as his champion, and finally decided on Njall Vollundsen. Njall was smaller than Gunther, but he was faster. Thor granted him a mythical blade to counter Ondesverd. This blade was called Maktdrikker, translated to 'consumer of magic'.

Anyway, Gunther and Njall fought in single combat. When Maktdrikker and Ondesverd first clashed, the magic Loki used to craft Ondesverd was absorbed into Maktdrikker. This angered him, and he began to cheat. He continuously funneled magic into Gunther to replenish the magic being siphoned by Maktdrikker. Though Maktdrikker was absorbing magic, Njall couldn't do anything with that magic, so the battle continued. Gunther wasn't fast enough to damage Njall, and Njall wasn't strong enough to get through Gunther's defense. The battle lasted three days straight before Maktdrikker finally broke.

When it broke, the magic that had been absorbed over the battle poured out in a beam. Njall pointed the end of the blade at Gunther, and the magic beam penetrated right through his armor and stopped his heart."

"That's a really cool story, but what's the deal with the blades?"

"Well, my sister told me something before the war broke out. She was dating this guy named Lee. Real piece of work. Didn't matter what I told her, Nikki just wouldn't leave him. He treated her like shit and she just stayed with him."

At the mention of Lee's deeds, Julius cut Laina off. "Sounds like the Lee that Dawn dated for a while. Did Lee beat Nikki too?"

"I think so, but Nikki's always been super clumsy so I don't know what's him hurting her and what's her hurting herself."

"Where's this guy from? I wonder if it's the same person."

"Braxton County."

"It's him. It's the same Lee. I know it is. God, I thought that bastard would've quit abusing women after I knocked out three of his teeth."

"That was you?"

"Yeah." Julius replied. "Back when Dawn was with Lee, my brother Adrian was dating her friend Robin. Dawn got beat up and Robin took her to our place. Lee tracked her down and showed up on my doorstep to get her back. Threw the door in my face when I answered it and just went to go grab Dawn."

"I don't see you taking that lying down."

"I don't see that either. An abuser comes to my home and hits me with my own door to try to abuse his girl some more? You know what my dad was like. He'd have beat my ass if I didn't hurt the bastard. Anyway, I knocked his ass to the floor and kicked him in his face. Then I broke a couple ribs and a couple fingers before I pitched him back out the front door and called the cops."

"Wow." Laina extended a hand as to give Julius a high-five. "I'd buy you a beer, but there's that whole zombie apocalypse thing going on. When I saw what happened to him, I actually said to myself, 'I need to meet the guy who did that to him and buy him a beer.'"

"Everyone, except my dad and my brother of course, always told me not to get involved in other people's domestics. Something about the woman's gonna defend her abuser. Didn't work that way here. I think when I stood up for her it made Dawn realize she's actually worth something."

"Good for you then."

"She promised me that night she'd find a new guy who actually treated her well. The next day she came back and wanted me to ride with her in her limo to the city."

Laina looked down at her book, and suddenly realized they had gotten off on a tangent.

"Oh, the whole reason Lee came up." she said. "He believed in magic when he was with Nikki. He was trying to make some kind of magic sword that could do what Maktdrikker does. I'm pretty sure he's dead, but I have to wonder how close he came. Braxton's not that far, I think you should look into it."

"Didn't the high priestess say something about Dawn needing a blade?"

"You're right, she did. It would qualify for that too." Laina replied. Suddenly, she jumped up and took off across the library towards a table with another tome on it. "The prophecy!" she shouted excitedly.

Julius caught up to Laina quickly even though she ran away from him. He noticed that Laina's strength did not translate to movement speed. To him, what Laina called a run was an awkward walk-jog. She grabbed the book, the same book she had shown to Dawn before, and opened it to the page with the prophecy.

"Aphrodite's strength has turned, replaced by the realm of Styx," Laina read. "Aphrodite's strength is love, and the realm of Styx is hate. Dawn used to love Lee, and now she hates him."

"Former allies part under no uncertain terms." Laina continued. "Nobody has any doubts about what they feel towards each other now."

"One, the Dawn of a new world, the other, the sadist of his own prison." she read. "We all know now Dawn is the 'Dawn of a new world' from the other prophecy. Lee is definitely a sadist."

"But together once more, they will be rejoined, on the fields of battle, against the world's greatest foe." Laina recited. "The world has never faced an enemy so formidable as Aaron and Stacie."

"His blade and her shield will guide the path to survival." she finished. "Dawn is going to use that blade to win the war. I bet the blade's still in Braxton County. It's probably still at Lee's."

"Laina, that information is critical. I'm gonna tell Dawn about it as soon as she wakes back up. Now I'm going back to bed. I'm still exhausted."

"Good idea." she replied. "I think I'm gonna go to bed too."

Chapter 12

The Spell-Drinker

Light's Bulwark Fortress, West Virginia
The next afternoon

Dawn finally awoke with Julius beside her, still sleeping. She cuddled him and kissed him awake.

"Hm?" Julius asked sleepily.

"Come on, we should get up."

"Mmh." Julius muttered as he sat up in bed. "How'd you sleep?"

"Good, once you helped me clear my doubts. How about you?"

"Not so good. I got up and walked around. Apparently Rick and the others are building some kind of laser weapon in the basement. Oh, and Laina deciphered the prophecy about Aphrodite and Styx."

"Oh? What did she come up with?"

"The blade it mentions is a real blade. The mentions of Aphrodite and Styx are love and hate. The Dawn of a new world is you, which we knew, and the sadist of his own prison is your ex Lee."

"Why bring him up..." Dawn asked, saddened by his mention of the past. "I told you to never say his name."

"It's important. The blade, the one you need to win the war, is probably at his house. We need to go and recover it."

"I'm not going out there. I can't. Not after what he did to me there." Dawn frowned and shuddered at the horrible memories.

"I'll take Nadia then. She knows how to fly the Helix, you said it yourself. But I'm going. We have to know if that blade exists."

"Fine. Go. I'm staying. And you're still an ass for mentioning him."

"Nadia, report to the Helix pad. Nadia, to the Helix pad." Julius announced over the intercom. Nadia surely would report, expecting Dawn to take her out on another mission. Nobody ever knew the missions Dawn had planned here, not even Nadia, until the Helix was in the air. One day, Dawn might take the Helix to raid supplies left over from before the war. Another, she might drench undead in gasoline from the sky and ignite them. The third, she might ferry naval personnel. Today, she wasn't even going.

Nadia found Julius awaiting her at the Helix pad. The Helix was being prepped by one of the prep teams brought over from the USS Abe Lincoln. The crew from the Lincoln was increments faster than the Light's Bulwark defenders, having trained properly in how to prepare a helicopter for launch. Occasionally, one would get tripped up by the differences in the Soviet-built Helix against the American Chinook, but these instances were few and far between. The last step, finishing the refueling, was taking place as Julius found Nadia.

"Nadia, it's just you and me today. Dawn's not going. Our mission is to retrieve a mythical blade that I think can help us against the undead."

"A blade?" Nadia asked. "But we have all this firepower, why do we need a blade?"

"It's the one mentioned in the prophecy. The first one was right about Dawn being a Solari high priestess, so I think we should believe this one too. Laina cracked the code and figured out about Lee's magic blade. We think it's a replica Maktdrikker."

"What's a Maktdrikker?" Nadia asked, confused.

"It's a legendary blade from Norse legends. Anyway, it absorbs magic from things it hits, so I think it'll give Dawn a good way to kill those flesh golems she's so worried about."

"Without punching holes in our walls too."

"Exactly. You know how to fly the thing, as soon as they finish refueling, take us out of here. I'll navigate."

Nadia seated herself in the pilot's seat of the Helix. The controls were familiar to her by now, but this is the first time she had operated the craft without Dawn at her side. Julius would be no help except in directing Nadia towards the weapon. The ground crewman removed the fuel hose from the Helix, giving the all-clear sign as he put it away.

"Spinning up engines." Nadia announced as the twin rotors atop the Helix started up. The helicopter started to lift itself off the ground unsteadily, rocking back and forth as Nadia struggled to stabilize it. As it reached height to clear the walls of Light's Bulwark, Nadia increased the speed of the rotors to maximum. The Helix climbed much faster now, getting to cruising altitude quickly. With a push forward on the yoke, the Helix nosed down and surged forward, reaching cruising speed with little trouble.

The eighty mile journey from Light's Bulwark to Lee's home in rural Braxton County was relatively uneventful. There were no sightings on radar, either undead or human. Parts of the land were killed off by some form of blight. The land nearest the houses was barren, all of it unseeded dirt. Away from the houses, crop fields were overgrown with weeds. This pattern confused Julius, who had been shut inside Light's Bulwark for the better part of the last year with Dawn.

"Nadia, do you know anything about this? Why's the land around the houses barren, but the crop fields overgrown with weeds?"

"Julius, they had toxin cannons. Don't you know about that?"

"Toxin cannons? Dawn and I locked ourselves behind Light's Bulwark's walls right after the war broke out. We didn't have much contact with the outside world."

"The toxin cannons. They first appeared in the Battle of Pittsburgh. It was there that we realized we had a chance, even though it seemed like we were facing certain defeat. We lost the battle, because of the cannons, but we decimated the mindless. I was the only survivor. I took a boat off the docks and drove it down the river, all the way to the road below Light's Bulwark. That's where I met up with the others."

As the Helix approached Lee's farm, Lee's things started to come into view. The ground around Lee's farm was littered with the slain corpses of undead. His truck, a big silver Dodge pickup, sat in the weeds. His home looked broken into. Burned up bones littered the area, as if charred by some form of energy blast. The house itself was charred and decaying. What used to be a cornfield lay burned up nearby.

"There. In the burnt-up cornfield. Can you land there?"

"Sure, hold on."

Nadia brought the Helix down, slowly easing off the throttle to set the chopper down gently. As she got close, she jerked the throttle back nervously, causing the Helix to jar against the ground. The helicopter was unhurt by the impact, but the force rattled their teeth. Julius exited the helicopter first, pulling his pistol as he turned toward the house. Nadia exited as well, also drawing a pistol.

"It looks like the undead already attacked this place. I wonder if they took the blade." Julius said as they approached.

Inside the house, much of the furniture was burned up. The floor was littered with skeletons, all charred and mangled. A door led into an unknown place, obstructed by a skeleton and a metal drum. Julius knocked the metal drum on the ground and pulled on the door with force. It didn't budge.

"Locked. Let's see if there's anything we can use to open it." Julius said to Nadia as she moved into what appeared to be an attached shed. Most of the tools had wooden handles and were thus useless after the fire, but Nadia was able to find a blackened crowbar amidst the ruins. "Try this!" she shouted to Julius as she raced back over.

Julius and Nadia placed the crowbar between the door and the frame. The crowbar was sufficiently long for both to pull on its end. Under their combined strength, the door frame separated from the wall, taking part of the locking mechanism with it. With the lock broken, the door swung wide open, revealing a basement level.

The basement level was vastly different from the outside. Down here, everything was in perfect condition. It seemed the battle never reached this level. A blacksmithing forge was still burning with a magical flame. An entire shop full of machining equipment, all seemingly undamaged, sat with metal filings and scraps all around. A book sat on a workbench, open to a page in a strange language. A finished sword, inscribed with a rune from the book as well as two other runes, stood in a corner propped against the wall. Papers littered the workbench written in English, detailing the spellwork of the runes on the blade. Together, the runes spelled out "consumer of magic".

"Consumer of magic," Nadia said aloud. "Is this the blade we came for?"

"It is. If this works the way we think it will, we might have the weapon that wins us the war." Julius answered. "The priestess told Dawn she needed a blade. I think we should give this one to her."

"There was a prophecy too. Laina solved it. We think this blade is the one from the prophecy, and that Dawn is meant to wield it."

The earth shook suddenly, as if a bomb had hit nearby.

"Now!" Nadia yelled as Julius grasped the handle of the blade. They raced up the stairs as the ground shook again. A third shake caused Julius to stumble. As they made their way through the charred house, they realized that the shaking was caused by artillery shells falling nearby. As the shells hit, green clouds of what could only be assumed to be poison expanded from the impact sites.

"Get to the chopper!" Nadia shouted at Julius. The pair ran to the Helix and Nadia spun the rotors up. The spinning rotors pushed the air away from the body of the helicopter, keeping the expanding clouds of poison at bay. Julius checked the minigun mounted in the nose of the helicopter. Its four thousand round magazine was full and ready to fire. As Nadia pulled the Helix off the ground, Julius grabbed the radio and signaled Light's Bulwark.

"Light's Bulwark Fortress, this is Helix One. We have the blade. We're lifting off and under heavy artillery fire! Repeat, we are under heavy fire! Minigun is fully loaded, moving to engage!"

The Helix took to the sky as artillery shells fell all around. Once above the treeline, Nadia and Julius could see clearly – three dozen artillery pieces firing shells towards the house that they were just inside minutes ago. Nadia moved the Helix towards the artillery pieces, diving towards them to allow Julius to fire. Julius fired the minigun in short bursts, aiming at each artillery piece before firing. As the lead fell downrange, the cannons turned towards the sky. They opened fire on the flying Helix, but attempting to shoot a flying helicopter with a cannon is futile at best. None of the shells even flew close to the helicopter.

The Helix strafing run was incredibly effective. In the first pass, Julius cut apart nine of the weapons, killed the mindless crewing the cannons, and killed the cavalier commanding the operation. Without the cavalier's command, the mindless stopped firing, unable to coordinate the necessary intelligence without the psychic link to the cavalier. Nadia pulled the bird around for another pass, giving Julius another chance to shred the remaining poison cannons. In this pass he shredded six more. In a third pass, he ripped apart another eight, bringing the kill count up to twenty-three.

A light on the control panel lit up amber, reading "minigun". The ammo counter read "424".

"We're low on ammo. Should we waste any more of these guys?" Nadia asked as she checked the new lights.

"Why not? We'll get to reload back at base anyway, and I guarantee the Helix can outrun those gargoyle things. You were at the second battle, you saw how easily Dawn outpaced them. Bring it around for another pass."

Nadia turned the helicopter around for a fourth pass. Julius turned the minigun on the remaining artillery pieces, exhausting his ammunition and killing seven more. With their kill count at thirty, only six remained operable. The minigun, having used up its supply of ammunition, made a dry clicking sound as the trigger was held down.

"Okay, I'm dry!" Julius called out to Nadia.

"Light's Bulwark Fortress, this is Helix One! We've got thirty confirmed kills on these artillery pieces. Ammo's exhausted, we're oscar-mike! ETA thirty-eight minutes."

"Helix One, this is Light's Bulwark. We read you. Excellent work out there." Rick's voice could be heard over the radio.

With the artillery silenced, the journey back to Light's Bulwark was uneventful. There were no sightings of gargoyles or any other undead along the way. The Helix arrived back at base at the predicted time. Nadia sat the helicopter down on the landing pad on the third attempt, botching the first two due to poor alignment. Dawn's eyes lit up as she saw Julius exit the Helix with the blade in hand.

"It... it's real? You recovered it?" she asked.

"Looks like it, but we won't know if the magic works until we use it in battle. It's called Spell-Drinker, and according to the plans, hitting an enemy with it will drain their magical energy and store it for later use. If it works, it's a one hit kill on the undead since they're animated with magic. It looks like it's supposed to be able to release the magic as a ranged attack too. If that magic blast is powerful enough, you can kill the flesh golems with it. Even if it's not, you can still hit the golems with the blade and drain the magic used to build them."

"This might be very useful. If it works, of course."

Chapter 13

Laying Siege

Flame Point Fortress, Peru
The next day

Stacie prepped her spell in front of the large viewing point in the fortress dome while Aaron stood by. She placed a box of matches alongside a piece of charcoal, a can of gasoline, and some dried leaves. Stacie placed the leaves in the bowl and the charcoal on top of them. She then poured the gasoline into the bowl over the charcoal and leaves, and placed the can on the ground. She struck a match and dropped it into the gasoline, igniting it.

"Tya vikzon rathiel eiyos, qapith adali gavetol!" she said as she pointed to a place on Aaron's map designating where the monastery in the Himalayas was. The view screen showed a monastery with Buddhist monks preparing for battle in the courtyard. The monks looked up and watched the demon's eye forming over their monastery. One hurled a stone at it, but the stone glanced off the side of the sight ward harmlessly.

Stacie placed her hand over the burning bowl and flexed it, turning the fire inside green. She raised her other hand towards the view screen. "Zyath Vieron Cthuuni!" she spoke, and the demon's eye burned green while the bowl was extinguished. The heat from the flame repelled the extreme conditions at the mountain's peak where the monastery was built.

"Rift stable. Eye operational. Protections active." Stacie reported as she controlled the eye. It showed her the monastery, its placement, its

85

population... and the trap door in the courtyard that led into the old tunnel used by the People's Army.

"Aaron, do you see that?" Stacie inquired. "There's a trap door on the ground. I'd bet it leads somewhere at the bottom of the mountain. That's probably how they're feeding themselves. We don't have the cavaliers there, so they're sneaking through and raiding the abandoned villages of canned goods. They're strong enough to beat up mindless, so mindless alone won't stop them. We couldn't figure it out because they weren't killing the cavaliers."

"So we just march up the passage and kill them all. Easy."

"No. Not easy. That's the same mistake the Chinese made. We're gonna find their tunnel, and we're gonna put flesh golems in front of it. We've got the parts for flesh golems already in the area, from the mindless they threw off the cliffs. We've even got necros in the area to build them. They'll all starve in days."

"I'll have Jiang do that then. Jiang!" The commander in the Asian theater appeared on the display.

Jiang was a dissenter from China who wanted to see the Communist regime toppled. Aaron and Stacie provided him the strength to overthrow it. The poisons they released into the waterways quickly crippled the People's Army, killing millions and creating an army of corpses to attack the villages with. Anarchy broke out as the army fell to the combined power of the poison and the undead. Jiang and his army stormed Zhongnanhai and carried the Premier from his palace to his death on what he now called Justice Day.

"Commander, what is it?"

"We figured out what's going on at Cloud Peak Monastery. They've got a tunnel through the mountain that leads down into the villages. They're raiding all the canned goods and leftover supplies, and killing your mindless with their fists. Round up your necros and set 'em to work on flesh golems. Round up your mindless and put 'em in front of the tunnel entrance. Stacie, give him a sight ward to follow."

Jiang ordered the necromancers under his command to the valley beneath the ridge from where the monks knocked the mindless off the ledge. After so long, the frozen bodies and bones of the mindless had accumulated. They were stacked atop each other in an unorganized heap from battles with the monks, forming a landfill of the dead. To the necromancers, this pile of mixed flesh and blood and bone was a nearly endless supply for flesh golem parts.

With a tendril of dark magic, one of the necromancers reached into the pile and extracted a femur with bits of rotten flesh still hanging from its sides. The other necromancers followed suit, targeting the bones as they sorted through the grotesque pile. Every bone extracted from the pile was placed in a pile. Occasionally a fully intact slain mindless could be pulled from the valley. These were sorted into a separate pile. The patches of flesh were sorted into their own pile, though the necromancers tended to extract either bones or intact and semi-intact mindless with their tendrils of darkness.

While the necromancers toiled in the pits of flesh-shaping, Jiang followed the sight ward Stacie had laid down. The demon's eye followed the cliff line along the Chinese side of the Himalayan range, looking for a road that could carry heavy People's Army military equipment into a cave. Though the length of the Chinese section of the Himalayas is immense, the Chinese were known for their efficiency before the outbreak. With no need for food, sleep, or even to rest from a full sprint, Jiang and the demon's eye were able to find the caves in the possible hundred mile stretch within six hours.

Stacie, with her vision from the demon's eye, plotted the caves on a map of the Himalayan range and the roads in the area. When compared to a map of roads in China from before the outbreak, the roads led to the city of Shigatse from only one cave. Another cave had a road leading to it, but it only led to farming villages. None of the other caves even had roads leading to them. With that information, she directed Jiang to which cave to assault.

"Follow the demon's eye," she directed Jiang. The demon's eye, though it could easily keep pace with a man in a full sprint, was unable to maneuver quickly. Stacie steered it in wide arcs when she needed to redirect it, and tried as much as possible to avoid changing directions. She sent the demon's eye back to the proper cave, Jiang in hot pursuit. Though the demon's eye could not fit inside the cave, once Jiang knew where the cave was, the trap was set. A nearby necromancer set up the first gate of a portal nearby. All that had to be done now is the creation of the flesh golems.

The necromancers worked consistently, having no need for food or sleep. They, like all the other undead creations of Aaron and Stacie, did not need the things the living needed. All they needed was the supply of magic, that which Tyadrig fed to Aaron and Stacie and they fed to their creations. In the hours it took Jiang and the demon's eye to track the caves, the necromancers had sorted some of the bones out of the pile of flesh. They placed some of the bones on the ground in an array. Two skulls were placed at the top. Two spines were woven into one and formed the creature's spine. It took two of each leg bone to make one of the creature's arms, and two of each arm bone to make one of the creature's legs. The reversal of the bones gave the arms the crushing power to break walls and crack skulls while still retaining mobility. These creatures were slow, but their massive frames compensated for this weakness through unparalleled fortitude.

Flesh was pulled from the pit in a torrent of grotesque bodies and dark magic. It formed around the bones the necromancers had assembled, forming into feet, legs, hands, arms, and eventually a torso and head. Eyes could be seen protruding from various places on the limbs. A tongue stuck from the creature's chest. A jawbone could be seen protruding from its knee. The fifteen foot tall amalgamation was covered in flesh of mixed age, giving it a partially rotten appearance. The creature reeked of disease and death. Teeth stuck from its mouth at odd angles, clearly not attached to a jawbone the way human teeth are. One of the necromancers held out a sharp hook and lifted it with dark magic, attaching it to the abomination's left arm.

With a wave of his hand, the necromancer started opening a portal, linking with the one near Jiang. The magic rippled as the mage wove the spell components together. Eventually a portal opened, one with a large enough opening to allow the newly-created flesh golem through. The first flesh golem took up its place at the mouth of the tunnel as Jiang stood by.

The necromancers at the flesh pit continued to lay bones in the array and pull flesh to them. Each completed flesh golem walked from the staging area through the portal, being directed into position by Jiang. Only the one was equipped with a metal hook, but many were built in the same way with sharpened jawbones, or fitted with teeth as claws. All were grotesque monstrosities, ugly creatures that stunk of rot. Though the flesh-crafting operation took all day and most of the night to complete, the army of amassed flesh golems stood at the entrance of the tunnel at the end of the night, fifty strong and ready for battle, with the ten necromancers among them.

"This is gonna be easy." Aaron said to himself as he observed the goings-on at the base of the mountain.

Chapter 14

Making Repairs

Light's Bulwark Fortress, West Virginia
Three days after

Dawn walked down into the basement, where Rick and the other engineers were gathered around a strange chamber about seven feet in diameter.

"What's this?" Dawn asked. "And you guys still need to fix the eastern wall. Remember how the flesh golems damaged it in the last battle?"

"It's something I call a Lens Chamber, or well, it's gonna be. We think we can build something similar to an ion cannon from it. But anyway, the wall. We'll stop this to go fix the wall since it's more important than our pie in the sky superweapon."

"Rally on me!" Rick yelled to the other engineers as he moved towards the lift. The other engineers fell into formation around him, and they all took the lift to the ground level.

They gathered on the eastern wall of the fortress near where Dawn sent the flesh golems into the moat below. These flesh golems, still unburned, were the only remaining undead in the area. The fall into the moat onto the blades crumpled the golems on top of each other, forming a disgusting mass of flesh and bone that occupied a portion of the moat. The engineers crumpled their noses as the stench from the decaying golems reached them.

Rick picked up the microphone for the eastern ramparts position.

"Julius, flush the moat with forge metal from the fourth flush point. We need to get rid of the golems in the moat before I can fix anything."

Julius, who was in the courtyard at the time, stayed seated at first. He was playing poker against a couple of the Navy guys and a few other defenders. He peeked at his cards, showing him the Jack and King of Spades. Laid down on the flop was the Ace of Spades, Ten of Spades, and Ace of Diamonds. Opposite him, a man bearing the insignia of a Seaman First Class sat, eyeing down Julius. He looked down at his cards. He had two Aces, the Ace of Clubs and the Ace of Hearts. His hand would have four aces. Surely he was unbeatable, but Julius called his extremely high bet. The turn came – the Three of Spades. Julius now had a flush, not strong enough to beat the seaman's four of a kind, but better than the three of a kind Julius thought the seaman had.

The seaman raised another five thousand. Even though Julius knew the odds were probably against him, he called. The seaman might be bluffing. His card might come up on the river. The seaman might just be playing aggressively, expecting Julius to just fold to go attend to his duties. The river card came up – the Queen of Spades. Now, Julius had taken the advantage. His hand, now Ace through Ten of Spades, would be good enough to beat four Aces. The seaman, not noticing the royal flush on the board, raised another five thousand. Julius raised his raise, going all-in at twenty-seven thousand eighty-four.

The seaman saw the royal flush on the board when Julius went all in. He thought for sure Julius was bluffing. There was no way he was holding a royal flush. He called, going all-in at twenty-three thousand even. Julius would still have chips left after the loss the seaman believed was imminent, but he would be down a lot of chips. The seaman flipped over his aces with confidence, smirking at Julius as he said "four aces". Julius slowly flipped his cards, showing his Jack and King. "Straight flush, ace to ten," Julius said with a smile on his face.

The burly seaman slammed his fists on the table as Julius calmly pulled the chips from the center of the table into his own pile. "Come on, it's not like we're playing for money. Or that money's even a thing any more." Julius remarked as the seaman stormed off and cursed under his breath. He started to sort the chips, stacking organized piles ten chips high based on denomination. When he finally had his chips organized as he intended, he spoke up.

"Check/fold me, dealer. I have to go figure out what they're calling me for."

As Julius stood and left the table, his organized pile of chips still at his place, the dealer took some chips and placed them in the center of the table. The player to Julius' left placed twice the number of chips taken from Julius' pile in the pot. The dealer began to lay cards around the table as Julius walked away. Once the dealer got back around to Julius, he checked to see if Julius owed the pot chips. Since he still owed the remainder of the big blind, the dealer swept Julius' hand up as a fold.

Julius walked down the stairs to the forge to B2F. The forge room was a full-fledged blacksmithing shop, a hobby he had taken up when he moved here with Dawn. She had given him this room as his workshop, and he used her father's money to fill it with tools. The workshop's forge was built into the wall, using pumps and pipes that formerly carried water to link it to the moat. Though Julius could hold metal in the heat with his blacksmithing tongs, he could also push it to the back and fill a reservoir with fully melted metal.

Julius started feeding metal into the forge, pushing it to the back with his tongs. The metal he fed into the forge came from the scrap pile Dawn had dropped into the catch point with the Helix magnet. He left the door to the forge open, tossing handfuls of metal at the open door. After a few handfuls, he would take his blacksmithing tongs and push the metal to the back, where it would fall below into the reservoir and begin to melt. Julius fed roughly eighty pounds of metal through the forge door in handfuls, filling the reservoir to about half.

He closed the forge door and the temperature began to rise again. With the door open, the forge lost heat to the workshop, but the closed door kept the heat in. Additionally, adding the room temperature metal reduced the forge's temperature greatly. He would have to wait for nearly an hour to get the metal to reach the proper temperature to melt.

When the gauge finally read the proper temperature, Julius turned his eyes to the five levers above the forge. Each lever corresponded to a flush point in the moat above, opening the valve for the pump to drive the hot metal to the right point. The levers were aligned with the points. The fourth lever was the one Julius needed to open the valve and pour molten iron across the flesh golems now occupying the moat.

Julius leapt and grabbed the lever, letting his weight pull the lever down. A valve opened on the front side of the golems. The pump kicked into action, pumping molten iron up from the subterranean forge to the moat level. Red-hot iron flowed in a slow, viscous flow from the valve to the flesh golems. The intense heat from the molten iron half-melted, half-burned what remained of the golems' bodies. The blades, made of a tungsten alloy with a far higher melting point, remained intact and did not even warp from the heat of the molten iron. Thanks to the downhill slope of the moat, the iron flowed only one direction – down the moat, over the flesh golems, and towards the exit point on the cliff face.

With the flesh golems gone, work could finally begin. However, one problem still remained. Even though the iron had flushed down the moat, the radiant heat was still too intense for Rick and his crew to descend down the face of the wall to make repairs.

"Julius, the flesh golems are gone, but now the heat's too intense for us to get close. Flush the moat with water and take the heat away so I can actually do something." Rick called to Julius using the intercom.

Julius returned to the freight lift, taking it to B4F where the water treatment facility existed. He raced through the narrow hallways and avoided the low-hanging pipes as he headed for the diversion chamber. To reach the chamber, Julius made a forward dive over a pipe at three feet off the ground. With a quick roll, he returned to his feet and ran once more. He finally reached the diversion chamber, the room with the levers that allowed him to divert water flow from the fortress to one of the dispersion points. Again, he threw the fourth lever, releasing a torrent of water through the pipeline that only minutes previously carried molten iron. The cold water steamed as it surged through the pipeline, at first only emitting pressurized water vapor. It finally poured from the drain point, rushing down the moat and driving the residual heat from the molten iron away.

"All clear Julius. You're cleared to restore water to the fortress."

Julius forced the lever back to its resting position. The torrent stopped pouring from the drain point, and soon after stopped falling from the face of the cliff down onto the road. Water was restored to the main functions of the fortress, such as toilets, sinks and showers. Julius left the diversion chamber at a fast clip, once again tumbling over the midsection pipe blocking the hall. Once past the midsection pipe, he continued to duck and dodge the pipes. He reached the lift and took it back to ground level. Julius never reported to Rick at the top of the fortress. He instead took his place back at the poker table. The bulk of his chips were still as he left them, minus the few that were taken as blinds while he was away. "I'm back." he said, as the dealer was about to take his cards for an automatic fold. "I'll play this hand." Julius laid his bet down, equal to the blind for the hand.

Back at the eastern ramparts, Rick was securing a few suspension cables. The engineers had already gathered the spare bricks at the top of the ramparts. They had also gathered bags of mortar cement, tools, buckets, and a platform that could be lowered with a suspension cable. The engineers were still running supplies from inside the fortress up to the ramparts.

"Listen up." Rick said as soon as he had all the engineers on the ramparts. "Dave, I want you to drop down on the suspension cable and determine how much damage the wall took from the golems. Emily, start mixing the mortar. Jason, I need you to help me prep the platform. We need to load it with bricks so we can lower some to the team."

Dave secured his suspension cable and started his descent down the side of the wall until he found the portion the golems had damaged. Their powerful strikes had cracked some of the bricks on the outer facing. This was the only visible damage. The cracked bricks would need removed and replaced, and Dave hoped that the damage didn't extend deeper into the wall. Surely the golems weren't strong enough to make that happen, especially given the limited time they had to beat on the wall. Eventually they might be able to damage it, much like a man with a sledge hammer, but Dawn refused to provide them such time.

Jason lifted the unladen platform while Rick lifted the suspension cable and fastened it to the four support cords. With this configuration, the platform could hold a load without tilting. Jason carried the platform over to the wall as Rick aligned the suspension cable with the pulley bolted into the wall for this exact purpose. Rick held the cable securely as he gave the command to drop the platform. Jason dropped the wooden platform over the wall of the fortress to the ground below, but Rick's strength ensured that it never fell. Rick pulled up on the cord, bringing the platform back to the edge of the wall.

Jason turned and looped the slack end of the cable through a loop on the inner side of the floor, and another on the inside wall. Jason held strong, giving Rick the signal to release his own hold. The platform, now secured with mechanical advantage, never fell despite Jason's loose hold on the cable. The platform was now ready to be loaded up with bricks. With the mechanical advantage the array had created, Jason could hold, raise and lower a load of bricks with little difficulty.

Dave returned to the top of the wall, hoisting himself through use of the cables.

"Okay Rick, looks like some of the surface bricks and some of the mortar joints are cracked." Dave reported.

"Alright." Rick replied. "I'm gonna grab a cable and go down too. Get a masonry saw and a grinder. We need to get this fixed before the undead attack again."

Jason dropped the platform to the level at which Rick and Dave were working. With their tools in hand, Dave and Rick secured their suspension cables and dropped down the side of the wall to where the golems had damaged it. The pair located any brick that had damaged mortar or cracks in its face, cutting around them with the saws. Every cracked brick was thrown into the moat, but the good bricks with bad mortar were placed on the platform instead. Jason continued to hold the platform stable, even as Rick and Dave placed bricks on it. A small section of the wall's face was removed, providing sight on the bricks underneath. None of the underlying brick was damaged in the attack, making the procedure far easier.

"Dave, go up and send Emily down. Have Jason haul the platform up and put some more good bricks on it."

Dave used his suspension cable to pull himself back up the cliff face. He detached himself from it and Emily attached herself to the cable Dave was formerly using. Jason pulled on the rope, lifting the partially laden platform up to rooftop height. Dave carried bricks, two at a time, laying them carefully on the platform as to not let any fall. Emily secured herself at work height as Dave finished loading bricks. Jason lowered the rope to Emily and Rick, providing them with bricks. Dave lowered the mortar bucket using a separate cable.

Emily and Rick got into a system, allowing Emily to lay down mortar and Rick to place a brick. The actual brick laying was the easiest part of the entire operation. Once everything was in place, this went quickly. The pair laid bricks at a decent clip, quickly fixing the damage to the wall. Once all the bricks were in place, Rick braced himself against the newly laid bricks. Holding them in place let Emily slide her trowel in to fill the top sections with mortar. Without mortar holding the tops of the new bricks to the bottoms of the old, the wall's strength would suffer and it would take damage more readily. This took Emily time, but the entire repair was done within a day. Thanks to the suspension cables, nobody needed to venture outside the walls to fix anything.

Dawn visited the repair site as the engineering team was cleaning up after themselves.

"Rick, how's it lookin'?" she asked.

"Excellent. All bricks are back to full strength. This wall should be able to continue to take a beating from those things. Just don't let them hammer the wall for days straight and we'll be fine," he replied.

"Great. And the moat systems worked as intended?"

"Yep. Julius flushed the moat with both metal and water. Everything seems to be working perfectly."

Chapter 15

Tracking the Survivors

Flame Point Fortress, Peru
A couple days later

Stacie was milling around her magic laboratory. She was awaiting a test to finish. Tracking living humans still evaded her, but she was modifying an ancient spell the shamans once used to track prey for their tribes. So far, she could get the spell to track plants and non-sentient creatures, but it wouldn't work through the demon's eyes yet. This time, however, Stacie called on her demonic allies for the power behind the spell. Using an integrated power source should, she believed, make the spell easier to relay through the demon's eye.

Currently, a demon's eye floated over what was once the city of Alice Springs, dead center of the Australian continent. Many of the buildings here still stood, but the entire city was devoid of human life. Sand had been blown in from the surrounding desert. The US flag still flew from the long-abandoned base here. Animals used the human-built roads to get around with ease.

The demon's eye rose into the sky, higher and higher, until Stacie finally stopped it. To climb to a sufficient height, Stacie would have to cold-proof the sight ward to prevent it from freezing in the high altitude. Just like before, Stacie gathered her reagents. She needed a bowl, dried leaves, a piece of charcoal, and her gasoline can. She placed the leaves in the bowl, with charcoal on top of them, then poured gasoline over the leaves and charcoal. Once Stacie carried the remainder of the gasoline away from the ritual point, she snapped her fingers to ignite the mixture with a magic spark. Orange fire burst to life in the bowl.

"Zyath Vieron Cthuuni!" she cried, and the demon's eye covered itself in green flame, warped from the nether transport, while the ritual bowl extinguished. Stacie took control over the ward again, allowing it to resume its climb. The demon's eye ascended through the clouds, expanding Stacie's view outward in all directions, until finally the entire Australian continent was visible with part of the surrounding ocean.

Formerly, Stacie had performed this spell using five candles, just like the ones she used at the Inca temple. These candles allowed her to summon the five elements to her call. Though the elements were powerful, and enabled her to obtain the power of death, they weren't calibrated for her demon's eyes. This time, she was going to power her spell with a different power source – the burning hearts of the brothers Tyadrig, Krovon and Aarix.

Stacie placed an orb that contained purple fire, symbolizing the empty heart of Tyadrig. Next to it, she placed one containing red-orange fire, serving as the fiery heart of Krovon. Forming a triangle with the other two, she placed one containing green fire, for the toxic heart of Aarix. When placed in the array, the orbs of flame held against gravity, staying perfectly in place instead of their natural tendency to roll away.

Stacie poured a powder from a cup in a circle around the orbs. She placed along the circle of powder a bit of fur from a fawn, another bit of fur from a rabbit kit, and a couple feathers from a chick. She set light to the powder with a magic spark, releasing a fragrant odor from early spring flowers. These emblems of spring would provide the essence of life the spell needed to synchronize with the world's life.

"Hearts of the Brothers, empower my actions!" Stacie shouted. "Channel the essence of life through the eye of the Watcher, and show me what still lives!"

Most of coastal Australia lit up green, with small patches and individual points of green scattered throughout desert Australia. Stacie drove the demon's eye higher, allowing New Zealand and parts of Indonesia to be encompassed in the field of view. Though the salty ocean water blocked the spell, the islands lit up green as well, still carrying their flora and fauna. Stacie drove the demon's eye lower, closing back in on the area around Alice Springs. The resolution improved as she got closer to the ground, showing individual animals and plants as green points once she got the field of view down far enough.

The spell test was successful. Stacie could locate non-sentient life through her demon's eyes. For Aaron, this could be a breakthrough, allowing him to cut off the food supply easily and efficiently. Though he had set the undead to work destroying the farmlands, grasses and forests already, a precision targeting system would give Aaron the ability to hasten the process. Stacie ran from her spell lab up to Aaron's command center.

A display from another demon's eye, the one in Tibet, was on the main display window. Aaron was somewhat watching it, but mostly paying attention to a book written by a voodoo priest from the Congo. The voodoo priest was from the time when King Leopold's Belgians attacked. The priest had attempted to negotiate with the Belgians, and had even learned Dutch to communicate with them. Once the Belgians understood him, they understood that he knew the magic of voodoo. To learn voodoo for themselves, the Belgians arrested the priest and demanded that he write an instructional book on voodoo. They threatened to annihilate his tribe if he failed to comply. The priest wrote the book, but the Belgians were unable to reproduce what the priest had described. The priest was executed and his tribe annihilated during the Belgian reign, and his skull was placed on display at the Belgian governor's keep. After the Belgians left the Congo, they left the skull atop the keep, where it still sits today. The keep is now owned by the Kinshasa government, as a reminder to the residents of the evils of white man.

Stacie immediately drew Aaron's attention. "Aaron, I've made a major breakthrough!" she shouted.

"This better be important, I'm looking for knowledge on how to find Damupanga." he snapped back.

"I have a spell that allows me to track non-sentient life through the demon's eye!"

"I thought you could already track non-sentient life. What we need is to track humans."

"Yes, but I could only do it up close. Now I can do it through the demon's eyes, so I can do it anywhere on the planet."

"And the application of this is..."

"Australia. Remember how you ordered Wellington to eliminate the plants and animals?"

"Yeah..."

"Well, Wellington has his command post at the old US base in Alice Springs. If I shift command of the demon's eye to him while it's tracking non-sentient life, he can use his psychic link to the cavaliers to dispatch mindless in a targeted fashion. It'll make the process go way faster."

"There's a use for it." Aaron answered.

Aaron called on his own psychic link to the Australian field commander.

"Wellington!" he shouted as Stacie switched off the main viewer. Aaron's psychic link took over the viewscreen, showing General Roger Wellington in clear view.

"My lord! What news do you bear?" Roger replied.

"You have any necros on you right now?"

"Yeah I have one, why?"

"Warp Stacie in. She's gonna shift control of a demon's eye to you."

After a few minutes, a necromancer entered the command post and appeared at Wellington's side. He began to focus energy through his hands, forming a ball of tainted magic. His unintelligible speech in Demonic projected a sickly green image of Stacie in front of Wellington. The green light enveloped the real Stacie back at Flame Point Fortress, pulling her through the nether and across the globe to Wellington's command post in Alice Springs.

Stacie appeared in front of what was once a working video call screen in the command post. Before the war, generals and commanders used this very screen to have conferences with each other from all over the globe. Alice Springs in its heyday was a base for US forces to observe China, the South Pacific, and Oceania. Its commander was one of the highest ranking US generals, and was informed of many of the strategic and tactical developments in any war. Now, the screen rested at the front of the room, unused and without power since the place was abandoned.

It was this screen Stacie focused her magic on. It would be the best surface from which to project the demon's eye sight. Within seconds, the screen displayed the demon's eye sight as if it were actually turned on. Though the power source was magical and unrelated to the device's former functionality, the final effect was the same. A picture showed on a screen, changing as Stacie moved the demon's eye around. She flew the demon's eye close enough to the command post for the post to be visible on the screen.

"Wellington, there's your command post. If you go outside and look up, you'll see my demon's eye. Right now, I control it because I am its summoner. But if you stand back, I can turn this old drone control into a panel for the ward."

Stacie focused another spell into a control panel in the room. This panel, back when Alice Springs was an active US military base, operated an MQ-1 Predator drone. These drones were used in the time of humans to watch areas of ground and attack enemy targets on them. These very drone controls had been used to attack Al-Qaeda operatives in Afghanistan and Pakistan during Operation Enduring Freedom. Now, they sat covered in spider webs, without power, as decrepit reminders of what was once here. As Stacie focused her magic into it, the panel lit up as if it had power.

"Try it out. I've fused the demonic thought magic into the controls of the panel. Use the buttons and sliders to operate the demon's eye."

Commander Wellington sat down at the old drone panel and brushed the dust and cobwebs away. He pulled up on the yoke and pressed forward on the old thruster control, launching the demon's eye into a forward climb. It still moved slowly, but the ward responded to Wellington's movements of the yoke, thruster and yaw. The limitations of the control panel prevented the demon's eye from moving any direction but forward. When Stacie controlled these wards with her magic, she could move them in any direction regardless of the ward's facing. In the heat of combat, this could be a detriment, but the wards were not intended for this purpose anyway.

"It works. This tracking grants me the ability to clean the continent. I'll report back when I've been successful. However, I have one question. How many toxin cannons can you spare? I had fifty, but I lost them all to the bloody grenadiers and rocket men in the battle of Perth."

"I have three dozen in West Virginia, but it'll take me a while to get them here. I'll need to send necromancers out there to warp them in. Since all my necros in North America are out west right now, I'll probably need to figure out how to generate portals remotely to access the damn things. The hundred or so I have in Russia might be easier to get to you. I actually have necros closer to them since Aaron wants the cannons to use on the Swiss. Surely I can send you some. Be on the lookout for a communique from me, that way I can warp them in to your necromancer."

"Thank you, my queen. I'll have this continent cleaned in no time."

Chapter 16

Powers of a High Priestess

Light's Bulwark Fortress, West Virginia
That same day

Dawn was training with her new blade in the courtyard. The Spell-Drinker was intended to be a light sword for Lee, to make quick but not exceptionally powerful strikes. For Dawn, it was heavier compared to her body, so she couldn't swing the blade with as much speed as it was designed for. Though the blade still felt comfortable in her right hand, her strikes were not as quick as they should be. *This will probably fix itself when I'm in angel form*, Dawn thought as she continued to swing the blade with her right hand. *The shield's too heavy for me when I'm not in angel form too.*

"Try letting your strikes flow into one another." a male voice said from behind her. Dawn turned around to see Julius standing behind her, holding a metal rod that was to serve as his sword for this exercise. Julius stepped away from Dawn, giving both room to swing their weapons without fear of striking each other. Julius swung his rod in a cross-body strike, allowing the rod's momentum to carry the end upwards on his left side and back down into a second strike in the opposite direction. As the rod fell back to his right side, he pulled it back up and into another right to left downward strike.

"It's a really effective technique any time you have to use a blade that's too heavy for you. You will never have to use your strength to impede the motion of your blade. Try it."

Dawn swept her blade right to left, letting the weight of the blade carry it through the back part of the strike. She used her strength once again to slam the blade through the second strike, letting the weight of her strike and the blade carry it up into position for a third. As she continued striking one after another, her strikes became stronger and more furious.

"This is easier, but what happens when I actually hit something? It'll stop my blade, so it'll stop my momentum." Dawn spoke up after a couple minutes of swinging her sword.

"Pull towards you and keep it moving. Watch me." Julius said, turning to face Dawn. "Raise your shield."

Dawn raised her shield in front of her body and braced herself. Julius brought the steel rod down, striking the shield with an echoing blow that rattled Dawn from the edge of her shield to the base of her back foot. As the blow landed, he pulled the rod back towards his own body, letting its weight lift it back around and above his shoulder. He brought the rod down again, and with a clang of metal on metal the steel bar hit hard against the bronze shield. He pulled the bar across the shield a second time, keeping as much of his downward motion as he could to carry the bar back into striking position. After the second strike, Julius lowered the bar, having no need to continue striking the Solari Aegis.

"Pass me your shield," Julius requested, and Dawn slid the shield off her left arm for him. Julius slid his arm through the back strap and grasped the handle, returning the steel bar to his right hand.

"Go!" Julius said, and Dawn swung the Spell-Drinker straight at the Solari Aegis. Just as Dawn had the Spell-Drinker raised, Julius raised the steel bar into striking position. Dawn brought the Spell-Drinker down in a crushing two-handed strike aimed straight at her own shield, which Julius parried with the iron bar at the last moment. His parry was barely strong enough to prevent the blade from striking the shield.

"Stop!" Julius shouted at Dawn as he leapt back. "Jesus shit!"

"What?" Dawn exclaimed, astonished at Julius' random freak-out. Then it hit her what she almost did. "Jesus H. Christ, we almost lost the entire war!" she exclaimed.

"What the hell are you talking about?" Nadia inquired as she ran over from across the courtyard.

"Julius and I were trying to train, and he was showing me how to use this sword. He used that iron bar as his sword, showing me how to keep my sword moving. Then I handed him my shield and went to use my sword to practice. I almost hit the Solari Aegis with the Spell-Drinker."

"Okay... won't the shield hold from a sword hit?"

"The shield will, but the magic wouldn't. The Spell-Drinker would have drank the Solari Aegis' magic, then I wouldn't have my Solari power."

"Oh hell Dawn! How did it not happen?"

"Julius noticed what was going on and parried my attack... barely. Thank you, baby."

"Don't worry about it. It was my fault too, I was the one who told you to do it." Julius added.

"We have a forge." Nadia mentioned. "Can't you build a shield instead of using the Aegis? It doesn't have to be any good, it just has to block attacks. So Dawn has her own shield and sword, and Julius can use the ones forged here."

"Good idea."

"Dawn, get up to the roof. This is major." a male voice rang out over the intercom.

"That can wait. Let's go." Dawn said to Julius as she took off towards the front doors.

When Dawn reached the rooftop where the comms array was, Laina was awaiting, seated at Rick's side as he manned the communications array. She had yet another book from Dawn's own library, a barely read volume on the Battle of Salamis. It detailed a part of the battle not recorded by most historians, the role of the Solari High Priestess and how destructive she was to the Persian ships.

"Dawn, this is a very interesting passage, and it might give you a huge advantage – the ability to fly off at hypersonic speeds and annihilate a lot of undead. Listen up." Laina started, then began reading from the book.

"And I launched from the flagship with my four wings extended, out over the Persian fleet. The shield of the Solari shone in the bright sun. The admiral attacked while the Persian commander was watching me. Themistocles was a brilliant commander, despite not knowing what we Solari were capable of. He had built a trap perfectly for us to exploit.

He lured the Persians into attacking both sides of the strait. His fleet surged ahead, directly into the Persians' weaker side. The Persians had many more ships than Themistocles, but bravely he fought.

It was in that moment that I was different from the other Solari, from the other High Priestesses. I, High Priestess Eleftheria, had the emblem of Hermes painted on the back of my Aegis. Hermes was the Mount's swift messenger, faster than any other being. I let Apollo's light surge through the emblem, and felt the messenger's speed in my wings. I pushed myself faster and faster, eventually hearing a loud boom. When I passed over the ships at this speed, the sailors spoke quickly when I approached and backwards once I passed. I pushed myself still faster, to speeds I couldn't even measure.

Themistocles' fleet slammed into the Persian fleet's disorganized flank as I passed back over both. With my speed, I crashed shield-first through the hull of one of the Persian ships. My body skipped across the ocean when I hit the water beyond. When I circled back around, the ship I had hit was no more than flotsam in the sea. The Persians aboard, now floating in the sea, bled from their ears and noses. Two nearby vessels had capsized, though the seas were not harsh and there were no Greek vessels nearby. I dove at another Persian ship and crashed through it. My Aegis crackled with power and beamed with light. I skipped across the ocean once more and sailed skyward. When I came around for another pass, I saw another ship reduced to flotsam and three more capsized. It was then that I realized that I, with my speed that no human would ever match, was flipping the boats with the force of my wings."

Laina closed the book. "Apparently this High Priestess Eleftheria used magic from both Apollo and Hermes. I think she was flying faster than sound, since she said the sailors spoke quickly when approached and backwards when she flew away from them. But the key was painting the emblem of Hermes on the back of her shield."

Rick added to Laina's observations. "Eleftheria used it to punch holes in wooden ships. You can use it to fly around the world. And we have gauges to see how fast you actually fly, and thus how fast Eleftheria was in the Battle of Salamis. Get the emblem on the back of your shield, then let us know. We need to do a test run."

Chapter 17

Upon the Wings of Hermes

Light's Bulwark Fortress, West Virginia
Shortly after

Dawn stood by at the Helix pad, watching with Nadia as the Navy team prepped the Helix. By now, they had gotten used to the Soviet-built chopper and the differences between it and the American Chinook. Their training and practice was truly making a difference in prep times. The addition of the avionics crew of the *Roosevelt* had reduced the prep time for the Helix by nearly half.

The commander of the avionics team finally marked the last check off on a checklist, the one Dawn used to run pre-flight. He held his clipboard in front of Dawn and Nadia as he informed them that the pre-flight checklist was done and they were ready to lift off. Despite Nadia's recent flight experience, Dawn raced up to the pilot's seat, leaving Nadia to slide her thin frame between an avionics crewman and the open door to enter the Helix.

"Clear the pad." Dawn shouted at the avionics crew. "We're lifting off."

The avionics men scattered in all directions away from the Helix, leaving Dawn to fire up the coaxial rotors. She lifted the Helix off the ground and up over the walls of the fortress, giving her a view out for miles around. There were no signs of undead anywhere nearby. Dawn brought the Helix out the back way over the main body of the fortress, over the road and out to the river. She followed the river the entire way, not bothering with her navigation equipment until she reached the river-port city of Charleston.

Charleston had fallen before the undead ever reached the city. A chemical plant between Charleston and Light's Bulwark had a tank near the river rupture while it was still operational. Thousands of gallons of a deadly toxin poured into the Kanawha River. This toxin flowed down the Kanawha into the Ohio and eventually the Mississippi, poisoning millions and wiping out soldiers by the hundreds right as Aaron and Stacie made their move on the United States. The timing of this terrible disaster of engineering could not have proved worse for humanity. Now, the banks of the river still leech traces left over from the toxic spill back into the river. Most of the fish in the river were killed in the disaster, and it still remains too toxic for most fish.

Dawn fired up her navigation equipment as the city came into view. Her navigation system was taking her to an abandoned art store on RHL Boulevard in South Charleston called Michael's. Finding the store in the abandoned city was easy. The undead here likely were expended in the first or second battle, leaving none back to defend the city. Dawn set the Helix down in the parking lot of the store.

"Why are we going to a Michael's?" Nadia asked, perplexed.

"Laina found something major. Apparently if I paint the emblem of Hermes on the back of my shield and channel the light through it, I can go hypersonic." Dawn replied.

The pair entered the unlocked store. Dawn walked through purposefully, with Nadia trying to keep up.

"No idea where that'll help us except to cover us all in golem goo. If you hit a golem at hypersonic, you'll liquefy it and blast parts in all directions. And isn't that sword already supposed to kill them?"

"If I can go hypersonic, I can cross the globe quickly. Maybe the Navy can pull an evac operation in Tibet. Based on their numbers Rick's getting off the scanners, there's no way they can hold out unless they've got supplies stockpiled like we do."

"Maybe you can go hypersonic and blast those cannon things apart too." Nadia contemplated. "Those toxin cannons Julius and I killed probably aren't the end of his force."

"Good thought. That might work too."

Dawn and Nadia reached the paint aisle. Dawn lifted a silver bottle of acrylic paint and a pack of brushes. "These should do," she said as she pocketed them. "The original illustration of Hermes' symbol on Eleftheria's shield was silver in color, so I'll follow suit. I don't know if it matters, but if it does, I'd have to come back out here again and waste time that isn't on our side."

"That's everything we need here?" Nadia asked.

"That's it. Let's get out of here. We shouldn't be in any danger, but let's not chance it."

Dawn and Nadia walked purposefully back to the Helix. Dawn placed the small items in the front holding tray, not having bothered to bag them at the checkouts. She fired the rotors up and lifted the Helix off the ground, steering it over the power lines and buildings of Charleston towards the river. Dawn followed the river along its course back to Light's Bulwark, not bothering with her navigation equipment. The trek along the Kanawha was uneventful, and Dawn laid the Helix on the pad with no difficulties.

She exited the Helix with the supplies in hand and immediately took off towards the library on the second above ground floor, only stopping at the nearest intercom microphone to summon Laina to the library. When Dawn arrived, Laina awaited her.

"What's going on?" Laina asked.

"That book, the one about Eleftheria. Where is it? I took the Helix to Michael's to get paint so I can copy the emblem."

"It's over here. I had it sitting and I was reading another book. Still open to the right page, too. You really should radio people from the location you want them to be, just in case they're already there."

"Sorry." Dawn apologized.

Laina handed Dawn the book, currently opened to the page detailing Eleftheria's Aegis, with the sigil of Hermes on the back. Dawn placed her own shield on the ground near the open book, stopping to remove the arm strap. She opened the drawer of a desk and found a Sharpie, and began to draw the sigil from the book on the shield. The toe of the sandal started to come into view, followed by the heel and the wing on the back. Dawn used the brush, dipped in the paint bottle, to trace the Sharpie lines on the shield in silver paint.

"Now I'll just leave the Aegis here in the library. Once it dries, I'll be able to set up for a test run."

Four hours later, nearing dusk, Dawn returned to the library. The silver paint on her shield was dry, giving the reverse side a sparkling silver winged sandal. She placed the arm strap back on the shield and picked it back up. The shield felt the same as it always did when she wasn't in angel form, heavy and unwieldy. She carried the shield from the library on the second floor up to the rooftop, looking out over the courtyard as the sun set. Dawn recited the battle oath of the Solari, invoking the magic of the shield.

"Under daylight we will stand, triumphant, bright and tall
Under our relentless strikes, the enemy will surely fall
Break their ranks, break their hearts, break their armor too
Solari strike and Solari live, for that is what we do
Outnumbered and outflanked, we will always stand up strong
They might think they can beat us, but they are sorely wrong
Solari light will always win, the sun can never die
Wings of angels carry us, let the Priestess fly!"

Dawn's angel wings returned as the light from the shield flowed through her. The defenders below scrambled from their seats, expecting another attack. Rick, who was at the comms array checking its functions, grabbed a microphone to speak to the defenders of the fortress.

"This is only a test. There is no undead attack." His words echoed through the fortress and into the land around. It was answered by the frightened cries of birds as they flew from the trees into the dark sky.

Dawn took flight, hovering over the fortress at the ready. Rick monitored the radar displays, ensuring that there would be no disturbances to the test. He quickly calculated something known only to him, then called out for Dawn.

"Dawn, you might want to go over the fortress at speed so we can measure it accurately. I don't want to pick your acceleration up in the test since it'll give you a lower speed."

"Sure thing, Rick. Just lemme get the sigil working."

Dawn held her arms out to her sides, feeling the light rushing through her body. With a thought, she channeled it back into the silver emblem of the shield. The winged sandal glowed bright yellow. Dawn could feel power flowing back through her, different power than what the shield normally gave her. This was a feeling of lightness, of freedom. Dawn used her wings to carry her out away from the fortress towards the north. A boom shook the fortress as she took off. The survivors had no chance to track her as she soared across the sky. Animals of all sorts from the woods outside fled the fortress from the low sonic boom.

Dawn looped back around in a sweeping turn at hypersonic speed. Rick hit a stopwatch as soon as Dawn appeared back on the radar. Dawn's kept her flight high over the fortress, allowing Rick to maintain radar tracking. A bird was caught in Dawn's flight path, and at the speed Dawn now traveled at, it was unable to evade. The small bird was killed by the leading edge of the shock-wave before Dawn's body even made contact. Dawn rolled her wings in flight to test her aileron roll. The motion of her aerobatic maneuver turned the flat shock-wave into a corkscrew, sending pulses through the air.

She passed back out of radar coverage only three minutes and change after she entered it. She looped back around and turned back towards the castle, maintaining her hypersonic speed for most of the one and a half minute journey. After the first minute, she slowed to what now felt like a crawl, just about the cruising speed of her Helix. She came in easily and touched her feet down on the top of the fortress roof near the comms array and the radar equipment.

"So?" Dawn inquired. "How'd I do?"

"Jesus shit Dawn, that was incredible!" Rick replied. "It took you three point eleven minutes to cross through radar coverage. That averages out to..." he grabbed a piece of paper nearby and scribbled a calculation down. "Thirty eight hundred fifty-five miles per hour – Mach 5. In hypersonic flight you're breaking five times the speed of sound. No wonder one hit from Eleftheria ripped the Persian ships apart and capsized others. Remember when you grabbed a necromancer and pulled a seismic throw on him? Now you can just fly straight through him and bisect him. The five golems along the wall? Bisect them too. You might even be able to wave clear with a shock-wave attack if you can slam the brakes on. There's so many possibilities I can't even get into them all!"

Chapter 18

In Pursuit of Justice

Light's Bulwark Fortress
The morning after

Dawn sat in the library, searching for books about ancient battles the Athenians fought in. She contemplated the ability to paint Hermes' sigil on her shield and absorb his power. This is what she searched for, instances of Solari High Priestesses wielding the power of other gods. She thought of some of the other gods of the Greek pantheon and what powers a High Priestess could wield through the Solari Aegis.

She was reading a passage about the first Priestess, called Meija. She came to the salvation of the Athenian farmers in one year of famine. The rains fell, but the crops wouldn't grow. Without their crops, the Athenians were unable to feed themselves and their livestock. The famine drove the price of what food there was so high that the peasants couldn't afford it, and so they were dying of starvation in droves. It was a disaster for Athens, and Meija recognized it.

Meija, the first wielder of a Solari Aegis, wondered what other things she could do with it. She could command the power of Apollo, but agriculture was not his realm. It was the realm of the goddess Demeter, and Meija was not her priestess. Still, she had to save her people. She painted the cornucopia, the sigil of Demeter, on the backside of her shield, calling upon the goddess to raise their crops from the ground. When that failed, she called upon Apollo to influence the actions of his aunt. She poured the light from her sacred Aegis through the sigil she painted on its reverse side, and the power of life surged through the first Priestess. With her new power of life, Meija raised her hands, and the crops rose from the ground before the eyes of the Athenians. The bountiful harvest breathed new life into the starving Athenians and livestock, and a great feast was thrown in her honor.

Dawn was inspired by this passage. For the second time that she knew of now, a Solari priestess had inscribed the sigil of another Olympian on the back of her shield and used the light of Apollo to reach the power of that Olympian. She began to envision other uses for this power. She saw the anvil of Hephaestus on the back of her shield, and the power of flame at her command. She saw the trident of Neptune on her shield as she stood atop a cliff calling the waves. She saw the lightning bolt of Zeus on her shield, and with it, she called lightning down from the sky. The owl of Athena gave her unerring logic.

A male voice broke Dawn out of her reverie. "Dawn, we need you on the roof," it said over the intercom. "Navy needs you."

Dawn bookmarked her page in *Ancient Athens* and stood. She left the library, taking the stairs up two flights to the roof level. Rick awaited her at the rooftop, on the line with the Navy captain.

"It's Captain White. She says it's major. Something about Tibet."

Dawn grabbed the radio from Rick's outstretched hand.

"Light's Bulwark." Dawn answered.

"Light's Bulwark, this is *USS Eisenhower* and there's a situation in Tibet." Captain Carrie White replied. "I think the monks are under siege fully now. They can't get out of their monastery. They'll starve in a few days without aid. *HMS Queen Elizabeth* is off the coast of LA, and *USS Lincoln* is off the coast of China. If you can get to *Queen Elizabeth,* we can fly you to *Lincoln* while you rest. Then we'll need you to fly to Cloud Peak and waste the zombies so we can extract the monks. Our Chinooks can't get high enough to reach the monastery, so we need an alternate escape. Think you can do anything?"

Rick looked over at Dawn. "Remember the Hermes sigil? You can hit mach five now. It won't be an issue for you to get to LA, but we can't go with you. Can you handle it on your own?"

"If not, I can jump jets outta there and take off across the sky at five times the speed of sound. It's not an issue. Besides, I needed a test for the Spell-Drinker. I'm going for it."

Dawn turned back to the radio. "I'll go for it. Make sure *Queen Elizabeth* and *Lincoln* are ready for me. I'll be there in a couple hours."

"What the hell are you flying, Light's Bulwark? A space shuttle?" the naval captain asked in disbelief.

"You don't know about the Aegis yet. Well, your boys on *Queen Elizabeth* are about to be in for a treat. Tell em to expect me in two hours, assuming it sustains over distance. Over and out."

Dawn grabbed the intercom mic. "Julius, you're in command. Don't lose my fortress, I'm going out for a couple days. That monastery in Tibet's under attack by the undead, and I'm gonna put a stop to it with my new hypersonic flight."

Julius was down in the basement level moving a skid of rations on a forklift. He knew Dawn after the two years he spent with her. He knew that he would never get to the comms array before she lifted off. That was how she was. If she said she was leaving now, she was on her way out the door and about to get in the car. By the time he got off the forklift, up to ground level, and up four flights of stairs to the rooftop, Dawn would be halfway to Huntington with that new swift flight she had. He simply touched his right hand over his heart, and his left over his right. "I love you." he whispered, barely even audible to himself over the drone of the forklift motor.

Dawn spoke the oath of the Solari and launched herself off the rooftop in clear view of the defenders in the courtyard below. She dropped a level and kicked into normal flight, soaring over the walls of the fortress and banking westward, towards Los Angeles and the *Queen Elizabeth*. Once well beyond the fortress, and thus out of shockwave range from it, Dawn channeled the Solari light through the winged sandal of Hermes. She kicked herself into supersonic and then hypersonic flight, reaching cruising speed quickly.

As she flew over the decimated nation heading west, she finally saw what had happened out here. Most of the nation was still farmland, but the cities and towns along her route showed the effects of the war. A few had been reduced to ash, a scorched earth policy of the fleeing survivors. Others had simply been abandoned, their denizens fleeing ahead of the zombie horde and leaving their elderly and disabled behind to die. Occasionally a wheelchair or other walking implement could be seen in the street from where a disabled person attempted to flee their demise and failed.

As she crossed the Mississippi River, she could see below her a sign. "You are now entering St. Louis, the Gateway to the West." The iconic Gateway Arch lay in pieces on the ground with its crown missing, presumably at the bottom of the nearby Mississippi. Impacting the side of the flight control tower was the remains of the President's doomsday plane, having crash landed here after exhausting its fuel supply. The district near the airport had burned. All that remained of the Hilton hotel was a pile of metal and concrete, and a broken sign lying across the freeway from the rubble. An explosion had ripped through the building from a gas line ruptured in the battle, tearing down the building and throwing the sign. Most of the buildings in the city had suffered significant structural damage.

Tanks and military vehicles could be seen on the roads throughout the city. Some showed damage from toxin cannon rounds striking their bodies. Others had been crushed by falling debris from the skyscrapers. Some had simply ran out of fuel. Around the armored vehicles, spent brass and empty clips covered the roads and sidewalks. The machine guns on the vehicles had partially been melted from constant use. Empty automatic rifles and combat knives littered the streets. Some of the rifles and knives had been broken after being used to bash and stab undead.

Wow, Dawn thought to herself, *those soldiers fought to the last round and then some.*

Dawn's entire flight path was devoid of undead. Though she thought this odd, she continued at top speed. She passed over the barren West, tracking her compass towards Los Angeles. At high altitude, she could see over the San Bernardino Mountains to the city. Dawn pressed on, clearing the mountain peaks and diving towards the city. In her dive, she let gravity aid her, pulling her even faster, past five times the speed of sound. The shield of light protecting her from the effects of air resistance and turbulence still held, clinging to her body like a second skin.

Dawn slowed her approach as she entered the city, back down to her normal flight speed. In Los Angeles, the lights in the buildings were still on. With their wind power systems still operational, even without human maintenance, the streetlamps in the city still illuminated the surface streets and highways. Though empty of cars and people, the city looked like it had before the war. The traffic lights below changed colors as they always had. The traffic alert billboards lit up along the I-10 corridor, displaying clear freeways.

The *HMS Queen Elizabeth* had lights aimed at the sky to give away its position in Los Angeles Port. Dawn noticed the great ship easily, and swooped down towards it. As she approached, she lit the Aegis up, signaling the crew members. She flew low over the deck, pulling up and touching her feet on the deck in a run. The flight deck crew cheered her as she touched down on the runway. The ship's captain awaited her on the bridge.

"Specialist." Captain Hermione Cole spoke in a clear North London accent. "I see you spoke the truth of your flight speed. Good to see, we'll most definitely need it. We're preparing a Harrier VTOL jet for you, not too far from where you touched down. We're gonna take you as far as the *Lincoln*. They're currently in the Bay of Bengal, about as close as they can get to the monastery. We'll have you spend the night on *Lincoln* while they're prepping the extraction vehicles. Captain Daniel Velasquez will brief you once you're aboard. Lieutenant Worthington, show the specialist to the Harrier."

A black man barely taller than Dawn rose from his chair next to the captain. "Come with me," he said to Dawn as he walked from the bridge back towards the flight deck.

"Wow, I'm glad to see you!" Dawn told him. "I thought the world's diversity died when the cities fell and Africa was overran. It's nice to see that there's still black people."

"You really thought all the black people died?" the lieutenant asked. "When the Queen Elizabeth is still afloat? You don't know much about Her Majesty's Navy, do you? Or your own, for that matter. There's more blacks on the Yankee ships than this one! Didn't you know that?"

"I didn't even think of that." Dawn replied. "I guess there's more than I thought. And the monks we're saving, they're Asian. Looks like we might be able to actually rebuild."

"None of the world's races are gone yet. As long as we survive, none of them will die out."

A sailor yelled to the pilot. "Brock, the jet's ready! Take care of her!"

"Take that shield off and stand on it when he takes off!" another shouted at Dawn.

Dawn climbed into the co-pilot's seat, placing the Solari Aegis on the floor. She fastened her harness on the lieutenant's command, keeping the Aegis pinned to the floor under her boots. The lieutenant climbed into the pilot's seat and performed the final steps of the pre-flight checklist before giving the all-clear signal. On the flagger's command, the lieutenant fired the jet's engines up. The catapult caught the wheels of the plane, throwing it from the deck at considerable speed. With all engines at full throttle, the jet soared into the air from the deck and turned towards the west.

The journey from the *Queen Elizabeth* in the Los Angeles Port to the *Lincoln* in the Bay of Bengal was a much longer one than her flight from Light's Bulwark to Los Angeles. Part of this was the distance – the trip across the Pacific was three times as long. Another part was the speed – Dawn's top speed was another threefold above the jet's. However, Dawn didn't want to test her ability that way. If her Hermes-given speed exhausted over the Pacific and she slowed back down from mach 5 to less than two hundred miles per hour, she could die of thirst before reaching safety. After using that speed for the entire distance from Light's Bulwark to Los Angeles, she considered that a likely possibility.

Dawn drifted off to sleep on the nine hour flight to the *Lincoln*. She only awoke from the sound of the flight controller's voice aboard *Lincoln*. "Harrier Five, this is *USS Lincoln*. Swing your approach around eighty-five degrees to land on the deck. You are cleared to land as soon as you are ready."

Lt. Worthington flipped his radio to transmit. "This is Harrier Five. Roger. Coming in."

The lieutenant was one of the best pilots in the Fleet Air Arm. He brought the Harrier in, catching the third cable with his landing hook and setting the jet down effortlessly. The lieutenant and Dawn both climbed from the cockpit, touching down on the *Lincoln* as the crew stood by. A seaman first class led Dawn and Lt. Worthington off the flight deck and up to the bridge, where Captain Daniel Velasquez stood at the helm. The bridge of the *Lincoln* had far more crew within than *Queen Elizabeth*, all watching different tracking radars and scanners to keep tabs on the Tibetan situation. Velasquez didn't even move when the trio entered, and only noticed when the seaman spoke up.

"So our specialist's here." Velasquez said loudly once he noticed Dawn. "I dunno what all ya can do, but Carrie says ya fly. Good, cause we're gonna need it. You're the only air asset we've got over twenty K, the choppers can't fly that high. Ya might need a coat though, it's colder than Aaron Murphy's black heart up there."

The captain continued. "We've only got four operational Chinooks, since they're mostly for Army and not us. All the Army ones are sitting grounded with nobody to fly them, but we can't get to them either with all the undead everywhere. It'll take us a bit to get the monks aboard and ready to lift back off, so Dawn, you and the marines will hold the staging area while the monks are being loaded up. Once the monks are gone, you'll have to survive three hours for us to come back and get the marines again. Once the marines are airborne you can lift off and join them."

"Captain, are there any art supplies aboard?" Dawn inquired.

"Maybe, ya gotta check with the quartermaster. Dunno why ya need 'em though." Captain Velasquez replied.

Dawn turned her shield to show him the winged sandal of Hermes still painted on the back. "That sigil is how I flew to LA so fast. But I need a different sigil for this battle. Hypersonic flight's great, but I think I'm gonna need to lay down fire or shake the snow loose from the peaks for this battle. To get those powers, I need to paint different sigils on my shield."

"Shake... the snow loose... from the peaks..." Captain Velasquez mused. "You're gonna bury the mindless in an avalanche?"

"Exactly. A thousand tons of snow should do some damage to the undead. Don't land the marines immediately. Let me bait a gathering and bring the snow down first, and I'll waste half their force."

"Jesus woman, you've got an answer to everything. No wonder your base is the only one still standing."

Dawn blushed at the commander's complement. "My fortress is manned with really good people. It's not me."

"Anyway, for your art stuff, check with the quartermaster, or ask around. Someone might have their own for downtime. I keep track of where the ship is and needs to be, I can't be messin' with nonessentials."

"Alright, will do."

Dawn left the bridge and reported to the quartermaster, who was at the supply warehouse. He was taking inventory of stockpiled food aboard, making note of various things on a clipboard. Dawn stopped him as he surveyed a skid of canned goods. At first, he only replied with

"Go away, I'm busy,", but on Dawn's second inquiry, he turned to see who it was stopping him from performing his duties.

"Oh, you're the specialist!" he exclaimed. "Sorry, I thought you were somebody else. What did you need?"

"I need some kind of paint." Dawn showed the broad-chested man the sigil of Hermes on her shield. "I need to change sigils for the battle."

"Oh. Well I don't have any, I mostly handle necessities like ammo and food. I do know Velez got some in the mail though. Might wanna ask her."

"Thanks."

Chapter 19

The Battle of Cloud Peak

Aboard *USS Lincoln*
The next day

Dawn awoke in a bottom bunk, below a Marine Sergeant just off night shift on radar duty. It took her little time to get ready, simply donning a lent Navy uniform and equipping the Spell-Drinker and Solari Aegis. She left her room to report to the mess hall, where sailors had gathered for breakfast. Dawn filled her plate with what non-perishable and easily storable foods the Navy had prepared for its sailors and took a seat at a table with other members of the strike team.

The large table sat Dawn, the four Chinook pilots, and another five Apache pilots that were supporting the marines. Dawn had the art supplies out, and was painting the trident of Poseidon in place of the winged sandal of Hermes on the back of her shield.

"What the hell are you doing?" one of the Apache pilots asked her.

"Unleashing a secret weapon." Dawn replied. "With this emblem on my shield, I'll be able to do some heavy damage before the battle even starts."

"How?"

"Basically, painting the sigil of Poseidon on my shield grants me abilities in his domain. He's the god of the sea, but he's also the god of earthquakes. So I'm gonna shake the ground and bring all the snow down off the peaks to bury the undead."

"This is gonna be fuckin' good." another pilot added.

"I can't wait to see this shit." a third replied.

Dawn continued. "The blade I have's an untested weapon. It's supposed to consume the magic the undead are animated with, which means it'll turn them back into a corpse with a touch. If the counter blast works, that's another factor in our favor."

"Ho-lee shit." one of the pilots responded. "Your sword eats their necro shit and blasts it back at them?"

"Exactly."

The intercom sounded off shortly after Dawn finished her meal. "All attack team members, report to the flight deck. All attack team members, report to the flight deck. Preparations are almost complete."

Dawn, the pilots, and the marines chosen for the mission stood from their seats and filed out of the mess hall and up above deck, forming an array on the flight deck in front of Captain Velasquez. The captain addressed the group of allied fighters.

"Alright, listen up. Our mission is to get those monks out alive. To do that, we need to secure the staging area at the base of their tunnel so we can fly them out. Our specialist's going in first, sending the monks down the tunnel, since she's the only one who can reach the monastery. After, she's gonna bait the undead into an attack. She's got a special attack that'll trigger an avalanche and bury a lot of undead. After the snow hits, Chinooks, you're gonna drop the marines in to help hold the point on the ground. Apaches, your job is to guard against enemy advance. After dropping marines, the Chinooks need to get those monks out of there. You'll come back for the marines once the monks are safe.

"All forces, move out! Get airborne! Go! Go! Go!" Captain Velasquez shouted. The pilots ran to their helicopters and got seated, awaiting the marines to file into the Chinook troop carriers. Once the marines were seated in the Chinooks, all the helicopters lifted off from the deck in a flurry of wind and steel. Dawn joined them in the air, Solari Aegis strapped to her back and Spell-Drinker at her side.

The flight from the *Lincoln* to the staging point, taking about two hours, was relatively uneventful. No enemies on the ground fired at them or even noticed them, allowing easy transit to the monastery. The helicopters broke off from Dawn as they approached the monastery, flying through the valley around to the staging area outside the monks' tunnel. Dawn touched down in the courtyard of the monastery as the entire force of monks watched in awe.

At first, Dawn attempted to speak English to the monks, who did not understand. "Get down the tunnel! We're going to fly you to safety!" she shouted, but the monks never moved. Eventually, one monk, a silver-haired Chinese man with his hair tied back, stepped forward.

"They do not speak English." he said to Dawn. "But if you are here to help, then let me translate for you. I am Ji Quan, leader of this monastery."

Ji translated Dawn's orders into Cantonese for the monks, who immediately started down the tunnel. As the monks filed down, Ji continued to address Dawn.

"This monastery has given us a sanctuary for a time. We already know the living dead have cut off our tunnel. You brought warriors to fight them. I thank you for saving us. But where will you take us?"

"We have a boat the size of a city floating in the ocean. That is where we will take you. The undead can never reach it, simply because they cannot swim. Your monks have finished using the ladder. Go. I will go back to the sky and meet you on the other side."

Dawn lifted back off the ground and flew over the other side, finding the pilots awaiting her next action. She touched down at the top of another peak nearby, raised the Solari Aegis, and channeled its light through the silver sigil of Poseidon on the back. The trident glowed silver at first, then took on a bluish tint.

"Poseidon, with your power, I shake the very earth beneath their feet!" Dawn shouted. "I will bury you, fiends!"

Dawn stomped the ground like a sumo wrestler before a match. With every stomp, the earth shook beneath her. Snow on the peaks rumbled, holding at first but then collapsing. Every nearby peak rumbled, their snow falling in great waves of frozen death. The waves of snow fell into the valley, combining into a roaring avalanche. The attack worked just as Dawn intended it to, burying and destroying undead by the thousands.

Immediately, the Chinooks moved in to drop marines near the tunnel's entrance. The flesh golems attacked, but were driven back by machine gun and missile fire by the Apache gunships. The marines established their positions, using their rifles to repel the mindless and allowing the pilots to take care of the golems. Monks started to exit the tunnel and were directed by their master to the transport helicopters.

Dawn leapt off the top of the mountain and spread her wings. Leading with Spell-Drinker, she flew straight at a flesh golem in level flight. The golem slashed at her with its bone weapon, striking against Spell-Drinker. The dark magic that gave the golem its life was sucked into the blade on contact, leaving the great creature motionless and slain.

"It works!" Dawn shouted as she turned to face another enemy. "The blade works!"

The marines formed a circle around the Chinooks to protect the monks. The Apaches held their positions in the air, forming their own circle farther out. Dawn was the only mobile fighter, using her wings to carry her from golem to golem. Against each target, she slashed with Spell-Drinker, consuming the magic that animated the horrific creatures.

The fast-moving cavaliers, mounted on the rotting forms of Mongolian horses, tried to slip past Dawn's guard to attack the marines. Though their maneuvers were successful, and Dawn never gave chase, the Apache gunships were able to rip the cavaliers and their mounts apart with heavy machine gun fire. Though the airborne gunners focused their rockets on the golems and their machine guns on the cavaliers, they still proved to be useful against mindless as well. The machine guns ripped the ranks of the mindless apart between bursts against cavaliers.

The necromancers who had previously crafted the golems now were opening portals from far beyond the battle zone, keeping the undead flowing into the area. One loosed a shadow bolt at one of the Chinooks as it lifted off from inside the circle. The bolt struck the metal frame of the helicopter harmlessly, unable to damage it. He instead turned his shadow bolts on the marines, finding them to be much more vulnerable targets. The body armor of the marines was effectively useless against the magic attack, and direct hits proved fatal.

Marines in the circle turned their rifles on the necromancers. Though they were far beyond the standard effective range of the M4s the marines used, a pair instead wielded Barrett fifty-caliber rifles. The rifles gave the marines the power to pick off the necromancers, though their snipers still struggled to hit their targets over the extreme distance.

The marines fought on, their assault weapons against the hordes of mindless, and their long-range rifles against the necromancers and their shadow bolts.

It took some time for the pair of snipers to finish off the necromancers and shut the portals down. During that time, the Apache helicopter gunships exhausted first their missiles, then their rocket pods, and eventually their machine guns. With no way to protect the marines, and being low on fuel, the gunships left the combat arena one by one until all were gone and the ground forces were without air support.

Dawn used the Solari Aegis to block shadow bolts when she could. Though the Kevlar armor the marines wore was useless against them, the Aegis was able to deflect the attacks. Dawn's main focus was on the flesh golems, moving and slashing to down each one, one after another. She continued this attack pattern until voices rang out from the marine circle.

"I'm dry!" one shouted.

"Out of ammo!" screamed another.

Dawn looked down at her watch. The Chinooks should be still fifteen minutes out. She looked at Spell-Drinker. It held a strong charge, enough to loose an area of effect blast. She decided she needed to save that for when the helicopters actually arrived. She looked at the tunnel opening. It was only three marines wide. It would be easy to defend with just her blade and shield.

"Into the tunnel!" Dawn shouted at the marines. "I'll hold the line!"

The disciplined marines did as instructed. They filed back into the tunnel, filling part of the path up to the monastery. Dawn removed her Aegis and planted it in front of the tunnel, forming a barrier of light in front of the marines. Holding Spell-Drinker in both hands, Dawn stood ready, facing down the horde of oncoming undead. She swung Spell-Drinker back and forth in front of the tunnel, cleaving the mindless three at a time as they marched up the tunnel. With each hit, Spell-Drinker absorbed magic from the undead and stored it within the blade. The stones on the hilt started to fill in purplish-black as she cleaved more and more undead.

The Chinooks came over the ridge and into Dawn's field of view. Dawn lifted the Aegis to remove the barrier. With a blast of light, she cut a path through the undead with the Aegis and raced forward through it. Undead closed on her as she made her attack, moving to fill the void. She raised Spell-Drinker high above her head. A mindless slashed at her with its clawed hand, striking the Aegis. Another slashed at her back, poking a hole in her shirt.

Dawn drove the point of Spell-Drinker into the earth. A wave of magic radiated out from her, blasting everything in all directions. The marines took cover against the walls of the cave, allowing the fragment of the blast to pass by harmlessly and strike the earthen floor inside the tunnel. The undead for a thousand yards around were instantly slain by the blast wave, clearing the landing zone for the Chinooks. With such a large blast radius, there would be no way for the undead to reach the clearing before the helicopters had the marines aboard.

The Chinooks touched down and opened their doors, allowing the marines to enter. The operation was successful. Only a handful of marines died in the extraction from zombie scratches and bites. Dawn re-equipped the Solari Aegis, allowing its purifying light to flow through her. The scratch on her back where the mindless had attacked her faded into her skin. Her wings re-formed, and she took to the skies once again with the allied helicopters, entirely clear of danger. Though the still-operational sight ward attempted to follow the helicopters, its flight speed was far too slow to even attempt to chase, and the helicopters got out of visual range quickly.

Dawn's feet touched down on the deck of the *Lincoln* just ahead of the Chinook transports. The returning marines and pilots were congratulated on an accomplished mission. The monks waited for them on the deck, with Ji Quan at the front. Captain Velasquez stood outside the bridge looking down on the flight deck, where the marines and pilots had moved into a formation.

"Sailors, marines, that was excellent work out there. We sustained a few casualties, but we successfully extracted all the monks from the monastery. They are grateful for our assistance. Specialist, we know you will have to ride back with the British pilot at sunrise, but we were very happy to have you aboard. We can't really afford to have them aboard, so we're gonna send them on transports out to your fortress. Be ready to receive them in the next couple weeks."

Chapter 20

King Leopold's Legacy

Flame Point Fortress, Peru
That same time

"What the hell?!" Aaron exclaimed from the viewing room. "About ten dozen cavaliers all went down outside the tunnel in China at once! Get a demon's eye up out there!"

"Sure thing. Initializing energy output."

Stacie focused on the large viewscreen in the room and channeled demonic power, forming the basis of the eye. Then, she spoke the oath that would summon the device.

"Tya vikzon rathiel eiyos, qapith adali gavetol!"

The ward's vision started to fade into existence. It watched outside the tunnel leading up to Cloud Peak Monastery. American Chinooks were dropping US Marines, probably the last ones still alive, in front of the tunnel. A handful of Apaches hovered in a half circle, protecting the tunnel entrance. The marines formed another semicircle inside the Apache one. A four-winged angel, the same angel as they witnessed in battle at Light's Bulwark, flew in low and fast along the valley and took a place ahead of the marines.

"So, the monks came to us, and the sailors at sea tried to rescue them." Aaron commented aloud. "And that damned angel from West Virginia's there too. Good. We'll get to wipe all three threats out at once."

"I'm pulling the demon's eye back." Stacie replied. "I think she's under too much fire to come after it, but I'm not gonna risk her coming through and blasting us. We'll still have front row seats, the eye just won't be so close to that angel."

The demon's eye pulled back, well out of range of the missiles and rockets from the Apache gunships. From this distance, they saw Jiang in the back with the necromancers, directing mindless into battle with a psychic command. The mindless shambled along towards the marines, who opened fire with their assault rifles. The flesh golems charged in too, and immediately fell under fire from the Apache rockets. The angel, too, took to the skies and attacked the flesh golems, felling one with only one strike of her one-handed sword.

"What the fuck was that!" Aaron shouted. "How did she do that?! She dropped that golem in one strike!"

"Could it be..." Stacie muttered. "Could that be Maktdrikker in her hand?"

"Maktdrikker? You mean from the legend of Ondesverd?" Aaron asked.

"Did you not listen to Olaf?" Stacie grumbled. "You moron!"

"Moron? Why you... whatever, what the hell's Maktdrikker?"

"Maktdrikker, translated from the Old Norse as Spell-Drinker or Magic Drinker, is a legendary blade." Stacie started. "According to the story Olaf told us, Gunther Sigurdsson was the champion of Loki. He wielded Ondesverd, which you recovered from his tomb. Gunther died in battle against Njall Vollundsen, the champion of Thor. Njall's weapon was Maktdrikker. It was said that, with Maktdrikker in his hand, Njall could slay any creation of magic with one well-placed strike. Maktdrikker would absorb the magic used to create the blade's enemy, in this case removing the animation spell and bringing our golems down. She has Maktdrikker!"

"Well then, you need to find a way to make us immune to it. Just in case you've forgotten, we're constructs of magic too. You're a warlock now, and I'm a lich knight. If she gets here and hits us with that blade, we die."

"I know that. But it won't matter if she dies here, now will it? Just watch."

Aaron and Stacie turned back towards the viewscreen and started watching the battle unfold. The Chinooks were able to extract the monks, despite the best efforts of the mindless, cavaliers and flesh golems. However, the Apache rockets had stopped coming. Dawn was still laying waste to the flesh golems, but it was clear the Apaches were running out of ammunition.

"That's it. Look, their helicopters are firing dry. See, that one's leaving the battle now cause they're out of ammo. We'll have those marines overrun before their transports get back."

Without their air cover, the marines were desperately holding onto their small piece of land. Though Dawn had slain the last flesh golem some time ago, the hordes of mindless were beginning to gain ground. One marine exhausted his ammunition, followed by another. More marines ran out shortly after, and with each marine exhausted, the kill line got closer and closer to the marines.

The angel shouted something at the marines, and they began to retreat into the tunnel. Dawn held the line, swinging Maktdrikker in a wide arc to cleave the mindless, just long enough to cover the marines' retreat. She then fell back too, just inside the tunnel.

"And that's game." Aaron said proudly. "They can retreat up the tunnel, but we can follow them. Those marines aren't monks. They can't hold the line with just their fists like the monks could. With enough mindless, we'll overrun them even in the monastery."

Stacie brought the demon's eye to a lower altitude. With Dawn pinned in the tunnel, she knew it was safe from her high-speed winged charge. The eye regained sight of Dawn and the marines just in time to see Dawn fling the Aegis into the snow and form a light barrier in front of the marines.

"What the hell is she doing?" Aaron asked the display. "She's gonna lay her life down for a handful of marines out in Asia?"

"I don't think so." Stacie said. "Look."

The Chinooks were starting to come back into view. Though their extraction point was full of undead, they continued on their path. Suddenly, the angel grabbed her shield back off the ground and dropped the barrier. She brought it up across her body, and with a blast of light, she cut a straight path through the undead about three wide. She took to her feet, racing down her newly created path, slashing wildly with Maktdrikker back and forth as the undead closed in on her.

"And now the angel falls." Aaron said matter-of-factually.

Dawn raised Maktdrikker high over her head. One mindless slashed at her front, clashing with the Solari Aegis harmlessly. Another slashed at her back, tearing her shirt and scratching her back but dealing ineffectual damage. She brought Maktdrikker slamming into the snow. A wave of darkness radiated out in all directions as she unleashed all the necrotic energy she had stored up throughout the battle. Every mindless around for a thousand yards was obliterated, turned to dust before Aaron and Stacie's eyes. Stacie managed to pull the demon's eye up in time to avoid the ground attack.

Aaron and Stacie looked on, stunned, as Dawn beckoned the marines from inside the tunnel. It was seemingly unaffected by the blast, as the same number of marines exited as entered. The Chinooks found their way to the rendezvous point quickly, and the marines were aboard before the remaining mindless could close the thousand-yard gap from the kill line to the helicopters. The choppers took to the sky, their marines safe for now. Dawn, too, re-lit her wings and soared away victorious.

"What just happened..." Stacie asked, bewildered.

"I don't... I don't know..." Aaron stammered.

"Maybe Olaf knows." Aaron said as he composed himself. "Falkenskold!"

The Norse barbarian appeared on the viewscreen where the battle for the monastery had just been.

"My lord!" Olaf replied.

"You're the one who knew about Ondesverd. What do you know about Maktdrikker? Specifically, can it unleash the magic it stores?"

"Absolutely. That's how Njall won even though his blade broke. When Ondesverd shattered Maktdrikker, the magic it had absorbed started pouring out of the broken blade. Njall aimed the end of the broken blade at Gunther, and the magic beam threw Gunther against a cliff and buried him in an avalanche. Why?"

"Because the angel has Maktdrikker, and she just wiped out every undead in a thousand-yard circle by unleashing the stolen magic."

"The enemy has Maktdrikker?"

"Yep. And she's pretty damn good with it too. She just used a tunnel to hold off a quarter mil for nearly a half hour. Then, she blasted a path, charged down it, and unleashed that damned holy hand grenade on everything. Anyway, that's all I needed. Now I'm sure that blade's Maktdrikker."

"But it can't be Maktdrikker. Maktdrikker was destroyed in the battle between Njall and Gunther. She had to have made a new one. The blade part of Maktdrikker was melted down into other steel, and the hilt was buried with Njall. We know where Njall was buried, so I can go check and see if the hilt's still there."

"Do so. I'm out."

An alarm sounded from the spell lab. Stacie immediately took off down the spire stairs into the lab. A magic device she had rigged was finally giving an output on the powered down television monitor. A skull was resonating and glowing purple in a containment unit, connected through a magic conduit to the monitor. On the monitor, various random bits of information appeared. Some was simple things that anybody knew, such as "1 + 2 = 3". Other bits of information showed more complex mathematics, like the "sin 0 = 0" that appeared on the screen shortly after. Still others were intimate details about Stacie's sexual prowess.

"It works!" Stacie shouted in excitement. "Aaron, get down here!"

Aaron slowly descended the steps, ducking his head to avoid contact with the bulkhead. He looked at the monitor, which was now cycling through thousands of concepts taught in American public schools before the war.

"What am I looking at?" he asked, annoyed that Stacie had even called him down.

"You are looking at how we're gonna find Damupanga." Stacie said proudly. "I've been working on this device ever since Kgosi told us about how we killed off all the voodoo priests and we needed a spell to read the minds of dead people. Right now I can get it to display on this monitor, but the monitor's not actually powered up so it's all magic. If I had electrical power, I could write it to a document and use a search function to find information quickly."

"So we get power." Aaron replied. "I can't bring power here, but I know somewhere that probably has power. Hoover Dam is a power station. Unlike all the coal-fired stations, it'll still be producing power long after we've summoned Tyadrig. If we go to Hoover Dam, and bring that device with us, we can use their own computers to process the data."

"There's still one hangup though." Stacie said. "Eric's skull only contains knowledge Eric had. That's why it knew trig and why it knew personal things about me, but it won't know where Damupanga is. We need a skull of someone who knew where the blade was to be able to find it."

"I have just the person – the voodoo priest who wrote the book on voodoo for the Belgians. His skull was placed atop the Belgian governor's keep in the Congo, and the Kinshasa government left it there when they took over. I don't think they took it down when we attacked, so it should still be there. I'm gonna see where Kgosi is. Move your ex's brain contents so I can use the viewscreen."

Stacie shut off the device, and Aaron tapped into his mental link to Kgosi. The lanky African appeared in his loincloth on the screen.

"How ya doin', boss?" Kgosi asked.

"Stacie has that spell you needed, but we need a certain skull to find the location of Damupanga."

"I know which one ya be talkin' about. Da Belgians, dey got it on a pike at dere mansion. I got it already, I knew ya gonna need it for da spell. Damupanga, it be almost yours. I got necros ready, I gonna warp one to ya wit' it."

Another tall man with bluish-black skin walked up behind Kgosi, holding a skull that had turned brown from exposure to the elements. "He be your target, lady. He got da skull."

Stacie channeled a spell, bathing the necromancer in sickly green light. His image appeared at Flame Point as a green silhouette, nearly transparent at first. It started to fade in as the real one faded out, until finally the one in Africa faded out entirely and the man appeared fully at Flame Point with the skull. After surrendering the skull to Aaron, a second necromancer came to Kgosi's side. He duplicated the spell that Stacie had just cast, pulling the first necromancer back to Africa.

"The second blade is almost mine." Aaron proudly stated.

Chapter 21

The Blade of Baron Samedi

Outside Flame Point Fortress, Peru
Shortly after

Stacie stood outside Flame Point Fortress. The black obsidian fortress was suspended by three paths over the open crater of a volcano. The bubbling magma below radiated heat, able to be felt this high up. It was this magma she focused her magic on. A beam of purple-black magic flowed from Stacie's hands down over the edge of the barrier and into the magma, causing some to separate from the rest of the reservoir and ascend. Stacie's magic beam formed the magma as it rose, creating the image of a bird. The magma bird's body was easily the size of an elephant, and its wingspan reached over a hundred feet.

"Ryzuul, Qaathi, Viceros!" Stacie shouted at the magma bird as she released the magic beam. The bird soared up out of the volcano's crater. Stacie's magic beam seized the bird again, turning its brilliant red flame to the same purple-black as the beam. The magma bird circled around the fortress, coming to roost on one of the connective bridges.

Stacie cast one more spell on her construct. With her final spell, she sealed the bird's internal heat, preventing it from burning objects around the creature's body. Finally, the creature was ready to bear weight. Stacie yelled for Aaron, then climbed atop the bird's large body. The bird easily held her weight thanks to the magic. Aaron exited the fortress, holding Stacie's device with the skull from the Belgian keep inside. He handed the device up to Stacie as she sat atop the bird, then mounted up himself.

The bird leapt from the bridge and took to the sky. It soared over the rim of the volcano, carrying the pair out over the Andes peaks north towards Ecuador. Stacie gripped the bird at its wing joints, pulling the bird to one side or the other by leaning her body as if driving a motorcycle. The bird was not very fast, only reaching speeds close to those of a helicopter.

"Can't this thing go any faster?" Aaron asked angrily. "It's gonna take us, literally, two days just to get there. And that's straight line! Then we have to come back! Why couldn't we just use a teleport?"

"We don't have that kind of teleport." Stacie said, irritated at Aaron's impatience. "Necromancers can only summon. We can't teleport. So if we had a necromancer already at Hoover Dam, we could have done exactly that. But we don't, so we're taking this bird. And, in case you've forgotten, we have our home teleport stones too. So we only need to fly there on the bird. We'll just teleport back."

The marathon flight was nothing for the pair of undead and their elemental construct bird. Since none of the three needed food, sleep, or bathroom breaks, the straight-line forty-one hour flight was exactly that, straight line and forty-one hours. The flight took them all the way from Flame Point in Peru to Hoover Dam on the Nevada-Arizona border. The bird touched down on the dam's walkway, letting Stacie and Aaron dismount before taking back to the skies and starting its journey back to Flame Point.

The pair of undead leaders walked to a door for entry into the dam's main power access. The door was locked, but a shadow bolt from Stacie was all it took to blast the door free from the hinges and open the path. They walked through, using a fire escape schematic to navigate the corridors and rooms of the power facility. Eventually, they reached one labeled "control room".

"The control room." Stacie mused aloud. "In here there's bound to be computers. Keep that thing steady, will ya? If you break it, we have to port back home, I'll have to build a new one, and we'll have to repeat that stupidly long flight."

Stacie turned from Aaron and charged a shadow bolt. She flung the shadow bolt at the door, hitting it with enough force to break the door from its hinges and fling it across the room. The broken door smashed into a computer terminal. Sparks flew from the terminal. The machine's screen cracked and went black.

Stacie located another terminal, one that was still functioning. In their haste to abandon the station when it came under attack, the control operators left the terminals in this room logged in with credentials. Stacie opened the word processing program on the computer and pointed to a spot on the ground.

"Put the device here, then hand me the cable running off it." Stacie ordered. Aaron placed the device down, then tracked the USB cable he had looped around the case while carrying it. Stacie inserted the plug into the terminal's drive. Shortly after, text started to type itself in the word processing unit. The entire document was written in a language neither could read.

"What the hell is this?" Aaron asked angrily. "I can't read this shit! What language is this anyway?"

"It looks like German. Could be Dutch or Norse though, I can't tell. They all have those vowels with the two dots over them." Stacie calmly replied.

"So how are we gonna read it? We can't even search for anything if it's in German. I don't know even enough German to know what to search for."

"Remember when we took Spanish at college together?"

"Yeah, the teacher's name was like Juan Carlos something. But what the hell's Spanish got to do with German? They're not even the same family!"

"Proper nouns don't change. Like, when the Mexican ambassador was going to Washington to meet the American president. Washington was still Washington, even though it's an English word. When we watched El Clasico at Camp Nou, the announcers spoke Spanish, but they still pronounced that British guy's name right that played on Real Madrid."

"Wasn't he actually Welsh?"

"You're missing the point."

"Which is...?"

"Damupanga, since it's a Swahili word, is probably still Damupanga. It's a Swahili word, but it probably is the same even in German, or whatever the hell language this thing is in."

"So try that then. Search it for 'Damupanga'."

Stacie typed control-F and searched "Damupanga". It showed a passage about Damupanga's location.

We begraven Damupanga waar de Belgen nooit zou hebben. Het plan was zo briljant dat alleen de priester zelf haarr visie had kunnen zien. We plaatsen het mes in de vloeistof steen de Belgen vroeger geboudwd met. Vervolgens verzegeld ze het mes in de steen zij gebruikten om hun fort te bouwen.

"Shit!" Aaron swore at the computer. "We still can't read it."

"Hold your damned horses, Aaron. Lemme just check something. This place was under the Comcast sphere. I'm betting they had things downloaded and saved to the hard drive for when service went out."

Stacie searched through the programs directory, finding a copy of Google Translate on the hard drive. This program was a widely used online translator, one that the operators of the dam had downloaded to allow use without service just as Stacie had suspected.

"Bingo." Stacie said as she opened it. She copied and pasted the passage about Damupanga into the first box in the translator. A question came up. "Language recognized as Dutch. Accept?"

"I thought you said it was in German. Decline it." Aaron said.

"It's not German, it's Dutch. That's why it says it's in Dutch. I'm accepting." Stacie replied. "You said they were from the Congo, right? The Belgians invaded there, and they speak Dutch. Accept."

The computer displayed the passage again, this time translated into English, at least partially.

We bury Damupanga where the Belgians would never have. The plan was so brilliant dad only the priest himself Haarr vision can zien. We put the knife in the liquid stone Belgians used to build. Then they sealed the knife into the stone they used to build their fortress.

"Well, it's not perfect." Stacie said. "But at least the gist of it is here."

"Liquid stone? What the hell's liquid stone? And why's it talking about a knife? I thought Damupanga was a sword." Aaron asked.

"As far as the knife thing, my guess is they used a word like 'blade'. The Dutch words for 'blade' and 'knife' are probably the same word, so the translator can't tell the difference. Liquid stone though is probably not a translation error. I'm thinking it's because the writer didn't know about technology. Remember, an African wrote this, not a Belgian."

"So what do you think it means?"

"I'd guess concrete. To someone who doesn't know what concrete is and how it works, it looks like liquid stone."

"And why is it translating "dad"? And why are 'haarr' and 'zien' still showing as Dutch words?"

"Because it's Google Translate. It's not that great, but it's good enough here to get what we need. We know what we came for. Let's get out of here. Use your home teleport."

Stacie pulled her home teleport stone, with its rune of home imprinted on its surface. She traced the rune, and light enveloped her. Aaron did the same, also being enveloped by the light. Within a few seconds, the pair arrived back inside the main viewing room of Flame Point Fortress. Aaron quickly called on his link with his general, Kgosi, and the loincloth-clad tribesman appeared on the viewscreen.

"Aah, it be da king! What ya say, my liege?" Kgosi inquired.

"I know where Damupanga is, Kgosi. The skull held answers, just as we thought it would. Turns out your ancestors are clever. We think they took Damupanga and threw it into just-poured concrete when the Belgians were building the governor's mansion. Go to the mansion and break apart every stone. Leave nothing behind but dust. You've got a handful of flesh golems. Their strength should aid you."

"I be on my way, my lord. Ya gonna have dat blade in no time!"

"Excellent." Aaron replied. "Excellent."

Chapter 22

Home Sweet Home

USS Lincoln
The next morning

Dawn only awoke in the morning when the girl she shared a cabin with woke her. Dawn showered at the shared shower room, then found her way to the mess hall to take advantage of the ship's breakfast. Brock, the pilot she had flown here with, found her at the mess hall and sat down across the table from her.

"Well, looks like we get to go back now. That was brilliant, by the way. The Americans talked about you. Something about putting your shield in the ground and blocking them behind a wall of light, and cleaving undead with a sword."

"Yeah. We retreated into the tunnel so I could keep the undead down to three at a time. The sword kills on contact since it absorbs the magic used to keep them alive."

"How are you using magic?" he asked. "I thought only the villains had it."

"No, we have it too. The difference is theirs is demonic and mine is divine."

"Divine? Like God? God gave you magic to beat them?"

"No, not Jehovah." Dawn answered. "Before the war, I wouldn't have believed there was a Jehovah, or any other gods for that matter. My shield's magic is from Apollo, and I don't even know what went into my sword."

"Apollo? Isn't that a dead god?"

"He's not worshiped any more, not since the Roman Empire went Christian. The shield came off a statue built before then. A high priestess of him built it and gave it her power when the Romans invaded Athens, trying to preserve the Solari order."

"And you said you don't know what magic your sword is?"

"No. The guy who forged it..." Dawn shuddered as she thought of him. "The guy who forged it worshiped the Celtic pantheon. So it's probably Celtic magic in the sword."

"More dead gods. Where's God in all of this?"

"No idea. All I know is Apollo and whatever gods this sword's magic is from have helped me so far. Jehovah so far has been absent, so I haven't really factored him in."

"My faith is in God. He will guide me through this tragedy."

"You have your faith and I have mine. Hopefully we meet again, once we win."

"Agreed. Anyway, we need to take off soon."

Dawn walked with Brock from the mess hall up to the flight deck. The same Harrier jet that Dawn took to get to the Lincoln was sitting on the catapult. People with green vests over their uniforms moved hoses away from the takeoff area. A man in yellow inspected the flight deck one last time, ensuring that there were no loose bolts or anything else that could get sucked into the turbojet and bring down the Harrier. Dawn climbed into the co-pilot's seat, placed the Aegis on the floor, and strapped herself in. She planted her feet firmly on the Aegis, keeping it on the floor.

"You are cleared for takeoff." a voice announced over the radio. Brock fired up the Harrier's engines. The catapult pushed the front wheel forward, carrying the entire jet behind it. The engines lifted the Harrier from the flight deck at over two hundred miles per hour, accelerating the jet to one and a half times the speed of sound for its supersonic cruise back to the British ship docked off the coast of Los Angeles.

The flight across the open Pacific was incredibly boring. There was nothing out the windows for Dawn to look at on the nine-hour flight but open ocean. She talked over the radio to random people from Lincoln and from Queen Elizabeth, but she still dozed off for part of the flight. Finally, a voice came over the radio for Brock.

"Harrier Five, this is HMS Queen Elizabeth. Please alter approach angle thirty-five degrees clockwise for final approach."

"Queen Elizabeth, this is Harrier Five." Brock replied. "Roger. I'm coming in."

Brock steered the jet downwards and to starboard side, going in low for his approach on the ship. He once again executed the practiced landing perfectly, his landing hook snagging the third cable across the deck. The tension on the hook wire brought the jet to a screeching halt on the deck of the carrier. The pair exited the jet, tired from their long flight. Dawn and Brock both walked down to the mess hall, where a few crew from the night shift ate a meal. Brock sat with the people he formerly sat with while deployed aboard Queen Elizabeth, while Dawn sat with a couple of women from the flight crew.

The three women discussed the war, Dawn's fortress, the ship, and everyone left behind while they ate their evening meal. Dawn made a point to drink coffee to wake back up after the battle the previous day and the flights back and forth. She played cards and games with other crew members, and re-painted the emblem of Hermes on the back of her shield before going to sleep.

The next day, Dawn got breakfast at the mess hall before leaving the ship. Her breakfast consisted of eggs made from the preserved egg product sold in cartons, canned beef, and potatoes grown aboard in a low-space farming area only invented a couple years before the war. Having filled up on this food, Dawn returned to the flight deck. She said the Solari oath while standing on the deck, and her wings regrew. The light surged through her body as she ran down the flight deck. She leapt off the edge of the ship, and her wings carried her into the air. Sailors watched in awe as she circled back around towards the mainland.

Dawn channeled the light from her shield back through the sigil of Hermes. She once again felt that absolute freedom her speed gave her as she crossed over Los Angeles. She pushed herself faster, breaking the sound barrier as she passed Staples Center. Banners supporting the Los Angeles Lakers still flew over the arena. She pushed herself even faster, reaching mach five far before she got to the San Bernardino Mountains beyond the city.

It took less than two hours at that speed to cross the immense width of the United States and reach the West Virginia border with Kentucky. Below her, as she finally entered West Virginia again, she saw the sign put up by the governor at all the roads leading into the state. The sign said, "Almost Heaven, West Virginia", naming a man called Geoff Klondike as the governor. Geoff had died, along with fifty thousand other West Virginians, when the toxin from the chemical plant reached the Charleston water treatment facility.

As Dawn saw the sign, she thought back to what it was like the first time she saw the sign. She was nineteen years old back then, driving her newly-inherited Acura down Interstate 77. Back then, a man named Earl Ray Tomblin was the state's governor, and the entry signs read "West Virginia, Wild and Wonderful". She had just buried her mother in Chicago, and now was driving to a property her father's lawyer told her was off US Route 60 in Kanawha County, West Virginia.

She had grown up in the ghetto area of Chicago. Most of her neighbors were in gangs or were affiliated with the gangs. The Bloods ran this section of the city, and very seldom did metro police even come here. Her own mother, Sarah Jenkins, was a prostitute. Most nights Dawn slept at home alone while her mother was out with some businessman, small-time politician, or whoever was lonely and wanted the company of a woman. She had to get herself up and catch the bus to go to school since her mother was sleeping in hotels with clients. She often ate crackers, cereal or toast for dinner, while her mom lay on the couch strung out on heroin. She never believed she would be anything else more than a part-time fast food worker who whored herself out on the side.

Sarah was killed when Dawn was seventeen. While buying her heroin from a drug dealer affiliated with the Bloods, a carload of Latin Kings rolled up on the scene. Gunfire was exchanged, and in an instant the scene turned from an everyday drug buy on the streets of Chicago to a bloody massacre. Sarah, her drug dealer, and the lieutenants with the dealer fell in a pool of mixed blood. Police chalked the murders up to gang violence, and only one of the Kings involved was ever charged and convicted for the murders.

Through her entire life, her father had searched for her. Her transition in and out of foster homes and her mother's constant movement and periods of homelessness made his search nearly impossible. With Sarah's death, however, Dawn's name entered the papers, and he tracked her down. He was Roger Cahill, a billionaire energy tycoon who owned most of the nation's coal, oil and natural gas. Dawn met him at the courthouse during the trial of her mother's murderer. The scene was reported on as a happy ending to a horrific tragedy. Dawn now knew her real father, a man she had never met before, and now had the kind of money she only thought socialites could get.

Having no guardian and being underage, Dawn moved in with her father. His home was a mansion in the rich district of the city, a beautiful residence with everything anyone could ever want. As the limo pulled up to the porch, Dawn saw the ornate marble columns and the hand-carved mahogany doors. Inside, there was a magnificent foyer complete with a crystal chandelier. The home had its own compliment of chefs, butlers and maids. When Dawn looked out the back set of doors onto the property, she could see past the tennis court, the basketball court and the pool all the way to the country club that Roger was a member of. When she walked down the stairs to the basement, she found a bar fully stocked with liquors that would have cost hundreds of dollars a bottle. This was Roger's man cave, where he would watch the seventy-two inch flatscreen while drinking from a bottle of liquor that cost more than her mother made in a month as a prostitute.

When she walked to the upper tier, she found it just as ornate and opulent as the rest of the home. Dawn's new bed was a hand-carved masterpiece that cost over thirteen thousand dollars. There was a rug from Iran on her bedroom floor that would have cost him another eight thousand. Another large flatscreen hung on the wall in her bedroom, and all the bedroom furniture in the room was made of mahogany and carved by artisans. Her bathroom fixtures were made of marble and had solid gold knobs and handles. Dawn found herself wondering how many years worth of rent it would take to buy a single doorknob in this place.

Merely months after, Dawn lost her father to cancer. In those months, she had grown to love her father, the man who rescued her in her darkest hour. He treated her like the princess that other girls always thought they were. Everything she wanted, she could now have. She learned to drive with his chauffeur. His maids and chefs cleaned and cooked for her. Her life was a dream until Roger's death, and it shook her greatly. The strain of so much turmoil in her life in such a short time deeply affected her. She dealt with it as best she could, by immersing herself in her new life as an heiress.

She bought and wore the clothes she never thought she could afford. She ate at the restaurants where society's elite dined. She slept in her new king-size bed. She joined her father's country club and played golf for the first time. She swam in his pool, shot hoops on his court, and played tennis against her new staff. Then, she went on a tour of her newly inherited properties. She flew to Los Angeles to see his Hollywood mansion. She flew to Miami to see his beach house. She flew to New York to see his penthouse suite in downtown. Finally, she drove his Acura to West Virginia, and she fell even more in love with Nethergarde than she did with his first home in Chicago. She sold off all three other properties and made Nethergarde her home. She even had her name changed from Jenkins to Cahill to reflect her new life.

Even the first speeding ticket she received, given to her courtesy of the Ohio Highway Patrol, was a happy memory. She remembered the fine, two hundred dollars, an amount that would have bankrupted her and starved her to death in her old life. And now, with the kind of money that dreams were made of, she simply laughed at the courthouse clerk as she handed over her bank card.

Losing herself in her memories broke the concentration she needed to maintain hypersonic speed. She slowed quickly from mach 5 down to less than two hundred miles per hour from the sudden loss of power. She still flew, not paying attention to what was around her, until her foot caught a freeway sign posted over the interstate. The sudden catch flipped her earthward and shook her out of her memory. A pair of spectral hands seized Dawn around the waist and carried her skyward, preventing the collision with the tarmac below.

Dawn came to a stop and turned around. Behind her, she could see the ghostly form of High Priestess Amynta, who still occupied the shield.

"High Priestess, the Solari Aegis can be dangerous if used improperly." Amynta said. "Pay attention when you're flying, otherwise you might crash."

"Sorry." Dawn apologized. "I just... got caught up in my own head. Thanks. For saving me."

"You're welcome. Be careful."

Amynta's spectral form phased back into the shield, and Dawn took off again, finally coming back to land on the rooftop at Nethergarde.

Chapter 23

Trouble in Paradise

Light's Bulwark Fortress, West Virginia
Two weeks later

Rick's voice rang out over the intercom. "Dawn, come up to the rooftop! You have to see this!"

Dawn, who was training in the courtyard with Julius, was already in angel form as part of the exercise. Instead of running up the stairs to the communications array, Dawn simply leapt skyward. Her four radiant wings took her higher, easily allowing her to jump the four stories from the courtyard to the rooftop. Rick had his back turned to the courtyard, facing a computer where he was still working. The *thud* of Dawn's feet hitting the rooftop floor visibly spooked Rick. He spun around quickly and raised his fists, only to lower them when he saw Dawn.

"Jesus shit Dawn, you scared me!" Rick half-yelled.

"Sorry!" Dawn apologized.

"Anyway, I hacked into an American anti-missile satellite and put it in geo-sync orbit over the fortress. It was designed to interact with a ground-based laser that was under construction out in Montana when the zombie attack happened. There's a few more of the things in geo-sync over our allies. Western Europe has one, Israel has one, South Korea, Australia... anyway. The original intent was for the Americans to shoot the Montana laser at the one I moved over us, and mirror it around the globe using the others to redirect it back down at any

147

missiles the Chinese or Iranians launched. But with it over us, I think you might be able to break the Swiss out of the siege they're under."

"But I don't have any kind of beam attack. So I can't do much with that."

"Yet. That's another project Dave and the others are finishing in the basement. It's something we're calling a "lens chamber". Basically, it's a chamber with a lens at the top and mirrors all around to redirect light. We think you can just radiate power in all directions, and the lens chamber will turn it into a laser I can shoot at whatever the hell we need eliminated."

"You want me to be the battery for your laser thing."

"Exactly. I could probably power the thing with a nuclear reactor, but I don't exactly have a nuclear reactor lying around.

"Once you finish that lens chamber, get it up to the courtyard. Julius can do it with the forklift. I have to imagine it's probably just a ball about seven feet in diameter?"

"Well it's more of a cone, but yeah, it's about that size. The forklifts can move it."

"This is gonna be epic. Find out where Aaron and Stacie are, and we'll just hit them with the laser. We'll probably still have to kill the rest of the undead, but without Aaron and Stacie directing them, they'll not be able to put together any sort of strategy."

"Will do."

Within a few hours, the lens chamber was finished. It was a simple design, using mirrored surfaces in an array to focus all the light into a lens, which would narrow it into a destructive beam. Julius carefully lifted the device using the forklift and drove it aboard the heavy lift, which carried it up into the courtyard. Julius sat the device down, lens end up, on the opposite side of the courtyard as the Helix and its pad.

"I don't have the satellite in position exactly." Rick told Dawn. "I need you to go into the chamber and close it up, then show me what you've got. That way I know where to put the satellite, and how much power we're talking here."

Dawn entered the newly placed lens chamber and sealed the door shut behind her. The latch was a small pin that she could rotate to lock and unlock the door. In its locked position, the entry side was mirrored too, preventing loss of energy in that direction. Dawn channeled light through all parts of her body, allowing it to escape at full power from every pore in her body. Though she couldn't see while radiating, the beam looked fairly wimpy to the observers in the courtyard. It was only about the width of a finger, not the beam of death with a radius as wide as the lens everyone was expecting. After a few seconds, Dawn stopped and unlatched the device to exit.

Rick simply stared at the display, mouth agape. He never noticed that Dawn even stopped firing and exited the chamber. On his display, a graph of power output from the emission point was showing Dawn's maximum power capacity – eleven hundred million watts. He continued to stare at the graph for a few more seconds before finally snapping out of his reverie and grabbing the microphone.

"Dawn, I think I'm a genius." Rick announced to the entire compound over the intercom. "When all your power is focused into one point, it adds up to about eleven hundred mil. That's as strong as the anti-missile laser we're replicating, since it's supposed to vaporize a missile in a less than a tenth of a second. I think it's because of how the shield works. It doesn't have any diminishing power curve. Emitting from one site or a hundred thousand gives the same power per beam. The Greeks couldn't harness it because they didn't know how to build lenses. We do, and now we've got a death laser. You ready for the second test?"

"Second test?" Dawn asked. "What second test?"

"The Swiss are under siege. They're able to repel the undead for now, but they've got all hands on deck right now. The undead have too many – they'll eventually overrun the Swiss if they keep pressing at the rate they are. I've got control over a spy satellite in geosync over Berlin left over from the Cold War. I'm moving it to see over the German border, where the undead are attacking from primarily. Scanners estimate they've got three million amassed, including flesh golems."

"Let's go for it then. I wanna see how long I can keep it up."

"Satellites moving into position. Dawn, you're cleared to fire."

Rick flipped a switch, relaying the signal from the Cold War satellite to every television in the fortress. Light's Bulwark's defenders filled rooms with televisions to watch through Rick's eye in the sky. Dawn re-entered the lens chamber, sealed the hatch, and released her energy again. Light poured from her pores in all directions. It shined through her clothes, coloring itself based on the color of her clothes. Her red shirt reflected the red light back into her body, amplifying her output everywhere by backfeeding power. Her blue jeans did the same thing to the blue light. All the light emitted was bounced around the lens chamber by the mirrors before finally exiting through the lens at the top. The finger-width beam struck the first satellite, then the second. A lens on the second satellite, one that nobody knew existed, expanded the finger-width beam into a circle of death the size of an average bathroom. The targeted flesh golem and everything immediately around it was vaporized within a hundredth of a second by the tremendous power of the makeshift ion cannon.

"Yeah!" Rick cheered as he started aiming the second satellite with his computer. As the undead forces attacked, Rick moved the beam back and forth, sweeping it across tracts of land quickly. It occurred to Rick that even one degree of movement that high off the surface of the earth translated to a lot of ground movement. He continued to sweep Dawn's beam across the surface of the earth, leaving a track in the dirt where the beam was. Every undead he caught in the beam's movement was instantly vaporized, from mere mindless to mighty flesh golem.

Rick's computer kept count of how many undead he vaporized as he moved the beam. Between the devastating power the beam held, the speed at which Rick could move it across the earth, and the size of the expanded beam, Rick could slay nearly twenty thousand undead in just over a second. Rick continued to sweep the beam across the undead, leveling them ten ranks at a time. Dawn powered the beam for just under a minute thirty before she collapsed to the floor of the lens chamber.

"One minute twenty-six seconds." Rick announced to the fortress through the intercom. "In one minute twenty-six seconds, our device killed over a mil and a half. That'll give the Swiss a break!"

Julius ran over to the lens chamber and rotated the pin on the outside, releasing the lock and opening the lens chamber. On seeing Dawn, he reached in and pulled her free. The overcoat Julius wore covered his arms, but by the time he had extracted Dawn from the chamber, his hands had third-degree burns on them. Despite the pain he was now in, he lifted her limp body and carried her into the castle. He carried her all the way up to their bed and placed her gently on it.

Back on the roof, Rick received a radio call.

"Light's Bulwark, this is Geneva. Do you read me? Over."

"Geneva, we read you." Rick replied to the French-accented voice.

"I don't know how to explain this. A... death laser... just wiped out the undead. About half their force was vaporized, and the ground's turned molten outside the walls! We have no idea of where it came from—"

Rick cut the radio operator off. "That was us. You're welcome."

"That was you? That was Light's Bulwark's weapon? What kind of weapon is it?"

"I call it the Solari Undead Nullifier. The SUN laser. We bounced it off an American anti-missile satellite."

"Thank you! You saved us! We were about to get overrun!"

"It was all we could do. Everyone's in this together."

"When will you be able to use that thing again?"

"I have to assume it's down for a while. I'll check on it and get back to you. Light's Bulwark out."

Rick paused for a moment, thinking about the Swiss position. *How are they still alive...* he pondered. *Why didn't the dead in their own country overrun them?*

"Geneva, this is Light's Bulwark. So, how did you guys manage to kill the dead in your own country?"

The French-accented voice replied. "We didn't have any dead in our country. They never got in."

"But what about the cemeteries in Switzerland? Why didn't those bodies get up?"

"I have no idea, and it's a really good thing they didn't."

"Thanks. Light's Bulwark out."

Rick left the communications array and walked down into the courtyard. The lens chamber was open, and Dawn was nowhere to be found. Upon inquiry, Rick found that Julius had carried Dawn up to their quarters. Nobody mentioned anything about the burns on Julius' hands from the superheated lens chamber.

Rick found Dawn's chamber on the second floor. When he entered, Julius was holding Dawn, kissing her forehead and whispering to her. She was completely unresponsive. Though the pain of his burns was intense, Julius seemed to not care about his own pain. He continued to hold her and caress her face, despite the unbearable pain the motion caused in his hands. Julius laid his head on Dawn's chest. He could hear a faint heartbeat, and he could feel a weak but steady rise and fall of her chest.

"You're alive..." Julius wept. "Please wake up... I love you, Dawn, please wake up..."

"What the hell happened to her?" Rick asked. "Is she okay?"

Lightning flashed in Julius' eyes. He released Dawn's hands and spun around to face Rick, a look of pure rage on his face.

"You..." Julius seethed. "You did this to her..." His voice reverberated through the room. His blistered hands clenched into fists. His jaw closed tight. His face turned red as blood rushed through his body, fueled by adrenaline. "HOW COULD YOU! YOU BASTARD! DIE!"

"I couldn't have expected--" Rick started, but stopped when Julius charged straight at him.

Julius was a strong man. He stood six feet even, weighed in at about two hundred pounds, and had years of mixed martial arts fighting under his belt. Compared to Rick's five foot six height and less than a hundred and fifty pounds, Julius was huge. Julius moved fast, closing the twenty feet between the men in less than three seconds. His steel-reinforced boots hit hard enough to crack ribs when Julius launched himself into a two-footed kick straight at Rick's chest. The kick sent Rick sailing backwards across the hallway and into the plaster interior wall. Rick slumped to the ground, unable to do much besides try to cover his face with his hands. Julius quickly dropped on top of Rick, furiously pummeling at his face with his undamaged elbows.

By this time other survivors had reached the second floor where Dawn had been taken. When they came to the top of the stairs, Julius had Rick pinned to the floor. Rick was desperately trying to cover his face. He had already flung his glasses down the hall in an effort to make sure Julius didn't break them. Jim raced over and tried to grab Julius' left arm, but Julius broke free of Jim's grasp and punched at Rick's face. Red grabbed at Julius' other arm while Jim tried to repeat his grab on the left. Nadia grabbed the back of Julius' coat and pulled. Between the three of them, despite much struggling, they were able to pull Julius off of Rick. Julius got one last stomp in as the three dragged him away, slamming his armored boot down on Rick's ankle.

"I'm gonna throw you in the forge, you bastard!" Julius shouted at Rick while being dragged away. "I'm gonna fucking kill you!"

Despite Jim's Army training and Red's farm strength, pulling Julius away was fairly difficult, but doable. Once the three dragged Julius away, a heavy-set girl with long black hair dropped down to Rick's side and started looking him over. Rick saw two of her. His nose had been broken and bloodied, his ribs were cracked, and he clearly had a concussion.

"Help me!" she shouted at the burly railgun shell loader. The former iron worker lifted Rick up. He cried out in pain as the man moved him, jostling his cracked ribs as he shifted Rick's weight. The girl opened the door to a room with a bed, ordering the shell loader to lay Rick down on it. "Don't worry, I'll take care of you." she said sweetly.

The girl turned to one of Red's crew. "Get the first aid kit! It's in the hallway! Now!"

"Yes ma'am, Kenzi!" he replied, then turned and ran down the hall to grab the first aid kit from its place mounted on the wall.

"You!" she yelled at another. "Go get Nadia! We're gonna need special medicine. She's the only one who can fly the chopper since Dawn's out. Take her place watching Julius!"

"Where do you need me, Kenzi?" one of the Army veterans asked. "I was a medic in Iraq."

"Go check on Dawn." Kenzi ordered. "Something major had to have happened for Julius to have flipped out like that. You treat her. I'll treat the others."

Chapter 24

Protecting Death's Fortress

Flame Point Fortress, Peru
That same time

"Excellent." Aaron stated as a demon's eye surveyed the three million under his command, ready to assault the Swiss defenses. "No way they've got enough ammo to repel my full assault. Switzerland's about to fall, even if that blasted angel gets in the way. There's no way she can kill three million, no matter what the hell she has."

"Aaron, don't get cocky." Stacie warned. "Remember Cloud Peak?"

"This is different, Stacie, and you know it." Aaron replied. "This is the final assault. It's do or die time. If this doesn't work, we're gonna have to play the waiting game unless you can figure out a way to get those demon's eyes to attack."

"I'm working on it, Aaron. I can only do so much. I'm also trying to figure out how to protect the fortress from attack, how to find the remaining humans living off the land, and how to attack that fortress out in West Virginia with their flushable moat that's too wide to cross and that angel protecting it."

General Pierre Du Couteau overlooked the forces he had at the German border with Switzerland. His force stretched out over fourteen thousand square miles, nearly a tenth of Germany's land area. Amassed here were three million undead in battle formation. The general used the psychic link to give the order to march. The flesh golems, cavaliers and mindless started towards the Swiss defensive wall.

"Watch as the defenders of Switzerland start wasting the front lines. They'll waste my minions for a while, but eventually their logistics will fail, just as everyone else's did. I can press the attack twenty-four hours a day for weeks on end. They'll fall – just watch."

A beam of yellow light came down from the sky, hitting and incinerating the leading flesh golem.

"It's that angel again!" Aaron shouted at the display. "But where is she?"

"Demon's eye looking up. I don't see her." Stacie replied. "Climbing. Still nothing, all I can see is an American satellite at the top of the beam."

"American satellite... those bastards figured out how to power up the American ion cannon!" Aaron exclaimed. "Oh well, they've only got ten seconds of fire then... they're still firing? What the hell is going on?!"

The yellow beam now swept back and forth across the undead lines, killing ranks ten at a time, over twenty thousand undead a second. The beam sustained itself far longer than the ion cannon Aaron believed it was. Twenty seconds went by, and it showed no signs of stopping. Thirty seconds, and the ground below was turning molten. Sixty seconds, and it still showed no signs of stopping. Finally, after eighty-six seconds, the beam stopped. Half the force was eliminated. Aaron grabbed his head in pain as the death signals from eighty thousand cavaliers flooded his brain.

"No!" he cried. "No more! Make it stop! Make it stop!"

When the signals finally were processed and sorted, Aaron looked up. General Du Couteau was retreating his forces. The ion beam had liquefied the rocky ground and set fire to the grass around. The area was now impassible. Worse still, the ion cannon had dropped the terrain level ten feet in all the places it hit. The entire sector now was impassible to undead for good, and bodies were incinerated as well, preventing recovery and flesh golem building. Though the necromancers at the back survived, and Aaron still had one and a half million undead in the area, the day was lost, as was his opportunity to blitz the Swiss defenders here. Now, the Swiss would get to regroup. They could move all the defenders from this area to other areas now that the undead would never be able to pass here.

"What the hell was that?!" Aaron exclaimed. "That damned ion cannon wiped out half my force!"

"I see that." Stacie replied. "The bigger concern is that they're gonna hit our fortress with it. We need to mirror the outside of the fortress."

"Well how the hell are we gonna do that?"

"We're gonna need paint. Lots of paint. We can use undead labor to paint the fortress reflective silver. That way the beam will bounce off and go in some other direction. We're gonna need the bird again. Do you know anything about the ion cannon, like when they'll be able to fire it again?"

"The American ion cannon can't fire for more than ten seconds at a time. Normally, they'd get to fire it once every twenty-four hours, but I don't think that's what they used. I think the angel did something, but I'm not sure what or how often she can do it. In any case, we need to paint the fortress. Probably the only reason they didn't annihilate us is because they don't know where we are. Let's hope they don't find us till we've mirrored the fortress."

"So how do you plan to get paint? We can't just buy it, we've killed everyone that sells it already."

"We're just gonna break in, duh. Just like we did at Hoover. Except this time we don't have to fly forty-one hours to get it. We're only flying to Lima. Surely that mirror factory still has some. It's a non-critical supply, so it would've gotten left behind."

Stacie and Aaron left through the helix staircase, going down through the spell lab and into the entry hall of the fortress before finally exiting through the front gate. Stacie faced skyward, forming a ball of flame in her hand. "Ryzuul, Qaathi, Viceros!" she shouted, and the bird flew down from its perch atop the fortress. The couple mounted and flew off across Peru.

This journey only took a couple hours. The villages they passed over had been completely ransacked by the undead. Rural farming villages with little technology proved easy prey for death's royal couple. They simply let their undead loose on the villages, and even without command, the undead wiped out the villagers. Armed with only farming tools, the villagers stood no chance. After the villagers were annihilated, the necromancers came in, absorbing the fallen corpses into the army of the dead.

Finding the city was easy, but navigating it was difficult. As the bird weaved through the city's streets, the royals could see the devastation they had wrought. Storefronts had been smashed in. Boards and glass littered the already dirty streets. Burned-out husks were all that remained of some of the buildings, primarily in the poor districts of the city where most structures were built out of scrap.

Stacie brought the bird low over the city's streets, but Aaron still had a hard time seeing the street signs and reading the map. He also struggled with the Spanish signs, finding it difficult to match up the street signs to the streets on the map. It took them another two hours of flying around the industrial district of the city to find the correct location. They flew over it a couple times not noticing, simply because of the Spanish language signs.

The warehouse for La Empresa de Espejo de Gonzalez was abandoned. It hadn't started falling into disrepair yet, having sat for only months and not decades. The employee parking lot, devoid of cars, was a perfect landing site for the great flaming bird. Stacie touched its feet to the ground, having it walk for a couple dozen feet before finally stopping to bleed off its speed without crashing. Aaron and Stacie dismounted, and the bird once again flew off back towards Flame Point. Aaron and Stacie entered the warehouse, finding it full of the raw materials required to make mirrors. Panes of glass were stacked up on skids. Other skids carried wood and metal used to build mirror frames. About seven skids held five gallon buckets, stacked five feet high and occupying as much of the skid base as possible. Though labeled in Spanish, there was little else the buckets could contain other than mirror paint.

"I'd bet those buckets are the paint." Aaron shouted at Stacie as she looked in another part of the warehouse. "But how do we get it back to Flame Point?"

Stacie surveyed the factory for a few seconds before replying. "Our home teleports can carry stuff with us if I do it right. If we can put the paint on the freight lift, we can warp the whole lift floor and everything on it back with us."

"Okay then. Let's use those forklifts over there." Aaron said as he pointed at the forklifts in the corner near a tank of diesel fuel.

Aaron and Stacie walked over to the forklifts and each started one up. The diesel-powered forklifts, still carrying fuel in their tanks, started up at the turning of the keys. Aaron immediately pulled his forklift out and drove over towards the wrapped skids of paint. He lined the forklift's tongs up with the holes in the skid designed for them and drove forward. With his tongs lined up, he pushed the lifting lever, lifting the skid into the air.

The skids were wrapped quite well. The metal bands that held the stacked buckets to the skid were attached with precise care by the factory workers, holding them in place for Aaron to lift the skids without spilling the buckets. He swiveled the forklift around to face the lift and depressed the accelerator with his heavy armored boot.

"Remember Eagle?" Aaron shouted over the drone of the forklift's engine. "Remember when we broke into that plant over Labor Day and played with their forklifts?"

"Yeah!" Stacie replied. "That was back when we were just punks. Before we learned what power really is. If someone told you back then what you'd be today, what would you think?"

"I'd tell 'em they were full of it!" Aaron shouted back. "I'd never imagined I'd be king of anything, let alone undead!"

"And imagine, that day led to this! If not for then, we wouldn't know how to drive these things!"

Aaron dropped the skid onto the freight lift and backed the forklift back out. "One down!" he called out as he spun the forklift back around. Stacie, by this time, had secured herself a skid of paint and was driving it across the factory floor towards the lift. Since the two were at opposite points on the floor, they never ran their forklifts together, despite having no formal training in forklift operation.

Placing the seven skids aboard the freight lift was a simple matter of time. The forklifts were limited to a very slow speed, but eventually Aaron placed the last skid down on the lift. Aaron waved at Stacie, directing her to abandon the forklift in a corner. With both forklifts in the corner, the couple walked back to the lift. They each pulled out their teleport stones, engraved with the sigil for "home", and placed them on the floor of the lift, sigil side up. In perfect sync with each other, Aaron and Stacie traced the runes on the stones. The stones began to glow purple-black, enveloping Aaron, Stacie, the freight lift, and the skids of paint.

The entire freight lift platform appeared in the main room of Flame Point Fortress, with the royals and the skids of paint aboard. Aaron immediately tapped into his mental link with Olaf Falkenskold, the undead general who helped him find Ondesverd, which now sat at Aaron's throne on his left side.

"My lord!" Olaf said as Aaron focused in on him. Olaf's face appeared on the viewscreen in the main room.

"Olaf, I need all your mindless for labor at the fortress. Stacie's gonna build a portal with one of your necros. Get one so we can. I need you and your mindless to funnel through the portal."

"On it, sir." Olaf replied, signaling for a nearby necromancer to come to his side.

Stacie focused on the necromancer, channeling void purple energy between her hands. The hooded necromancer channeled similar energy. The energy links grew wider in the center, expanding outward to form a noticeable circle at the middle of the channel. The circle grew oblong, longer in the vertical plane, and started to expand. The necromancer and Stacie both moved their hands out to wider positions, allowing the portals to expand to a full seven feet high and five feet wide. Stacie focused on the portal and stepped aside, just as the necro on the other side did. Undead started to walk through the portal on the Norse side, appearing on the fortress side. Olaf directed the undead to unload the skids of paint, and groups of two carried the buckets down the helix stairs towards the first floor.

Chapter 25

Treating All Wounds

Light's Bulwark Fortress, West Virginia
Shortly after

Julius sat on a bed in a guest bedroom with Jim and Red guarding the door. Kenzi stood over him, rubbing burn cream on his badly blistered hands. With his adrenaline rush gone, the full effects of the pain were starting to take effect. Every touch from Kenzi made him wince in pain.

"I'm almost done. This cream will help your burns heal. Now I just need to bandage you up."

Kenzi held a roll of gauze over Julius' left hand. She stretched it out and placed the end in his palm, wrapping it between his finger and thumb and bringing it back around his hand. She carefully wrapped each finger in gauze, as well as the palm part of his hand, before cutting the gauze from the roll and taping it down. She repeated the process on his right hand, sealing the burn cream on his hands inside the bandages.

"Now, what happened out there?" Kenzi asked Julius. "Why were you hitting Rick?"

"Did you see what he did to Dawn?" Julius asked angrily. "He damn near killed her!"

"He couldn't have known what that device was going to do. He only saw the good part from his seat at the control desk. You missed it because you were watching the lens chamber."

"The good part?" he asked. "What good part?"

"That device killed a million and a half undead over in Switzerland and blocked the pass. Now Aaron has to find another pass to assault, and regroup more forces."

"That makes it a little better, but if she doesn't make a full recovery I'm still gonna kill him. He's an engineer, he should've known better."

"Engineers don't know everything, Julius. Neither do doctors, or generals, or anybody else. And besides, as brilliant as Rick is, he doesn't actually have an engineering degree yet. He's only a senior, he wouldn't have graduated until May and the outbreak hit in March."

Kenzi stood up and walked towards the door now that Julius had been treated.

"Make sure you drink lots of water. Jim, Red, help him with that. I'm gonna go out to the helicopter pad and wait for Nadia to come back with the medicine from CAMC."

Charleston Area Medical Center, or CAMC as it was known to the locals, was the best hospital for a hundred miles around. In the time of the living, there were only two comparable hospitals in the entire state. Before the war, anyone with life-threatening injuries would have been taken there by helicopter. When the zombies attacked, the hospital staff were mostly unarmed. They knew they wouldn't be able to hold the hospital, and so they fled and abandoned the patients to their fate. They left the majority of the medicines behind, locked in the pharmacy behind a door. It was a simple matter for Laina to break the door down with a sledge hammer, allowing her and Nadia to load up the Helix with medicine.

The sound of the helicopter's rotors reached the fortress before Kenzi saw the helicopter coming in from the west. With the medics clear, Nadia sat the Helix down on the pad, turned off the engine, and pulled the manual brake to stop the rotors quickly. While Nadia and Laina simply started to unload the pilfered medicine, Kenzi quickly sorted through the medicine to find the anesthetic to put Rick to sleep. She carried it up from the helicopter pad to Rick's room and fed him the medicine. It took effect quickly, putting the engineer to sleep so his wounds could be worked on.

Kenzi first fixed Rick's damaged ankle. The stomp had damaged bones, so it had to be set and put in a brace. As for his ribs, she coerced the bones into their proper places with small movements, then bandaged his torso tight to prevent the broken bones from moving. Rick would have to stay here for six to eight weeks to allow healing, but there was little more she could do. With a proper facility and doctors, surgery may have been an option, but here in the middle of a losing war, this would have to do.

After the medics were finished with Rick and were watching him, waiting on him to wake up, another Light's Bulwark defender entered Rick's room with urgent news.

"Dawn's awake!" he shouted. "Dawn's awake!"

"Watch Rick. If he doesn't wake up within two hours, let me know. I need to go."

Kenzi left the room Rick was staying in and went to Dawn's room. She was awake and sitting up in her bed, with no visible wounds or other illness besides her current state of weakness.

"Dawn, you okay?" Kenzi asked. "How are you feeling?"

"That was too much." Dawn yawned. "Never again..." she trailed off.

"Tim, get her some water." Kenzi ordered. The army medic who helped Kenzi earlier walked out of the room.

"Thank you." Dawn said in a weak voice.

"You did amazing." Kenzi said. "You wiped out half the attacking force and saved the Swiss. It was amazing. You wanna see it?"

"Sure."

Kenzi flipped on a television. All the televisions, when on, now displayed a looping feed from Rick's hacked satellite. Dawn watched as her own beam hit the ground, amplified by the lens on the satellite. As the beam moved across the ground, everything caught in the beam vaporized, from undead to trees to abandoned homes and vehicles. Even the ground beneath liquefied, turning to molten magma in places.

"Wow..." Dawn said, impressed. "Hey, where's Julius, anyway?"

"Um..."

Kenzi told Dawn the story of how Julius carried her from the lens chamber to her room when she passed out. She also told Dawn about Julius blaming Rick for her state, and how he flew into a rage and pummeled the engineer. She spoke of the burns on Julius' hands, and how he seemed to not care about them when he carried her away.

"He did all that?" she asked. "He fought Rick... because he thought Rick hurt me?"

"Yeah. Can't figure out why either."

"Awww..." Dawn replied. "That's actually kinda sweet of him, to fight for me like that. He's wrong, but it's still sweet."

"Any idea why he flipped like that?" Kenzi inquired.

"I think it's because of Courtney."

"Courtney?"

"Courtney was his first love, before I ever moved out here. He's showed me pictures of her. He's told me I look like her in some ways. He dated her from when he was a junior in high school until his sophomore year of college. They were gonna get married when he graduated college. Then there was an explosion in the apartment complex she lived in. Turns out some jackass was cooking meth there and blew the place sky high. The cops said she burned up in the fire."

"Wow... that's so sad..." Kenzi replied, depressed.

"It's kind of strange," Dawn commented. "He trusts me to fight at his side against clear enemies like undead, but he's more protective of me towards people who don't call themselves enemies. He's always been that way, ever since we got together. I don't get it."

"He knows you're strong, so he knows you can fight on your own. He just wants to make sure there aren't enemies hiding in the shadows. It makes perfect sense."

"Oh... okay, I think I understand... but what about Rick? We can't have Rick and Julius wanting each other dead or we'll never win this war."

Dawn stopped for a second. "Where's Julius?" she asked.

"He's down the hall under guard. I put burn ointment on his burns and wrapped his hands in gauze."

"I want to see him, and I bet he wants to see me too."

"He does. Come on, I'll help you."

"I'll be okay. I can walk on my own."

Dawn eased herself out of her bed. After the laser attack, she was still exhausted. It took considerable effort for her to move out of the room and down the hall. Kenzi walked along Dawn's left side, Tim at her right, both ready to catch her should she stumble. Though it took a while, Dawn finally reached the room where Julius was staying. Kenzi reached out and knocked on the door.

"It's Kenzi. Let me in. I've got Dawn with me."

Jim opened the door, letting Julius see Kenzi, Tim and Dawn, all standing in front of the door. Dawn still looked pale and weak, but she was conscious and walking around again.

"Dawn!" Julius shouted as he leapt from the bed. His burned hands shot pain through his arms when he lifted himself up with them. "Damn it!" he swore.

"Julius, are you okay?" Dawn yawned. She walked towards him, and he cradled her in his arms. He tried to not press his hands against her with his hug.

"I was going to ask you the same thing. How bad are you hurt?"

"I'm not, just exhausted. My question is, what the hell were you thinking?"

"He hurt you, Dawn. Nobody hurts you and gets away with it, not since that first day when you came to my home."

"Julius, I love you, but you're an idiot! Rick's not Lee, he's an ally! Without him, there wouldn't be a hundred Tibetan monks in my fortress. They'd be part of the undead army trying to knock the walls down."

"Dawn, when I pulled you from the lens chamber, I thought you were dead..." Julius was visibly shaken emotionally by now. "I thought I lost you. I didn't know you were gonna just take a nap and be fine. I thought you were gonna die, or stay unconscious long enough for the undead to overrun us. I thought he had killed you with his contraption, that's why I attacked him."

"But he didn't. The lens chamber worked perfectly, I just overexerted myself. I can't sustain the prism attack forever. It was my fault I collapsed, not his. He did nothing wrong."

"Okay. But that means..." Julius stopped. "But that means I hit him for no reason." He covered his face in his hands. "I don't know what I can do to make it up to him, we're in the middle of a war here."

"One of the prophecies said I would be able to heal. If I can figure out how to heal, I'll be able to fix what you did to Rick. I wonder if it has anything to do with the divine emblems I can paint on my shield. Just stay here. I'm gonna see Laina and see if she has any insight on it. Probably we'll also check out the library."

Chapter 26

Repairing Bodies and Minds

Light's Bulwark Fortress, West Virginia
Three hours later

After drinking some coffee and eating food, Dawn was feeling mostly better from her ordeal with the lens chamber. Now, she sat in the library, reading through a book that had been translated from the ancient Greek by a historian many years ago. The book was originally written in Greek, and told the supposedly mythical tale of Pherenike, the second High Priestess of the Solari order. Now that Dawn carried Solari magic, she realized that the myths were true.

It was fortunate that Roger Cahill was interested in mythology. He greatly enjoyed reading epic tales of battle, gods and magic, so much so that he stocked his private library with any and all books on the subject he could find. When he lived, he got enjoyment from these books, but now, the massive library he had amassed was giving his daughter the power to save the world. This was something Roger would never have imagined. Never in his wildest dreams did his books provide anybody anything useful.

The book Dawn was reading told of a battle between Athenians and Phoenicians, where the two sides were evenly matched and neither commander wanted to surrender. Pherenike and her Solari came upon the battle shortly after it ended. There were no standing soldiers, either Athenians or Phoenicians. Many of the soldiers lay on the battlefield, impaled by spears or stabbed through by swords, bleeding to death.

Pherenike turned her shield over and drew a sun on the backside in the blood of one of the already slain Athenians. With the sigil of her own god on the back of her shield as well as the front, she was able to amplify the power that Apollo lent to his Solari. Instead of simply adding divine power to her attacks as she previously did, Pherenike was able to turn Apollo's sunlight into healing energy.

Pherenike strapped her spear across her back and used her now-empty weapon hand to channel sunlight. With her touch, she could close the wounds of the bleeding soldiers and restore them to their former states. Though she was unable to raise those who had already died, she still was able to add a sizeable force of Athenian hoplites to her Solari squad. With her force of Solari, now reinforced by the Athenian hoplites, she was able to assault the reserve camp of the Phoenicians and win the battle.

"Dawn?" Julius's voice pierced the quiet of the library. "Are you in here?"

"Over here." Dawn replied. Julius maneuvered through the stacks to reach her.

"I thought you were going to talk to Rick."

"He hasn't woken back up from Kenzi's makeshift surgery, but I think I've found something better."

"Oh?"

"I guess Dad had some fascination with mythology. There's so many books on it in here he had to, and it's good he did. I've gotten a lot of information on the shield from his books. Anyway, the better thing. This book talks about when Athens fought the Phoenicians. Remember how everything Solari is based on Apollo?"

"Yeah, the Solari worshipped him and got their power from him."

"And remember how the High Priestess can inscribe sigils of Olympians on the back of the shield to get more powers?"

"Yeah..."

"I guess Pherenike painted the sigil of her own god, Apollo, on the back of the Solari shield. I think that's how the prophecy expects me to heal, since Pherenike healed bleeding Athenian soldiers that way."

"So does that mean you can heal?"

"I think so."

"If you can, go heal Rick. That'll go a long way towards making him forgive me."

"Hey Dawn, we found something major!" a male voice sounded over the intercom, clearly excited. "I think it's their base or something!"

"Dawn, go heal Rick." Julius asked. "Nadia or someone can see what the engineers need."

"You're right, healing Rick is more important. Lemme go get my art supplies and send Nadia to the roof."

Dawn placed her book down and picked up the library's intercom microphone. "Nadia, go check the roof and see what the engineers have for me. I've got healing to do."

Dawn retrieved her art supplies and painted on the back of the Solari Aegis, forming the circle with rays emanating in all directions commonly used to symbolize the sun. Though finished, the paint was wet and would get on her skin if she tried to equip the shield immediately. Worse still, the paint would smudge and disrupt the sigil, preventing the effect from working.

Not wishing to waste time, she tried to think of something that would make the paint dry faster. She noticed a fire extinguisher sitting on a table, overlooking it at first while she considered everything else that was in the room. She stopped and turned back to the extinguisher, looking at its type printed on the side. The type was exactly what she wanted, a B-C type fire extinguisher that would spray pressurized carbon dioxide.

"Here we go!" she said to herself as she picked up the extinguisher. Dawn pulled the pin and tossed it aside, then aimed the nozzle at the shield and squeezed the clamp. A cloud of cold carbon dioxide rushed from the fire extinguisher and hit the shield. Dawn only maintained pressure for two seconds, but this was more than sufficient for the carbon dioxide to freeze the paint. With the paint dry, Dawn picked up the shield and placed it back on her arm. Though the shield was now quite cold from exposure to the extinguisher, it would not harm her. The paint held and did not run, having been frozen to the shield.

She carried the shield up to where Rick was barely awake and in pain from his injuries. Laina sat at his side, holding his hands in hers.

"Hey Dawn." Laina said as she entered. "What's going on?"

"Stand back, I think I have a way to fix him." Dawn answered.

"Sweet, go for it." she replied, releasing Rick's hands and stepping away.

Dawn spoke the oath of the Solari, allowing her wings to emerge and activating the light magic of the shield. She turned it back on itself, sending it through the sun she painted on the reverse side. The light from the shield intensified, and Dawn redirected it back into her free hand.

She placed her free hand on Rick's bandaged chest. The bones rejoined and grew back together. She moved her hand to Rick's damaged ankle, undoing the damage that Julius caused with his steel-reinforced work boots. She placed her hand on his face, and his blackened and swollen eyes returned to normal. Rick's fatigue from the medicine also faded as her magic accelerated his recovery.

"How... how did you do that?!" Rick asked, dumbfounded.

"Remember how I painted Hermes' wings on the back of my shield? Well, I did it with Apollo's sun this time. Since I'm already a priestess of Apollo anyway, I just backfeed my own light through my own sigil, and it intensifies it. Apparently, so much that Pherenike could heal sword and spear wounds... and I could heal you."

"Thank you!" Rick exclaimed.

"You're welcome. Now I need to go see what Jason and Dave wanted. I guess they found something on your comms panel."

"Hey Dawn, hold up." Rick said as she started to walk away. "What the hell happened to Julius anyway that made him flip shit on me?"

"He's super protective of me, especially against our friends oddly enough. I think he's like this because of how his last girlfriend died. She was killed by her neighbor when his meth lab blew. Nobody even knew the asshole made meth."

"I can see why that messed with him." he replied as he looked over towards Laina. "I don't know what I'd do if something happened to you."

"I already talked to him. He's really sorry. He kinda jumped to Courtney and how she died. She knew the guy who cooked meth. She used to drive him across town to get his kids for the weekends. From all accounts, he was a nice guy. He saw parallels between that and what happened to me with the lens chamber, that's why he went crazy and hit you. Can you forgive him?"

"I lost a girlfriend to foul play too. Her name was Andrea. She drove home from my place around when all the bars closed down. Someone ran a light and hit her on her side. Found out later he was twice the legal limit, driving on a suspended license, and had lost his license for drinking and driving.

Laina moved back to Rick's side and kissed him on the cheek, pulling him into a hug.

"Alright, I need to go see what Jason and Dave found." At the mention of the comms array, Rick turned back to look at Dawn.

"I'll come with."

Dawn and Rick walked up the stairs to the communications array on the roof. Dave, Nadia and Jason had a display of a black stone compound. It was a rectangular shape at its base, but about a third of the way up the structure it changed to a cylindrical shape with a domed top. Undead swarmed around the outside and top of the compound, covering it with what looked like silver paint. On the top third, a strange hole had been cut in the side of the structure, reaching just under half the distance around the dome.

"Hey Dawn... Rick? How are you standing?" Dave asked.

"Dawn healed me. She figured out how the prophecy wanted her to heal." Rick replied.

"Turns out I just have to put the sigil of Apollo on the back of my shield, just like I did with Hermes to fly at hypersonic." Dawn added.

"Glad you're feeling better, dude. So like, what the hell's the issue with Julius?" Dave asked.

"Dawn told me about the girl he used to date. I guess some jackass in her building made meth and his lab blew up, and that's how she died. He saw some kinda weird link between that and the lens chamber."

"That's weird as shit, but okay. Check this out."

"What the hell are they doing?" Rick asked.

"I haven't the foggiest." Jason replied. "Looks like they're... painting some weird base... built over an active volcano?"

"Wait a second." Rick said as he looked at the paint closer. "That's mirror paint. The kind they use to make beauty mirrors. It reflects light, that's why mirrors are reflective."

"So... they're trying to make their fortress reflective?" Dave asked, not putting the pieces together in his mind.

"Exactly. You do realize we just fired a laser and wiped out a lot of their forces, right?"

"So they're trying to stop us from hitting their fortress with it?" Nadia asked.

"Precisely."

"Absolutely not." Dawn interjected. "I'm not firing that thing again if we don't absolutely have to, and besides, I couldn't power that thing now even if I wanted to. It's gonna take me days to get back to where I can do that."

"So if we don't annihilate the base with the laser, how are we gonna attack it?" Rick asked.

"We could storm it." Nadia suggested. "Just fly there, march in, and blow whatever they've got left of their brains out."

"Storm it." Rick repeated. "You want to storm the fortress of a necromancer, one who can teleport undead in to defend it, and one who has attack magic. You realize we have to leave Light's Bulwark and make ourselves vulnerable to do that, right?"

"What about nukes?" Dave asked.

"Where the hell do you expect us to get nukes from?" Jason replied.

"What about the Navy? They've got some."

"Bad idea." Dawn answered. "You realize their base's over an active volcano, right? If we nuke the fortress, we'll set off the volcano and probably cause a quake and a tsunami too. As if we don't have enough problems, let's add a global radioactive ash cloud and a major earthquake to our problems."

"So what do you think we should do?" Dave asked Dawn.

"I vote we storm it, like Nadia suggested." she replied.

"And I vote you fire the laser again and wipe it out before they finish painting."

"No!" Dawn replied.

"I've gotta agree with Dawn here, if only from an engineering standpoint." Jason added. "They've already got a lot of paint on the fortress. If we fire the laser at the fortress, at least some of that laser's gonna reflect back up and hit the attack satellite. Except it's gonna be at some caddywhompus angle and it'll hit wrong. That's just a good way of melting the satellite and making sure we can't use the laser later."

"There's also the risk of the laser setting off the volcano." Dave mentioned. "If I can't nuke it cause of the volcano, won't the laser be bad too for the same reason?"

"Okay fine, we won't use the laser." Rick conceded. "But we're gonna need help from the Navy people to hold out that long without walls. And we'll need weapons that won't run out of ammo."

"Hold on. I don't actually think so." Dave replied as he started moving the intelligence satellite. "Yep. See that mountain down the pass with a flat top?"

"Yeah, but what's that got to do with anything?"

"The undead can't climb the cliff face, but we can. Especially if we put a team with ropes at the top. We blast a trail for Dawn to get in the building, then we retreat there. Dawn can handle herself against them, even with their magic... wait a second, hold on. That's strange."

"What?"

"There's a strange window in the dome. It couldn't have been built that way. That hole had to be cut there after it was built, and it looks like there's some kind of burn marks. If I zoom in I can see what looks like a giant TV through there. It's showing undead moving through what looks like France."

"A TV?" Jason asked. "Could they be doing something with the satellites like we are?"

"No, it's those eye things." Dawn answered. "Remember the one Dani blasted with the railgun? And the other one I blasted? I'd bet that's how they see what's going on at a battlefield."

"That makes sense." Rick said. "Huh. Dave, move over. I need to check something."

Rick entered a few lines of code, and the computer measured the angle of the hole that was cut in the side of the enemy compound. He joined the feed from another satellite alongside this one, choosing a satellite much further along the curve of the earth than this one. This satellite was measuring the dome more from the side, giving him a better view of the viewscreen on the inside. He entered the same code to this feed, giving him another measurement.

"The hole in the side of the fortress is at precisely the angle of the viewscreen." Rick reported.

"What? The hole... is the same angle as the viewscreen? Do you think the viewscreen somehow put the hole there?" Dave inquired.

"I don't know, but it looks like energy of some sort came through the screen and cut the hole. My guess is one of their spells misfired somehow. Like maybe Stacie tried to shoot a spell through one of those eyes and it went horribly wrong."

"So what did we decide? Are we storming it?" Dawn asked.

"Since you *refuse* to use the laser," Rick answered. "I guess we have to storm it."

"That road across the crater would make a good staging point. That's where we land our forces, and we cross the bridge and attack that way." Jason suggested.

"Excellent idea. But what about ammo?"

"Ammo? We've got all the ammo we need."

"But we can't take it anywhere, remember? Most of it's for the big guns that we aren't taking."

Rick looked back at Dawn, who had Spell-Drinker in a sheath strapped to her back and the Solari Aegis fastened over it.

"What about melee weapons?" Rick suggested.

"Melee weapons? You mean like my sword and shield?" Dawn inquired.

"Yeah. They don't run out of ammo, so there's no limit to how much we can carry. If we use our guns, we get weighed down by all the ammo and we'll still run out. If we use melee weapons, we can keep fighting for as long as we need to, provided it doesn't last so long we get exhausted."

Jason added a thought of his own. "Also, that means ideally we'll have shields, which the undead can't do shit to. So we just make a shield wall at the top of that mountain once we're all up. They can't climb, so we'll just hold out there till Dawn comes back and wipes the floor with em."

"But how do we get melee weapons?" Jason asked.

"I know." Nadia chimed in.

"I remember a place." she added. "They sold real metal swords and battleaxes and the like. Their weapons were blunted, but surely this place has some kind of grinder we could use to sharpen them. It's in Pittsburgh, but we're close enough to fly there by helicopter. And when the zombie war broke out, the stingy bastards who owned the place boarded it up and locked it down. I bet the weapons are still there."

"Excellent. Tomorrow you and Dawn can fly there in the Helix and check it out."

"If it's locked, I'm sure I can just blast my way in. It'll be easy."

Dawn started to walk back down the stairs, but then she stopped and took the intercom mic.

"Julius, come upstairs to the comms array." she called out to the entire fortress. Minutes later, he walked up the stairs and onto the roof.

"Hey Dawn. Oh, looks like you were able to heal Rick," he said.

"Hold still." she ordered him. She placed her hands over his bandaged ones and channeled her healing light through both. The burns on his hands disappeared and stopped hurting.

"Thank you." he said as she started to unravel the gauze Kenzi wrapped around his hands.

"Rick, come over here."

"Rick..." Julius started. "I'm so sorry. I just..."

"Dawn told me already. About Courtney." Rick interrupted. "We're cool. I know what that feels like. I lost a love to foul play too. I'd shake your hand to seal it, but Dawn's blocking."

"Hold on guys, I'm almost finished. Kenzi's damn good at this."

When Dawn finally finished unraveling the gauze, Julius reached his right hand out towards Rick. The men shook hands.

"We're good now." Rick said. "And I promise not to make Dawn fire that thing again."

"Don't break it though." Dawn replied. "Just in case I have to."

"And I'll do anything to make sure you don't have to." Julius answered.

Chapter 27

Into Position

Flame Point Fortress
That Same Time

Aaron sat at his throne, watching undead in Siberia sort through the snow and ice to find holdouts. These Russians he searched for now were the hardiest members of an already resilient people. These were the hunters and trappers that lived in a place very few would even venture. It seemed everywhere he looked with the eye, undead were doing the same thing. They scoured the land, but found very little. Occasionally, tracks in the snow made by human boots would show up, but these would be blown over by the winds quickly.

Aaron felt his mental link tingle. He was being messaged by Kgosi, the lean African bush warrior he had placed in command of his African forces. Aaron flipped the display to show the eye over his African forces, where Kgosi sat out in the open holding an evil-looking blade.

"Kgosi, why do you call me?" Aaron asked.

"Ah, my king, I found it! I found da blade of da Dark Baron!"

"Is that it? The blade you're holding?"

"Dat be it, my liege! I gonna get a necro to warp it in!"

"I'll get one from Stacie since she pulled a few back to help with spellwork. Be ready."

Aaron walked down the helix stairs into the spell lab where Stacie was preparing her altar. Only one necromancer remained in the lab with her, and he sat idle in a corner. Without saying a word, Aaron crossed the room and took the necro by the sleeve of his robes. He completely ignored Stacie, who was placing the orb of Tyadrig's empty heart on the altar. By the time he got back upstairs with the necromancer, Stacie was placing the second orb, the fiery orb of Krovon.

"Warp Kgosi to me." Aaron commanded the necromancer. Without speaking, the spellcaster began to channel evil magic. The magic bathed Kgosi in sickly green, giving his already blue-black skin a coloring that made him look like some sort of troll. An image of Kgosi appeared in front of Aaron, towering over Aaron despite his own height. As the image on the screen faded out, the one at the fortress intensified, until finally Kgosi stood before Aaron. The African warlord handed Aaron his blade. The necromancer on the screen duplicated the spell the one at Aaron's side just cast, recalling Kgosi to Africa, bladeless.

"My liege, dat blade got some wicked voodoo in it!" Kgosi warned. "It was made to kill da other tribes, da ones dat worship da same dark gods as us!"

"I know that, Kgosi. Why do you think I wanted it?"

"Ya don't understand! Da Nyeusi Chui tribe, dey use a magick dat drain all da other magicks! Damupanga be made ta stop dem! It gonna make all da magick resist drain effects!"

"Wait a second... you mean Damupanga can stop Maktdrikker?"

"Dat be exactly what I mean!"

"This is excellent news. You're free to go, Kgosi."

With that, Aaron closed off his mental link to his general and shifted the display back to showing the demon's eye over Australia.

Meanwhile, Stacie stood over the main altar in the spell lab. She already had the orbs of the three brothers in a triangle in its center. Her spell component pouch sat on a table off to the side of the main altar. She walked over to it and withdrew a white candle, set flame to its wick, and placed it on the east side of the table. "Air, I call on you once more. Hasten my spell and increase its range, so with one cast I can see all that lives and breathes."

She walked back to her spell component pouch and withdrew a red candle to symbolize fire. "Fire, I call on you once more. Empower my spell and increase its strength, so I can track the intelligent beings that still live and breathe." She placed the lit candle at the west side of the orbs in the center.

She withdrew a third candle from her pouch, a blue one, and lit its wick. "Water, I call on you once more. Clarify my spell and increase its precision, so I can remove that which does not think from the effect of my trace." She placed the candle at the south end of the altar.

With a green candle in hand, she walked to the north side of the altar and set flame to the wick. "Earth, I call on you once more. Ground my spell and make it permanent, so that the lab's display will always show me the sentient beings that still live and breathe." She placed it directly in front of her at the north side of the altar.

She walked back to her pouch and withdrew a fifth candle. This one, unlike the others, was not a solid color. Instead, purple and black wax were mixed to form this candle. To Stacie, this candle was where spirit merged with death. It would serve as the dark side of spirit, making it closer to the demonic magic she already used in the altar. She placed it between the three orbs and lit its wick. "Spirit, I have merged you with Death, so that you may blend with my new powers. The orbs that surround you are the dark hearts of the Brothers. I call on you to mix their power with your own, and to spread it across the circle."

Stacie poured a white powdery substance on the ground around the entire altar. She crossed the room and picked up several objects. One was the rattle that belonged to her sister's daughter before the war. The second was the cheesy "kindergarten diploma" given to the sister's son that same year. The third was a paper tracing of the key to the car Stacie drove as a teenager. The fourth, the US Selective Service card that Aaron had to register for when he turned eighteen. The fifth, the business card for a Dr. Hsu Chen, the doctor she saw before the war. The sixth was her grandfather's Medicare insurance card, and the final one was the death certificate of her other grandfather, who had served in Vietnam and died in battle.

Using due north as noon, Stacie placed the objects around the circle. She tried to place them as near as she could to the real place they would fall in a 12-hour condensed life. At midnight, the death certificate lay on the floor. Alongside it, the rattle. Then the kindergarten diploma, then the key, then the draft card, the business card, and finally the Medicare card. These symbols of the stages of life all lay in their proper places in the circle.

With a spark, Stacie lit the flammable powder. The flames jumped to life around the altar. The powder smelled like decaying bodies. It was milled corpse flower, mixed with a flammable powder to make it burn. Stacie could no longer smell the horrible stench of the corpse flower. Her sense of smell had been destroyed when she gave up her life and took on the powers of undeath. She raised her hands into the air and began to chant.

"Aveth Novari Ryzion! Aveth Novari Ryzion!"

A circle formed on the altar around the mixed candle in the center.

"Aveth Novari Ryzion! Aveth Novari Ryzion!"

Three lines emanated from the circle, reaching under the gaps where the orbs met.

"Aveth Novari Ryzion! Aveth Novari Ryzion!"

The lines encircled the orbs.

"Aveth Novari Ryzion! Aveth Novari Ryzion!"

The lines now reached out from the outer circle in four directions, each towards one of the cardinal candles.

"Aveth Novari Ryzion! Aveth Novari Ryzion!"

The lines encircled the four cardinal candles. The entire pattern burst upward in burning purple flame. Stacie turned her hands at the display in the lab. On it, a map of the world appeared. Green dots appeared on it, showing the locations of all living humans. The living at Cloud Peak Monastery had been evacuated, so no green dots appeared in Tibet. The entire nation of Switzerland was covered in green. There was a concentration in southern West Virginia, where the current greatest thorn in their side lay. Other green dots populated some of the rural parts of Africa, Australia, Canada, America, and Russia. There were also five concentrations of living in the sea. Occasionally, one of the dots in the rural areas would vanish when the undead would catch one of the living.

"Aaron!" Stacie yelled. "Come down here!"

Aaron came down the helix stairs and into the spell lab. When he entered, he saw the map on the display with green dots on it.

"What the hell's this?" he asked. "You called me down here over some weird map?"

"This 'weird map' tells us where the rest of the living are."

"How?"

"Those green dots? They all represent living people. We just need to kill them all, and the planet's ours. We don't need to cast as wide of a net now."

"Excellent. I'll send some mindless squads and cavaliers to take out the isolated ones."

"What about the angel's fortress and the Swiss?"

"Piss on the angel's fortress. Now we know she's holed up in some castle. She'll run out of food eventually. I'm pulling all forces away from the Swiss borders and warping them around the world to hunt down the rest of the holdouts. Then we'll amass everything we've got and overrun the Swiss. The angel? Piss on her, we'll just let her starve to death."

"What happens if they counterattack?"

"The Swiss defenses took a beating from the attacks I've already launched. They won't counterattack, they're gonna fix their walls and build up defenses. As far as the angel and her fortress, they don't have many troops. There's what, a couple hundred green dots there? Either they can use the laser again, assuming they can fire it again, or the angel can strafe us. But if I spread my forces out, both are gonna have limited scope. Even if they do counterattack, it won't do much."

"And what about those ships?"

"Easy. Animate some more gargoyles. I'll just have them dive bomb the ships and send 'em to the bottom. Maybe we can animate some dead whales or something to harass the ships too."

"I've got something better." Stacie said as she started down the lower staircase. "Come with me."

Stacie and Aaron exited the fortress through the front door on the lower level. By this time, the black stone fortress was now reflective silver, having been painted by Olaf's legions. The reflective silver paint gave the fortress a less evil appearance, but also protected it from energy attack. The lake of magma lay below, deep in the crater of the volcano they built their fortress over. Stacie walked to the edge of the fortress island and began to channel magic. The purple-black beam of magic hit the lava lake, and lava rose from its surface into the air. The beam shaped the magma into a second bird, identical to the first one.

"Ryzuul, Qaathi, Viceros!" Stacie called out, and the bird took flight out of the crater. She focused the beam back on the bird after releasing it, and the bird's body turned void purple just like its twin.

"This is how I'm gonna get rid of the ships. I'm gonna send these birds to dive bomb them, the same birds we rode to Hoover and Lima."

"Excellent." Aaron replied. "Get some more summoned and we'll waste 'em."

"Aaron, I can't summon these often," she replied. "It takes a lot of magic to summon them. It takes me a day to gather back enough magic to summon another."

"Fine then. Summon one tomorrow, but hold 'em back. Once you've summoned a handful, we'll unleash 'em."

Chapter 28

Enough Swords to Go Around

Light's Bulwark Fortress
Two days later

Dawn and Nadia were ready to fly by 9 AM. The military prep crews for the Helix were ready to fly even earlier, having been on the early military schedule before their reassignment to Light's Bulwark. The fuel hoses were away, and the air team was awaiting their pilots.

"Dawn!" one of the crewmen shouted as she approached the helicopter. "What's your mission today?"

"We found the enemy base." Dawn replied.

"Yeah, we need special stuff to attack it." Nadia added in.

"Yeah!" another crewman responded. "Sounds like you're gonna end this shit!"

"Soon." Dawn replied. "We're gonna end it fairly soon."

Dawn and Nadia climbed up in the cockpit together for the first time since Dawn first held Spell-Drinker. With the signal from the ground crew, Dawn lifted up on the stick. The Helix lifted itself off the pad and over the walls of the fortress. The rotors kicked up ash and dirt from the burned field beyond as Dawn steered the Helix north.

Below, the girls could see undead crawling the forests and rural areas. It was almost methodical, the way they searched. Cavaliers sat every so often, directing the undead in their search.

"Why are they so organized?" Dawn asked. "It makes no sense."

"It makes perfect sense, if you know their plan. They're trying to eradicate all humans on the planet so they can summon some demon." Nadia replied.

"How do you know that?"

"Back in Pittsburgh, we caught one of their necromancers. He was trying to raise St. John's Cemetery. We interrogated him, found out their plan. I guess they're trying to 'kill all the sentient life on the planet' so they can summon someone called Tyadrig. Tyadrig wants to 'torture the Lord Jehovah for all eternity', whatever that means. I guess he has brothers too."

"I guess their demon lord needed sacrifices. I think that's something demons do, they want sacrifices."

"Well no. Demons do like sacrifices, but the necro said something about our brains messing with the magic. That's why I think they could've summoned him a better way."

"How would that even be possible?"

"Just take one of those Virgin rockets to the moon and summon him there. It's a different planet, our brains couldn't screw with the magic there. Then they wouldn't have had to kill us all."

"Do you think they would've killed us all anyway?"

"No way of knowing. I think we were just a means to an end, but I have no idea. Maybe after they summoned their lord on the moon they'd have killed us anyway."

The southwestern boroughs of Pittsburgh were relatively untouched. It looked as if the people here had retreated in a hurry towards the interior of the city. Some of the buildings showed the aftermath of shelling by the toxin cannons, but most of them were still intact. As the Helix approached closer to the interior of the city, it started to tell a different story. Rock falls obstructed the lanes of the Liberty Tunnels. Nadia, the only remaining survivor of the city, pointed out things as Dawn flew near them.

"Those tanker trucks, trapped under the rubble. We blew them up to bring the tunnels down. It kept the undead out of the city center for quite some time. We also burnt the bridges down to keep the undead from crossing the rivers. Every bridge in the city's out, and it helped us hold out for weeks."

Nadia pointed out the remnants of tanker trucks near the collapsed tunnels and the remaining pillars of the destroyed bridges.

"The place is on the North Shore." Nadia directed. "Fly over both rivers, then keep flying north."

Dawn pointed the helicopter towards the north, passing alongside the pillars that once supported Ft. Duquesne Bridge. There was a time that Ft. Duquense Bridge was one of the three largest bridges in the city, the route over which commuters traveled from the residential western boroughs to the commercial Ross Township. Now, the pillars that held the roadway are all that remain of this once vital bridge.

"See the hospital?" Nadia asked as she pointed out the largest structure in this section of town. "Follow that major street to the west of it. It should be Federal Street."

Allegheny Hospital was the most imposing building in this section of the city. It had sustained minimal damage, despite being the refuge for most of the residents of the ghetto to the hospital's east. The front doors to the hospital had been blown open by cannon fire, but the rest of the building hadn't been shelled.

"One of the doctors escaped out the back when the undead hit this place." Nadia said as Dawn approached the hospital. "He told me the junkies from the ghetto got into the pharmacy once the building was locked down. Didn't even try to fight back, they were so stoned."

Dawn located Federal Street below and guided the Helix along the road.

"Bank left on Lang. It's the next street." Nadia directed, and Dawn brought the Helix in a ninety-degree banked turn to take it down the side street. "It's on the big block on the right, between Arch and Saturn."

While Dawn watched the now-useless power lines to avoid crashing the Helix into them, Nadia scoured the street for the store.

"There it is. Land the Helix on top of the red brick building." Nadia said as she pointed out the building. The first floor of this building was the sword shop.

"I can't land there, there's some sort of air conditioner blocking my landing site." Dawn replied.

"Hold it steady then, I'm gonna rip that air conditioner off the bolts with the minigun so we can toss it off the roof."

Dawn held the Helix steady, using precise maneuvers to keep the helicopter from wobbling as Nadia tried to line up the minigun. Nadia hit the trigger, and rounds sprayed from the barrel of the gun towards the unit. The fast-firing bullets cut the metal base apart, detaching the air conditioner from the bolts that held it to the roof. It fell to the ground with a hard thud as Nadia turned the minigun on the edge of the roof. The bullets chewed up the brick of the safety ledge as easily as they ripped through the metal. In under a minute, Nadia had enough of the safety ledge reduced to dust for the air conditioning unit to fit through the gap.

"Good job." Dawn said as Nadia stopped firing the minigun. "You've got the aircraft, I'm going down to push that thing off. You won't be strong enough to, and I'll have to go angel form to do it."

Dawn said the oath of the Solari and bailed out of the Helix. Her wings caught her and carried her down to the roof. Though it took considerable effort, Dawn was able to use her divine strength to push the heavy air conditioning unit through the hole in the safety ledge Nadia created. The air conditioner fell to the alley below with a great crash, followed by a pressure burst as the refrigerant inside blew through the damaged lines.

Nadia sat the Helix on the building's rooftop now that the air conditioner was out of the way. Dawn helped by directing her minute adjustments, allowing Nadia to perform a flawless landing.

"You're getting better at that." Dawn complimented.

"Thank you." Nadia replied, smiling.

The building had a roof access door, formerly used by maintenance personnel to repair the air conditioner that Dawn had just thrown off the roof. Dawn and Nadia opened the unlocked roof door and descended the staircase into the apartment. The highest floors served as apartments that occupied the space over the weapon shop. The doors to the apartments were left open, allowing the girls to see inside. The insides were cluttered and disorganized, as if people searched through them in a hurry. Though the floor was littered with clothes and books, and the furniture was askew and sometimes flipped over, little else seemed to occupy the apartments.

The door on the first floor did not lead into the sword shop. Instead, the staircase door led to the outside of the building at street level. The storefront was boarded up and its door locked. When Dawn and Nadia found themselves outside instead of in the shop, Nadia swore.

"Shit! That didn't work. How are we gonna get in now?"

"Relax." Dawn replied. "I'm just gonna blast the plywood."

Dawn charged power in the front of her shield and released it forward as an energy blast. The attack hit the wood that covered the windows and splintered where it hit. Part of the board held, but there was a clear hole in the center.

"Shit, it's gonna take more than one blast. Stay back."

Dawn charged another blast and fired again, this time at the corner. The blast hit the nails used to hold the corner in, but still the board didn't fall. Nails still held the other three corners. She turned a blast at the opposite corner, and it too disintegrated from the attack. She turned a blast on the remaining top corner, separating the wood from the nails and bringing the entire board into a forward fall. Nadia walked over and jumped into the air, landing on the sloped surface of the board. The last corner splintered away from the building, leaving the shattered window wide open.

Dawn and Nadia climbed through the window into the shop. Inside, metal weapons based on medieval designs covered the walls and floor. Swords, axes, flails, lances and bows were displayed prominently. Though none of the weapons were sharp, that could easily be remedied with the grinder they had at the fortress. The shields in the store wouldn't even need modification. They were made of metal and would protect the defenders of the fortress from the venomous claws and bites of the zombies.

Dawn unlocked the front door to make carrying the weapons up to the Helix easier. Nadia lifted a two-handed battleaxe. The heavy weapon was difficult to swing, even with two hands. It was clearly designed for a large, strong man.

"These heavy weapons are gonna be useless for us," Nadia suggested. "I can't even use them, and we're planning to use shields anyway. I vote we just leave them behind."

"There's really no reason not to though." Dawn answered. "The Helix can carry it all, and there's no undead around, so we might as well take it and see what we can do with it. At the very least, it's scrap metal we can flush the moat with."

"Alright, where should we put it all?"

"In the cargo hold."

Dawn and Nadia started collecting weapons of every shape and size, carrying them by the armful out the unlocked front door, back up the stairs, past the apartments and to the cargo hold of the Helix. The girls threw the weapons in the cargo hold haphazardly, not bothering to organize anything. The flight back to Light's Bulwark would, if the Helix hit any turbulence at all, disorganize the cargo and undo all the work put into its organization. It took the girls three hours to pack the store's stockpiled weapons into the Helix.

"Man, these people had to be stingy." Dawn commented. "How useful do you think this stuff would've been in that battle?"

"It's on the wrong side of the river, but someone would've brought it downtown." Nadia replied. "That's how we eventually fell, we ran out of ammo. We'd have still lost, but we'd have felled a lot more before then."

"So how did you end up at Light's Bulwark anyway? You made it sound like everyone got pinned downtown between the rivers."

"When ammo supplies got low, I sneaked off. Took a gun and as much food as I could carry, and stole a boat off the docks. Only took my brother with me, and he got caught letting the boat through the last locks at London."

"Letting the boat through the locks?" Dawn asked. "How did you manage that?"

"Basically I'd stop the boat on the side of the river. We took turns going into the locks. They all had power for some reason. Anyway, we'd use the panels to let the boat through the locks, then get back aboard on the other side. Ivan had the last locks before I met up with Rick and his group. He tripped over some roots and they caught him. He had the gun, I couldn't save him."

Nadia's voice was devoid of emotion when she talked about the things that happened to her. She was nothing like the other defenders of Light's Bulwark. Most of the fortress's defenders were students at the engineering college. They fled the town when the undead reached it, living off the wilderness for a while before finding safety at Light's Bulwark. Some of the others had similar stories, fleeing their farms and rural hometowns and living off the land. Dawn and Julius were the most lucky of all, having walled themselves behind Light's Bulwark's impregnable outer barrier and not needing to experience the war.

Nadia was different. She was there when the last thousand in Pittsburgh blew up the tunnels and bridges to keep the undead out. She ran with her siblings all the way from Allison Park to downtown, and saw the undead catch her youngest sister. She fought with the last survivors of the city to hold downtown. She ate the rats, and the fish from the rivers, to help make the canned food last longer. She watched from the boat as the survivors ran out of ammo and the undead overran them.

Once the girls finished loading all the weapons aboard, they closed the cargo hold and got back in the cockpit. Nadia radioed back to Light's Bulwark of their progress.

"Light's Bulwark, this is Helix One. We've got the weapons, we're inbound now. ETA seventy minutes."

Dawn powered up the rotors on the Helix, and it lifted off the rooftop. She steered it towards the south, cutting across downtown and flying over the collapsed Fort Pitt Tunnels. Nadia's estimated time was fairly accurate, as Dawn was able to maintain cruising speed the entire distance from Pittsburgh back to Light's Bulwark.

When they landed the Helix back at Light's Bulwark, the girls passed weapons from the cargo hold out to the others. The others stacked the weapons in the former first floor den, which quickly became an armory. When tasked with this, many of the Light's Bulwark survivors questioned Dawn's motives.

Dawn explained the discussion she had with the engineers and the decision they had arrived at. The response from the rank and file was mixed. Of everyone there, Nadia was one of the most supportive of the plan. Many of the hunters and animal wranglers were okay with the plan, as well as the naval crewmen, but most of the former Tech students opposed it.

"Why can't we just hit it with the laser?" one inquired.

"Yeah, it worked really well in Switzerland!" another mentioned.

"Did you guys see what happened to me after we used the laser?" Dawn asked. "It drained my strength. I passed out in the lens chamber. Julius had to pull me out and carry me upstairs. It sparked a fight between Julius and Rick. I'm not doing it again unless I absolutely have to. Just listen."

The crowd hushed as Dawn explained the plan.

"We're gonna use the Navy helicopters and my Helix to fly us up to the volcano where they've built their fortress. I'm gonna cut a path through any undead they bring to stop us, and you'll help me. Once I'm in, we have a retreat planned. We're gonna put a team on a cliff with a flat top and give them ropes. You'll retreat to there and climb the ropes, then you're safe since they can't climb. I'll kill their leader, come back out, blast them all back to hell with the Aegis, and we'll take the choppers back out."

"I don't know," one of the former students replied.

"That might actually work." another commented.

"I still don't buy it. How's she gonna get in?" another inquired.

"Remember Rick's satellite feed from Asia?" the first responded. "You saw it too. She'll get in."

Dawn hushed the crowd again to explain the timetable.

"We need to train with these weapons, at least somewhat. Figure out who's wielding what, and who's any good at what. Then we need to spend some time training with them. Based on the feed from the satellites, it'll take the undead another week to maneuver into position in France along the Swiss border to attack them. We'll train five days with the weapons, from sunrise to sunset. We can't wait any longer or I'll have to fire the laser again to save the Swiss. We'll radio the Navy and get some choppers for the assault. Everyone okay with that plan?"

The majority of the crowd looked back and forth at each other. Nobody seemed to have any real objections to the plan. Thanks to the intelligence satellites, every one of Light's Bulwark's defense force had a front row seat to Dawn's heroics in Tibet. This tipped the scales in her favor, winning her the respect and faith of her troops.

"Then it's settled." Dawn replied. "We'll call it Operation Enduring Life. We attack at sunrise a week from today. For Light's Bulwark!"

"For Light's Bulwark!" the crowd shouted back at her.

Chapter 29

The Reaver of the Moon

Light's Bulwark Fortress, West Virginia
Two days later

Rick sat at the communications array, watching his satellite feeds and keeping them in position. He was watching the remaining forces from Germany, as the necromancers formed portals. He could see the mindless moving through them, disappearing from view.

"Dawn!" Rick called out over the intercom. "Dawn, come up here!"

Dawn climbed the stairs from inside the building and came out on the roof by the comms array.

"What's going on?" she asked. Rick pointed to the satellite feed, where the undead were being marched methodically through the portals.

"They're... moving the undead away from Switzerland. I can't figure out why. Wouldn't they move to attack instead?"

"You're right, something else's going on." Dawn replied. "Call all hands to battle stations. They might be warping in on us somehow."

"I don't think so." Rick responded. "Nothing's coming up on radar. The last time they warped in on us, there were necromancers here. If there's no necromancers, I don't think they can warp. Nothing's showing up on radar for a hundred miles."

"Let's keep an eye on it anyway. If anything shows up, tell me about it."

Meanwhile, Julius was down in the basement at the forge level. He was shaping a piece of iron into a shape similar to a question mark. He pounded away at the iron, holding it with blacksmith's tongs into the forge as the iron cooled during work. He pounded the iron thinner and thinner over time, maintaining the question mark shape. When the iron achieved the desired thickness, he placed it back in the forge to heat it up, then turned and dunked it into a sink of cold water. Steam rose from the sink on contact with the red-hot metal, quenching the iron to make it brittle enough to hold an edge. It took him most of the day to bend the metal into the proper shape.

He left the blade in the water for a couple hours to make sure all the extra heat left in the metal could dissipate. With the metal cold again, he took the blade to his grinding wheel to sharpen it. The wheel ground the metal surface into a sharp edge, an edge that would stay sharp for quite some time because the blade was quenched. The curved two-handed blade would now need a handle. For this, he had a drilled-out steel cylinder, sized for his hands to grip in combat. He placed the handle on the blade and secured it with a pommel made from a rounded ball of steel. For the grip, he would use a piece of leather from his supply. He wrapped the grip in leather, using glue to hold it on. To hold the pieces together, he used a welding torch to weld the blade and pommel to the grip.

As the day came to an end, Dawn found Julius in his forge, finishing the welds that would hold his blade together. Dawn saw the blade and reacted immediately.

"Julius... where did you get that blade?"

"I just finished forging it. Why?"

"I dreamt about that blade a while back!"

"Really? Tell me about the dream."

"Well, it was ancient Greece. Athens, I think. I had the Aegis, and a sword, and I was fighting off Romans. There was some kind of wind reaver beside me, like my partner or something. He had a blade like that one, except it was able to cut through the Roman armor and shields. The Romans killed him with the ballista bolts. Then they turned the bolts on me. My shield blocked them, but the impact threw me over the wall and into a building. That's when I woke up."

"Athens, you said? And Romans were attacking? I don't think that was a dream. Let's find Laina, she probably knows more. Come on, let's go back upstairs."

Dawn and Julius walked from the forge to the freight lift and used it to access the above ground levels of the fortress. Once back above ground, they then called for Laina using the intercom. Though it was getting close to bedtime, she would likely be reading somewhere in the fortress.

"Laina, where are you?" Dawn asked over the intercom.

"I'm in the library. If you need me, just come here." she replied

Dawn and Julius walked from the courtyard to the library on the second floor. Laina was seated in one of the oversize chairs, reading a book. The book's cover was decorated with an American flag and an eagle, and was titled "The Eagle's Talon". She looked up from her book when she heard the pair enter.

"Hey Dawn, hey Julius. What's up?" she asked.

"Julius thinks there's some significance about a dream I had." Dawn replied.

"I'm a historian, not a dream reader. Why would I know anything?"

"It involves ancient Greece."

"Oh? Tell me."

Dawn explained her dream to Laina, describing the part where the wind reaver ripped apart the Roman legionnaires with a curved two-handed blade. When Dawn finished, Laina immediately jumped in.

"You're describing the Battle of Athens," she answered. "In the Battle of Athens, Amynta had an ally, Partheos. They called him Krýo Fengári, or Cold Moon. He wielded a blade like the one you described. It was inscribed with two sigils – the crescent moon in honor of Artemis, and the harsh winds of Boreas, the god of the north wind. I think we should try to remake that blade with its magic."

"You think we can do that?" Dawn asked. "Do you know how to do the magic?"

"I know how Partheos did it," Laina answered. "I think we can replicate the environments here too, or at least somewhere within flight distance."

"What do we have to do?" Julius asked.

"Well, first you need the finished blade."

"Already got it," he replied. "The finished welds are sitting to cool now."

"Next, you'll have to inscribe the crescent moon onto the blade. You got the stuff you need to do that?"

"Yeah, I have a computer controlled laser. I can just put the symbol in the computer and let the laser inscribe it."

"Then we'll need to leave it outside at night when the moon's visible. I'll say the prayer to Artemis for her blessing since it's in Greek and I'm the only one who speaks it. Then we'll have the blessing of Artemis."

"And for Boreas?"

"For Boreas, we need to inscribe his sigil. His is harder to find, but if your computer has like Photoshop on it I'll be able to design it for your laser to inscribe. After that, we'll need to find a cold place with high winds, like a mountain peak."

"I know a good place." Julius replied. "The highest mountain around here is called Spruce Knob. It's the highest peak for a few hundred miles. It's on the other side of the state, but it's not that far by helicopter. It's about five thousand feet from sea level, and the winds are very high and constant there. Will that work?"

"Partheos did his spell in the dead of winter, at the peak of a mountain twice that height. But I don't have any data on how strong the winds are on Olympus. If the winds at Spruce Knob are stronger, then it'll make up for not being as cold."

"Okay, thanks. I'll inscribe the sigil of Artemis now so you can do the prayer tonight."

"Thanks, Laina." Dawn added. "I really hope this works."

Dawn and Julius walked back down to the forge, where the blade's welds were cool enough to place the blade on the inscription table. Julius opened the inscription program on the computer and displayed the crescent moon on the screen. The blade sat underneath on the computer display, directed by a camera looking down on the inscription table. On the screen, the sigil was bigger than the width of the blade, and positioned off center. Julius resized the sigil on the computer to make it fit the blade, and moved the blade on the table to put the sigil in the right place.

"Dawn, get your safety goggles." Julius said as he donned his own. After Dawn walked across the room and put on a pair of protective glasses, Julius clicked the "Inscribe" button at the bottom right of his screen. The laser powered on, cutting a crescent moon shape into one side of the blade. The laser was set to low power, preventing the beam from cutting all the way through the blade and causing weaknesses in the steel.

When the laser shut off, Julius removed the blade from the table and quenched it in the sink again to cool it. With the blade now ready for prayer, Julius and Dawn walked to the freight lift and took it back to the courtyard, then using the flights of stairs to reach the roof. Dawn stopped on the mezzanine to use the intercom to summon Laina to the roof.

Laina met Dawn and Julius on the roof, where the sun had faded over the horizon. The waxing moon was in full view from their position near the communications equipment. Laina took the blade from Julius's outstretched hand and laid it across her lap, placing one hand on the hilt and one over the crescent moon. She stared at the moon and began to speak in a tongue not understood by any watching.

"Ártemis, na akoúsei tin ékklisí mou
skotádi échei pései páno mas
me tin evlogía sou boreí na exorísei
Ártemis, écho mia lepída
mia lepida pou aníkei se sas
I lepida afti tha patáxei to kakó
Ártemis, kópste to skotádi me to fos tou fengarioú
férei to kakó vasiliá sta gónatá tou
afíste ti gi na anapnései gia mia akómi forá"

As Laina completed her prayer, light began to shine from beneath her left hand. As she lifted it up, the crescent moon Julius had inscribed on the blade was glowing white, just like the moon overhead. The glow dispersed throughout the entire blade, fading away as the spell took effect.

"That should do it. Tomorrow, I'll draw the sigil of Boreas for you on the computer. Scribe it, and we'll fly to Spruce Knob to do the second part of the spell."

Chapter 30

The Reaver of the North Wind

Light's Bulwark Fortress, West Virginia
The Next Day

Julius and Laina went down the freight lift to the forge, where Julius had stowed the blessed blade awaiting the second spell. The blade sat in the quenching tank, where it was out of the way of anything else. The computer was left running, open to the inscription program.

"So Boreas. What's his sigil even look like? I've never even heard of him before."

"His sigil is very rare to come across in Greek mythology. There was hypotheses among scholars that Partheos was the one who created a sigil for Boreas, and that he never had one until he blessed that blade. Aeolus was the Greek god of storm, and the four wind gods answered to him. Boreas was the god of the north wind. They had gods for the other directions of wind too – Notus for the south, Zephyrus for the west and Eurus for the east. None of the other wind direction gods have sigils. Boreas is the only one, and it only appears in the legend of Partheos."

"So what sigil did Partheos use for Boreas then?"

"I'll show you."

Laina searched on the computer for an art program. This computer had no such programs, having been set up to operate the inscription laser and little else. However, as a Windows computer, it came with Microsoft Paint as a default program. Laina opened the program and used the curved line tool to make two wavy lines across the center of the window. With the arrow tool, she simply drew an arrow pointing straight down through the lines.

Julius looked at the display, puzzled. "Isn't down traditionally south? Why did you use a south arrow?"

"Well, the north wind means it comes from the north. So it's blowing towards the south. Thus, the south arrow." Laina explained. "Done."

"Okay, now save it as a j-peg and open it in the inscription program. I'll go grab the blade."

Laina saved the file on the computer and re-opened it in the program that controls the laser. The symbol she drew on Paint appeared over the image of the table. As Julius placed the blade on the inscription table, the blade's image appeared. The symbol Laina drew was far too large to fit on the blade, so Julius shrank the image on the screen to make it fit within the blade's image.

"Goggles on," Julius said as he put a pair of protective glasses over his eyes. Laina picked up the pair Dawn had previously worn and placed them over her face.

"Firing," Julius said as he pressed the "Inscribe" button in the bottom right corner. The laser began to draw on the blade's surface, first drawing each of the wavy lines and finally the arrow. The image from the screen was perfectly burned into the metal.

"Excellent," Julius said as he admired the work. "And it's only ten AM, we'll easily be able to lift off by noon, get there around one thirty, do your prayer and be back before three thirty. I'll quench the blade and grab some food, you go tell Dawn so we can get the bird in the air."

"Sure thing," Laina replied.

The crews had the Helix ready to take off by eleven thirty. Once all three people, the blade, and food for the trip were aboard, Dawn fired up the rotors and allowed the Helix to pick itself up off the pad and take to the sky. The helicopter flew along a straight line path towards Spruce Knob, the Allegheny range's highest point. Though it was only October, and snow hadn't started falling for most of the state, at this high of an altitude the ground was already snow-covered. The rains this fall that came down for the eastern part of the state fell as snow at this height, coating the Allegheny peaks in white.

Dawn relied on height to avoid collision with terrain. By staying at altitude above five thousand feet, she would keep the Helix high enough to avoid any terrain for hundreds of miles around. The nearest point above this altitude would be two states away. The Helix cruised effortlessly over the peaks of the Alleghenies, taking just over an hour to reach Spruce Knob.

The harsh winds at the peak of Spruce Knob, having blown in the same direction for thousands of years, had warped everything around. The evergreen trees here had no branches on the windward side. Their windward branches had been bent and wrapped around the tree by the wind and made to face the leeward side. The peak and the pines were covered in sparkling white snow.

The pure white snow that covered the area sparkled as the sunlight hit it, reflecting light in all directions. The snow-covered pines reflected the light too, creating a scenic view. Occasionally, a log cabin could be seen, its roof covered in snow. Had there been no war, these cabins would have been inhabited. Smoke would have risen from their stone chimneys, evidence of the fires that would have burned in the fireplaces inside. Tourists from everywhere from Portland to Atlanta would rent the cabins, light fires in their fireplaces, and drink cocoa and cider around the dancing flame. Now, the cabins sat empty as grim reminders of the revelry that once happened here.

"I can't land on that," Dawn said to Laina and Julius on seeing the peak. "Laina, think you can go down the ladder and do your prayer? I'll circle around so the wind from my blades doesn't mess anything up."

"Actually, keep hovering over me. Your downdraft should help the spell, not hurt it. The downdraft applies a downward force on us and helps us stay on the mountain."

"Sure thing. Julius, go put the ladder down."

Julius attached a rope ladder to the floor of the cargo hold and threw the door open. He cast the ladder off, letting it fall and dangle below the aircraft. Dawn moved the chopper while Julius looked out over the side, letting Dawn align the ladder with the ground properly.

"Hold it there." Julius said as he started down the ladder. The sheath that would hold his blade was already fastened to his back, giving him full freedom of movement as he descended. Laina followed Julius down the ladder and sat cross-legged on the snow. Julius unsheathed his blade and placed it in her hands. She placed her right hand on its hilt and her left hand on the sigil of Boreas that Julius had just inscribed, then broke into prayer.

"Boréas, to krýo to fengári sas chreiázetai
págoma lepída tou me ágrio voriá sas
étsi tha diaspásei kai na pagósei"

The winds Dawn was generating with the blades of her Helix started to whip into a vortex. Dawn moved her Helix from the site, but the winds remained focused on Laina and Julius. Julius sat across from Laina, placing his hands over hers on the blade and hilt. Laina visibly shivered as she continued to pray. Julius, thanks to the heavy coat he wore, did not shiver, but still felt the cold winds against his face.

"Boréas, Ártemis eínai mazí sas
to kynígi eínai kai eímaste oi kynigoí
na kynigísoun tous, na pagósei tous, tous skotósei"

The winds swirled faster and snow started to fall. Though Dawn's Helix was nearby, the winds did not affect it, and snow did not fall on it. The strange weather only affected the blade and what was centered on it. Julius was able to weather the cold. His armored overcoat served not only as protection from physical attacks but from most non-physical threats as well. Laina, however, was ill-equipped for this mission. The cold wind and harsh snow bit at her exposed skin. Still, she continued the prayer, as Partheos before her did in harsher conditions with less clothing than she now had.

"Mas voithísei na férei píso ti zoí ston kósmo mas!"

Lightning flashed in the sky over their heads. Dawn moved the Helix back in above Laina and Julius, providing a lightning shadow to protect the others. Though the Helix would take any lightning strikes aimed at Laina or Julius now, the winds intensified as the rotor blades added to the already fierce weather.

"I hope that lightning shield thing works..." Dawn muttered to herself.

"Dóse mas ti manía tou voriá!" Laina shouted. The sigil of Boreas on the blade glowed blue under Laina's hand. Julius removed his hand from hers, and Laina removed hers from the blade. The sigil shined bright, but the storm raged on. Julius lifted his newly blessed blade and slashed away from Laina, and the storm calmed as if at his command.

"Yeah!" Julius shouted as he slashed again. "This is gonna be great!"

"Get back in the chopper!" Laina shouted back as she started climbing the ladder. Julius strapped the blade on his back and climbed up behind her. Once back in the cargo hold, Julius pulled the ladder back up into the Helix and slammed the door shut for their journey back to Light's Bulwark.

Chapter 31

Operation Human Spirit

Light's Bulwark Fortress, West Virginia
Two days later

Dawn stood with Rick on top of the roof near the communications array. Below in the courtyard, almost the entire force of Light's Bulwark was training with the weapons they had just acquired from the abandoned shop. People struck everything from empty crates to each other's shields to even the castle walls with swords, axes and spears. The clanks of metal on metal echoed around the courtyard up to the rooftop.

"USS Eisenhower, this is Light's Bulwark Fortress." Rick spoke clearly into the radio microphone. "Over."

"Light's Bulwark, this is Eisenhower, we read you. What's your status? Over," the radio operator aboard the aircraft carrier replied.

Dawn moved up to Rick's side and spoke into the microphone. "This is Dawn Cahill of Light's Bulwark requesting the captain on radio. Over."

"Stand by," the radio operator replied. A few minutes passed before a female voice came back over the radio.

"Dawn Cahill of Light's Bulwark, this is Captain Carrie White of the USS Dwight D. Eisenhower. Please state your business." the female voice replied.

"Captain, my technicians have located the enemy compound." Dawn answered. "We have a plan to assault it, and we think we've got a good chance of victory, but we need help from your Chinook pilots."

The American command and control systems had been wiped out months ago when Washington fell. Without a standing American president, there were effectively seven nations acting independent of each other despite four of them sharing a common homeland. Each aircraft carrier at sea could now refuse orders from any of the others. The three American carriers, the one British carrier, the one Russian carrier, Switzerland and Light's Bulwark all acted independently of the others, though each tried to help the others whenever possible. As such, Captain White now had the full authority of a standing President, and was a world leader in her own right.

"I'm gonna need some details on the plan of attack," she replied. "Do you have satellite uplink capability?"

"I do." Dawn replied before whispering to Rick. "*Get the uplinks ready, we're gonna need to send some data to Eisenhower.*"

"Good. Send the data US-44-AHA so it can't be intercepted, then tell me what I'm looking at."

"Already on it, Dawn." Rick answered as he sent several still images to the Eisenhower's bridge displays.

On the bridge of the Eisenhower, some still frames taken by the hacked satellites showed up on the main display. Rick's voice came over the radio.

"Eisenhower, this is Rick Sylvan, chief engineer. You're looking at satellite images from defunct intelligence satellites I took over. That silver building's the enemy compound. It's over an active volcano, so nukes are out of the question. It's also painted reflective silver, so I can't fire the ion cannon either. Down that road from it is another mountain, one that's been flattened at the top by mining. We're planning to land a squad on top of it, and land the rest of the force near the enemy compound. Their fortress is only manned by the royal couple, but they can summon undead to defend it. The main force is gonna punch a hole to get Dawn inside with her magic augments, then retreat to draw the undead away from the compound. We'll retreat to that flat top mountain and have help from the squad on top to get up the cliffside. We'll keep the undead locked in battle long enough to defeat their commanders."

"A chance to kill their commanders and turn the undead mindless? It's worth the gas."

"Excellent. My men still need a few days more training." Dawn added. "We need your Chinooks at Light's Bulwark three days from now. We'll stage a day on your ship, then fly out the next morning on the attack."

"Slight problem with that. We need three days to stage, since we need to sail the ship close enough to the enemy compound to fly there and back by Chinook. There's also the issue of the Panama Canal being powered down. We can't get through a powered-down Panama Canal."

"So how are we gonna do it?"

"If we can power it back up, we can get through. The canal used to be powered by a coal-fired plant. We can't fire the plant back up. It might be possible to run lines from the ship to power the canal, but it'll take us a week to get through that way. Do you have a better idea?"

"Are you sure it's powered down?" Dawn answered.

Rick answered first. "It has to be powered down, why would you think it wasn't?"

Captain White answered just after. "There's no way it can be running, nobody's alive to power it."

"When I flew to LA, all the lights were still on." Dawn replied. "If LA still has power, other places might too."

"Los Angeles has power?" Captain White asked. "How?"

Rick paused for a second. "Green energy. They have power because of green energy. Same reason Nadia could sail down the rivers. All the locks had power since they have hydroelectric plants attached. LA had power because they use wind turbines. They don't need people to run."

"So does the Panama Canal have power or not?" Captain White asked.

"I don't know." Rick answered. "Panama was a poor country compared to the US, so chances are most of its power came from fossil fuels since they're cheaper than green energy. But it's also a locks and dam, so they might have hydroelectric. It's more expensive to build, but cheaper to operate since the fuel's free."

"I think they are hydroelectric. If all the hydroelectric power in the world's still working, then we can get through the canal."

"Good." Dawn answered. "If we can get through the canal, then the operation can happen. If you can fly out here, we can give you a full fuel load for the ride back. That'll extend your range a lot."

"It definitely will. We can put the ship in the Gulf and fly the whole distance on one tank of gas if we can refuel when we get there. That'll make the journey three days by ship instead of four."

"So the operation's good to go?"

"Just one last thing. Every good operation needs a name, and I'm finally in a position to name it. Let's call it... Operation Human Spirit."

"Sounds good. Seventy-two hours from now, Navy helicopters should be coming over the horizon here. Light's Bulwark out."

Dawn and Rick turned away from the array and walked down the stairs to the courtyard, where the Light's Bulwark defenders were training. They were arranged in pairs, each partner giving the other time to practice both offense and defense. Laina was practicing against Danielle the railgun operator, while Julius practiced against Jim the army veteran.

Though it was now known that Dawn could use healing magic, the warriors still trained with blunted weapons. Partially, this was because Julius hadn't informed anyone of the grinder's location yet, but this was also to prevent injury in training. Nobody knew of the extent of Dawn's healing, and even if the wounds could be magically healed, they would still be painful until then. Still, impact injuries from the blunt weapons left bruises on the training warriors and caused them pain.

As Dawn watched, warriors would receive injuries that wouldn't cripple them or endanger their lives, but still caused pain sufficient enough for the untrained to stop training. To remedy this, Dawn walked to the center of the courtyard and assumed her angel form. Once in angel form, Dawn channeled light through the Apollo sigil painted on the back side of her shield. The light fed back into her body, which she pushed into the ground. The entire courtyard of the fortress lit up, and all the bruises on the warriors faded and blended into their skin. Though Dawn wouldn't be able to heal the entire two platoons' worth of grievous injuries this way, she could heal minor wounds from everyone at once.

With their wounds healed and their pain gone, everyone thanked Dawn for her efforts collectively and resumed their training. Dawn walked across the courtyard to where Nadia trained with a light sword by hammering the heavy shield of another female.

"Hold!" Dawn shouted at the pair to get their attention. Both girls lowered their weapons and turned to face Dawn. "Nadia, I need you. We're gonna need bags to pack our gear in, so we're going on a Helix ride."

"Fine by me. I was getting tired of training anyway," Nadia replied. "Where we gonna go to get gear bags?"

"Let's break into the mall. It's abandoned now, since Aaron's ported his mindless out of the cities. There's a Macy's and a Dick's, both are gonna have bags we can steal."

"Good idea. Lemme go get ready."

"Sure. I'll get the flight crew prepping the Helix."

Dawn walked back into the building and used the intercom mic near the door.

"Attention flight crew, this is Dawn. Please prep the Helix as soon as possible for takeoff. Again, please prep the Helix as soon as possible."

Once the pre-flight checklists were done and the Helix was ready to fly, Dawn and Nadia entered the cockpit. Dawn started the engine and the rotors began to spin, lifting the helicopter off the pad and into the air. She brought the Helix in a wide arc south to west, over the main part of the fortress, to fly towards the city of Charleston.

The trip to Charleston along the Kanawha River was uneventful. They saw no zombies beneath them for the entire duration of the trip to the Charleston Town Centre Mall. They landed the helicopter in the empty bus lanes near the mall, where the Kanawha Regional Transport bus routes all converged before the war. The sliding doors had been forced open, and without power, they now would not close. Some of the doors still were smashed, probably from when the survivors first entered the store. The rains that had come since had washed away the blood and glass from the sidewalks and parking lots.

Most of the store was as it would have been, but the path from the door to the hunting section was ransacked. Clothing racks were thrown on the floor and displays were knocked over in the rush to get to the guns and ammo. The glass case at the gun counter was smashed and all its contents had been removed. The hunting and hiking boots were gone, as well as all the protective hunting gear. All the bows and crossbows were gone, as well as the arrows. The store was devoid of most of the shopping carts that formerly occupied spaces near the entrances, having been taken by the survivors to transport their looted gear. However, most of the athletic supplies were untouched, with the exception of the baseball and softball bats near the edge of the athletic department. Off in a corner on the opposite side of the store as the hunting section, the section where athletic supplies and clothes were sold had nothing of use to the refugees. Blood had been spilled throughout much of the store. Bloody footprints led all over the store in all varieties of foot size and gait.

It was here that Dawn and Nadia would look for bags. Before the war, athletes used various types of bags to carry all their athletic needs to and from the gyms and fields. The bags were designed to carry the athletes' sports uniforms, workout clothes, sports balls, any sort of tools needed on the field, and water bottles. They had sufficient space for what the refugees needed now.

"Over here." Nadia called to Dawn. "Here's some tennis bags. These should work."

"I've found some basketball ones too. Grab a cart so we can take it all. I've already got one."

Dawn had one of the few carts left in the store in front of her, and she was currently throwing the stock of basketball bags into it. Nadia left the tennis bags to search through the store to find a cart. She found one near the mall entrance, covered in dried blood. She took it anyway, pushing it back to where she found the tennis bags.

By the time Nadia returned with a cart, Dawn had already thrown the basketball bags into her cart and now was piling football bags on top of them. This Dick's had more football and basketball equipment than any other sports, but it still had some bags in stock for other sports. By the time the girls had filled their carts, they had bags from almost every sport, including somewhat obscure ones like lacrosse. To extract the carts from the store, the girls simply pushed them through the open sliding doors back to where they left the helicopter.

The two carts were stuffed full of sporting bags by the time the girls left the store, so it took a fair amount of time to pull the bags from the carts and throw them into the Helix's cargo hold. Once finished, Dawn flung the cart with a mighty heave, allowing it to roll down the bus lane and across Quarrier Street. Nadia followed suit, flinging the cart at Dawn's cart. The cart came to rest in the middle of Quarrier, but Nadia entered the helicopter without care. Dawn sealed the cargo door and entered the cockpit.

The twin engines came to life with a roar, and the Helix leapt from the pavement into the darkening sky. A fall rainstorm was coming, and it was approaching quickly. Dawn wasted no time pointing the nose of the Helix east and pushing the aircraft to full military power. She pushed the Helix to go as fast as its engines could carry it, attempting to outrun the storm at her back. The Helix's shadow below raced up the river as the helicopter powered through the air. She currently flew against a crosswind blowing from the south, and she had to account for the wind to keep her aircraft headed at the right angle to reach Light's Bulwark.

If the storm reached Light's Bulwark before the Helix did, she would struggle to land the helicopter without crashing it. With the wind direction changes that happen often during mountain storms, Dawn would fly counter to a wind and it could suddenly change, blowing her into the fortress or its defensive walls. Dawn pointed the nose of the Helix down, keeping it from climbing as she closed distance towards safety. The storm rolled in behind her, dousing the ground with rain. Lightning streaked across the sky behind her, striking trees and power lines.

"It's a good thing Julius cut down all the incoming lines!" Dawn shouted to her co-pilot over the combined sounds of the rotors and the storm.

"In this storm? Wouldn't that fry like everything if it came in off the grid?"

"Yeah! We've got lightning rods up to stop lightning from hitting us directly, but if it hits the lines somewhere else we'd be screwed!"

When the helicopter finally reached Light's Bulwark, Dawn hurried to land. The crosswind was already making this difficult, but if she waited any longer, the winds would start to shift and make the landing nearly impossible. She partially powered down the rotors, allowing the helicopter to slowly fall as its engines barely failed to keep it aloft. She landed by making subtle alterations to the rotors' speed, allowing the Helix to slowly fall without crashing into the ground. Once she dropped below wall level, the walls filtered and buffered against the wind, making her task far easier.

The Light's Bulwark defenders were nowhere in sight. They had presumably taken shelter inside the building against the storm. As soon as the Helix touched down, Dawn and Nadia exited the cockpit at a hurried pace, also fleeing the exposed courtyard and ducking into the front doors of the building. The bags were left in the cargo compartment of the Helix, where they would be safe from the elements. The rotors would, without power, stop spinning on their own eventually. Lightning flashed across the sky as Dawn and Nadia slammed the grand doors of Light's Bulwark to wait out the storm.

Chapter 32

Dawn's Landing

Light's Bulwark Fortress, West Virginia
Two days later

The Light's Bulwark defenders scrambled around the castle like ants in the rush to beat the Navy. They now had bags to pack things in, and so they packed what weapons and food they could. The Navy helicopters Dawn asked for would be here soon, and Dawn had asked all defenders to be ready for them to evacuate in short order. She didn't want to chance another attack on her castle while she was away, and so the evacuation had to happen quickly. Emily and Jason were not going with the rest of the team. Instead, they would cover the evacuation with the triple-A points to ensure no sight wards witnessed their exit.

Danielle lifted one of the fortress's many liquid carbon dioxide fire extinguishers from its place on the wall and stuffed it in her bag with her weapons, clothes and food. Laina, who was nearby, questioned the logic of the fire extinguisher.

"Dani, why are you taking that?" Laina asked as she pointed at the fire extinguisher.

"We're going to a volcano, aren't we? You never know when we'll need it."

"We're fighting undead. They're immune to cold-based attacks." another bystander commented.

"You're just gonna waste energy carrying it." a second mentioned.

"I just... think we'll need it. I'm gonna take it." she replied. "You don't have to take one if you don't want, but I'm taking this one."

"Fine by me." Laina answered. "Just don't expect me to carry it."

Meanwhile, Rick and Dave took the freight elevator to the third basement level, at the level of the road below. At that level was a switch that would turn on the landing lights placed along the roadway. They would signal to the Navy pilots where they were supposed to land. Additionally, the cliff face would block sight on the demon's eyes. If summoned on the upper tier, the demon's eyes would be unable to see the helicopters down on the road through the rock, but if summoned on the lower tier, the demon's eyes would be unable to see into the fortress. It was a clever maneuver only realized as Rick went to throw the switch.

"Dave, you realize you can't see the fortress from the road and vice versa, right?"

"Yeah, but what's that got to do with anything?"

"Those sight wards we've got Emily and Jason repelling. If they're summoned topside, they can't see the Navy down here. If they're summoned down here, they can't see the fortress."

"Okay, that's cool if they summon topside, but if they summon down here they still see us."

"That's the thing, they won't summon down here." Rick replied as they took the freight elevator back up to the courtyard. "They think the fortress is the threat, not the road. They'll want sight on the fortress, so they'll summon up there. They won't see us leaving before the others have them blown out of the sky."

"Jesus, Dawn's brilliant!" Dave replied.

"I don't think she even realized it. She probably just thought that was somewhere they could land."

After most of the Light's Bulwark residents had their items packed, the whirr of helicopter engines could be heard coming from the south. The USS Eisenhower had finally sent their contingent of helicopters from their ships. The red landing lights along the highway signaled the landing zone, but the helicopters were coming in from the wrong direction. They needed to come in from the east to properly land on the east-west highway. Rick radioed the incoming choppers on the secure channel.

"Eisenhower chopper pilots, this is Light's Bulwark Fortress. You are approaching from a difficult angle. Please adjust course thirty degrees from due north until aligned with the highway, then turn due west to land in a line."

"Light's Bulwark actual, this is Eisenhower-Charlie-1. Adjusting course."

The helicopters coming in adjusted course away from the fortress to the east, lining up their westbound turns with the roadway below them. This section of the road was four lanes total with no median, thanks to the renovation project paid for by Massey Energy seven years prior. The renovations made it a viable landing point for the Navy helicopters, since before the Massey project it was a winding two-lane country road.

The first Chinook touched down at the far end of the landing lights. Each helicopter touched down behind the last one, leaving enough space for the rotors to spin. Six helicopters in all landed, and in conjunction with Dawn's Helix, they would provide enough transport for the majority of the defenders and their gear. A handful stayed behind, merely enough to operate the gun emplacements and ground-level flamethrowers. The flight prep crew borrowed from Eisenhower also stayed behind, as they were needed to refuel all the Chinooks at Light's Bulwark for their return trip.

Dawn lifted the Helix off the pad after receiving the clear signal from the flight prep team, and steered it out to the highway. She landed the Helix on the highway, facing opposite the Navy Chinooks, at the back end of the line. One of the flamethrower operators now used the radio, directing the first Chinook to the internal helicopter pad. It landed on the pad inside the complex where the Helix normally sat. As the flight crews refueled and prepared the Chinook, the forty-three Light's Bulwark defenders that would ride in this Chinook loaded their bags of gear aboard and took their seats. After refueling, the Chinook took to the skies, leaving the rest of the team behind on US Highway 60 as it made a beeline for its mother-ship.

The second Chinook followed in behind it as directed by the new flight controller. Just like the first, it was refueled, inspected, and prepared for takeoff as the defenders loaded their gear and took their seats. It, like the first, flew in a straight path for the Eisenhower. Each Navy helicopter performed this maneuver, and each was loaded with a contingent of forty-three Light's Bulwark soldiers and their gear. As the sixth took off, Dawn landed her own Helix back on the pad. Julius and Nadia served as its crew.

Aboard the Helix was Rick, Laina, and Danielle, as well as a couple of the bystanders in the hall where Danielle took the fire extinguisher from. Still they troubled Danielle about her choice of weaponry.

"Why a fire extinguisher?" one asked. "What possible use could you see for it?"

"It's just a gut feeling, okay?!" she responded, clearly agitated by the constant pestering.

"What's going on?" Julius asked from the flight engineer's seat.

"Everyone's bugging me about what I packed!" Danielle responded.

"Knock it off." Julius commanded as Dawn checked her instruments. "Unless she packed bombs that'll blow up in flight and shoot the Helix down, leave it alone."

"But she packed a fire extinguisher!" the second one responded.

"I don't care." Julius answered. "I don't understand either, but she can carry a useless item if she really wants to. Who knows, we're in a volcano, maybe it'll help somehow."

"Ha!" Danielle replied to the other occupant. "Julius says I can carry it."

After her helicopter was fueled and ready to go, Dawn lifted it off the pad and turned it to the south. She used the radar to locate the nearest Chinook and plotted a course to match it. The flight took just under four hours to go from Light's Bulwark to outside Tampa where the Eisenhower was docked. Because of the delays in takeoff times, the helicopters arrived distant enough from each other to allow the landing pad to clear for the next helicopter to land. Dawn's Helix arrived with more distance between than the other Chinooks, simply because of the faster cruise speed of the Chinook compared to the Helix.

The first two days aboard Eisenhower were fairly droll. The Light's Bulwark forces were being called "the specialist team", though they did not seem as physically strong or adept as the Navy personnel aboard the ship. They ate with the sailors, slept in bunks, and did what they had done at Light's Bulwark when not fighting undead or working – played cards and other games with the sailors and each other. Over the journey, the Eisenhower sailed from Tampa to the Panama Canal.

During the journey, Dawn brainstormed with Julius, Rick, Nadia and Laina about which sigil to bear for this battle.

"So, what sigil should I put on my shield?" Dawn asked the others.

"Well, it has to be one of the Twelve." Laina answered. "I don't think any of the High Priestesses ever used lesser gods like Boreas. So you're limited to the main gods of Greece – Ares, Aphrodite, Artemis, Apollo, Athena, Poseidon, Zeus, Hera, Hermes, Hephaestus, Demeter, and Dionysus."

"Well," Julius added in, "I think some are gonna be kinda useless. Aphrodite for example. She's the goddess of beauty."

"Exactly." Laina answered. "Aphrodite would be useless. So would Athena, Hermes, Demeter, Hera, and Dionysus."

"Poseidon would be a bad idea." Rick added. "Remember how we didn't nuke the place cause we didn't want to cause an earthquake? Using Poseidon would trigger one. So he's out too."

"That leaves Ares, Artemis, Apollo, Zeus and Hephaestus." Nadia mentioned. "So which should we go with?"

"I like Ares." Julius suggested. "I think the sigil of Ares will make you a better all-around fighter, which will help when you're fighting Aaron."

"I'd suggest Apollo." Rick offered. "Apollo's the one that improves your elemental attacks and gives you healing abilities. That's gonna make a big difference if there's a fight outside."

Laina chimed in as well. "I was gonna say Hephaestus. If he has anything metal as a weapon or armor, Hephaestus lets you sunder it. That, and he also gives you fire attacks and immunity to fire."

"Ooh, I forgot about him being god of the forge." Julius replied. "I was just thinking of the fire attacks and the fire immunity. Yeah, if you'll be able to break his weapon too, go with Hephaestus. Plus, you won't die if you get knocked in the lava somehow."

"That sounds like a good idea." Rick added. "Go with Hephaestus. Break his weapons and armor, and he's only a touch away from death. You don't need a good blow with Spell-Drinker to kill him since he's undead, you'll just drain his animation and kill him that way."

"Okay, I'll go with that. Thanks for helping me, guys."

Dawn used the art supplies she packed in her gear to paint the anvil and hammer of Hephaestus on the back of the Solari Aegis. Once finished, she channeled the light through it and tested her forge power on an old piece of pipe lying around the ship. She could repair it to full strength, as well as sunder it to the point that any attack would break it.

Thanks to the third canal lane built in 2015, the Panama Canal was now wide enough for the Americans to take their great aircraft carriers through. The new canal also used less locks, allowing for swifter travel through the canal. The Navy used their Chinooks to ferry personnel from the ship to the control buildings at each lock. These personnel would activate the systems that would raise the carrier to the proper height, allowing it to pass to the next lock. With the systems activated, they could fly back to the carrier and prepare to activate the next one. It took the carrier eight hours to pass through the narrow waterway and come out the other side in the Pacific Ocean.

While the Light's Bulwark personnel slept, the ship continued to move, navigated by its night crew. The third day gave the ship time to move along the Peruvian coast, as close to the position of Flame Point Fortress as possible. By the time it arrived, it was night and the Light's Bulwark people were tired again, so it remained docked here overnight to give the strike team sleep time. In the morning, Dawn and her people awoke and took their weapons to the flight deck.

They loaded into the same Chinooks they used prior. A seventh joined them, replacing Dawn's Helix in the formation. Each helicopter had the same passengers as before, with few minor adjustments. Over the time they spent at Light's Bulwark, the refugees had formed cliques among themselves and tended to associate with one another. This extended to who boarded which helicopter in preparation for the attack.

The ride to the volcano Flame Point was established it took less than two hours by helicopter. Dawn's team was the first dropped, on the near side of the path to the enemy compound. Dawn stood at the front with Julius, protecting the only path of enemy attack. Of notable change to the ride roster was Rick, who rode with the team in the back instead. By putting the entire force of Light's Bulwark between himself and the enemy, he enabled himself to call for help from the Navy if they found themselves in dire straits.

The enemy fortress had three bridges that approached it from the west, east, and south sides of the crater. Dawn's forces had landed on the south side, providing quick retreat down the southern path to the mountain with the flat top. One of the Chinooks was currently landing a team on top of the mountain. This team would lower ropes to the ground forces, providing them retreat up the cliff face and out of reach of the undead.

As Dawn and Julius approached the enemy compound, undead began to emerge from it. At the back was a monstrous man, larger than Julius by a lot. He wore black metal armor similar to that of his king, and had long blonde hair and a blonde beard. The mindless moved down the bridge at their standard slow pace towards Dawn and the rest of the Light's Bulwark force.

"Shield bearers, to the bridge!" Dawn shouted. The warriors with shields rushed to Dawn's side, forming a shield wall across the bridge. Dawn formed the center piece of the shield wall, aligned perfectly down the center of the bridge. The mindless continued to charge at her, but Dawn charged a blast of light from the shield. The light blast cut a path through the mindless, but more filed out from the fortress and filled in the gaps. Dawn fired again, slaying more of the hideous creatures, but the flanks along the bridge closed the distance to the shield wall and now attacked with claws and teeth against the humans and their shields.

The shield bearers pushed with their shields and stabbed with their weapons at the mindless. Dawn cleaved with Spell-Drinker across the entire approaching force. Dawn's anti-magic blade de-animated all the undead it touched, dropping them instantly. Dawn continued to cleave, cutting a path across the bridge towards the Norse barbarian at the helm of command. He charged at Dawn, swinging his great axe in an overhead smash to crush his smaller opponent. Dawn raised her shield to deflect the mighty blow, channeling the light through her sigil of Hephaestus as she did. The sigil formed a red barrier around her shield, one that clung to the axe on impact. The energy of the barrier wormed its way into the cracks in the axe's head and its tenuous connection to the handle. The bolt that held the axe head on the axe rusted instantly. When Olaf swung the axe at Dawn again, the head flew from the handle and out into the lava below.

The catastrophic failure of Olaf's weapon gave Dawn the chance to finish him. With a slash of Spell-Drinker, she bisected his torso and absorbed the magic used to create him. Without his animation magic, Olaf fell just like the rest of his warriors. The mindless under his command now simply shambled in a straight line towards Dawn. The ones on the outside of the bridge fell off the side in droves and into the lava below. Dawn called on the power of Hephaestus once more, to ignite the body of Olaf the barbarian. The burning body of Olaf ignited the other undead as they crossed it.

Upon realizing that the undead weren't smart enough to use the bridge, Dawn quickly retreated and walked along the left side of the crater. The undead tracked her, stepping off the bridge in their attempt to use a straight line and falling into the lava. Only a few managed to cross the bridge, and these were quickly cut down by Julius and the other warriors. Julius brought the last mindless remaining down with a slash of Reaver's Claw across its neck, severing the head and sending it to the ground. After the head was severed, Julius kicked it with his armored boot and sent it to the bottom of the volcano crater.

Chapter 33

The Winged Magma Demon

Flame Point Fortress, Peru
Just after

"We've done it!" Dawn shouted at the victorious Light's Bulwark forces. "We've wiped out the guard!"

"Dawn... look up. We're not done yet." Julius said softly.

Dawn looked up. A flaming bird the size of an elephant was coming in from the north, wings spread and diving fast. If it remained on its path, it would slam into the Light's Bulwark ranks. The Light's Bulwark defenders scattered in all directions to avoid the impact. The bird's magma body would splash on impact, killing most of the army despite their attempt to scatter.

"Dawn!" someone shouted at her as they noticed the bird. "Do something!"

Dawn rocketed herself skyward, drawing the bird's attention. The creature angled its flight up, away from the scattering army, to chase after Dawn. It lowered its head and charged in fast on an intercept path against Dawn's. She raised the Solari Aegis against the attack. The creature's head slammed into the shield. Its body stayed intact despite the impact. Though the creature's attack failed to burn Dawn, the force of its impact knocked her backwards through the air. She stabilized with her wings, then turned her own attack on the flaming beast. She flew at the bird, veering left as she approached. She slashed at the bird's wing joint with her blade, but the blade merely passed through it. The construct's magic did not drain on touching Spell-Drinker.

The bird turned and attempted to chase Dawn, but Dawn was able to gain ground on it. The slow flight speed and poor maneuverability of the bird gave Dawn an advantage. She raised her shield again to block the bird's next attack, striking back with Spell-Drinker and again passing through its fluid body. It seemed to her that her melee attacks failed to damage it. Instead, she flew backwards and raised her shield to charge a light blast. Light leapt from the face of the Aegis and struck the bird square in the beak, but the energy was absorbed into the creature's body. It pulsed with energy as Dawn looked on.

"I can't damage it!" Dawn shouted as she dodged the bird's ramming attack.

"Kite it over me!" Julius shouted from below. "Maybe I can!"

Dawn flew low over the bridge where Julius stood, Reaver's Claw at the ready. The blade, inscribed with the sigils of Artemis and Boreas, gleamed in the sunlight. The bird chased Dawn, bringing its flaming talons within range for Julius to strike at them. He slashed at the talon, and the cold winds of Boreas released on impact. The talon turned from fluid magma to hard stone.

"I can... petrify it?" Julius said questioningly as the bird chased Dawn back around the lower levels of the fortress.

"Julius!" Laina shouted as she realized what was going on. "Boreas is the god of cold wind! Your blade's dealing cold damage! Keep hitting it with cold and it'll freeze!"

Dawn quickly reversed direction and dove under the bird's body, striking at the talon with the concussive force of a charged shield bash. The stone talon shattered, showering the Light's Bulwark army below in volcanic stone. The bird slashed at Dawn with the other talon, but the attack missed entirely. Dawn soared away behind the bird, and it turned to give chase again.

The bird held itself still in the air as magma flowed from its body to where the flaming talon once was. A new flaming talon formed in place of the old one. The bird's burning interior changed ever so slightly as the talon reformed, a change not noticed by any of Light's Bulwark's warriors.

Dawn drew the bird into another charging attack, flying a circle around the backside of the fortress. She kept her speed low as to keep the bird at the same distance from her. She circled fully back around, appearing once again on the left side of her allies. The bird stayed close, but was unable to reach her to attack. She flew low once again over Julius and his enchanted blade. He slashed at the bird as it followed, and once again the icy winds of Boreas froze the talon Julius struck with his blade. Dawn performed a quick Immelmann and came out low, intercepting the bird and striking the frozen talon with a charged shield bash. Again, the talon shattered from the force of the impact. The bird funneled the magma from its body to the site of the shattered talon, re-forming the magma talon again.

"Keep it up!" Rick shouted at Dawn and Julius. Dawn circled back around, keeping the bird on her tail as she flew in a circle around the back side of the fortress. Danielle, who stood near the back, opened her pack, extracting a bright red fire extinguisher. Dawn kited the bird back over Julius and his wind blade, allowing him to land another blow against the re-formed talon. His strike released the freezing winds of Boreas, cooling and solidifying the magma into stone. Dawn dove beneath the bird again, shattering the talon and sending the stone splashing into the magma far below.

The path across the bridge from Julius to the crowd was empty by now. The warriors of Light's Bulwark had moved back to the mountain road that led to the volcano crater, leaving Julius alone on the bridge and giving him room to swing his blade. Danielle jostled her way up to the front as Dawn circled back around with the bird giving chase. Danielle couldn't reach Julius before Dawn did, so she ducked down as her commander passed overhead. Julius struck the bird again with the Reaver's Claw, freezing the reforming talon. Dawn reversed direction and shattered the talon with another blow from the Aegis. Once again, the bird drained magma from its fluid body to re-form the destroyed talon.

By this time, the bird's body seemed slightly less fiery. Dawn kept the bird at her back, circling the fortress as Danielle moved into position and raised the fire extinguisher's hose to the sky. Julius didn't notice her as he tracked Dawn, coming in from the west with the bird still on her tail. As the bird flew over the pair, Julius slashed at it once again with his blade. Danielle squeezed the extinguisher's trigger with the hose pointed at the sky.

Icy carbon dioxide rushed from the extinguisher's nozzle at high pressure, freezing the bird's entire left leg and turning it to solid stone. Dawn turned back on the creature, slamming the frozen section with her shield to shatter it. This time, more stone fell free from the bird. It again funneled magma from its body to reform the leg, but the volume of magma clearly made a dent in the bird's physical size. Its body and wings shrunk in size as magma was pulled in to form a new leg.

"Yeah!" Danielle shouted as Dawn blasted the stone free. The bird again moved to attack Dawn by charging at her, but Dawn raised the Aegis to block. The bird's charge attack was knocking Dawn back a shorter distance now, with part of its mass gone. Dawn stabilized herself in the air as the bird attacked again. Dawn dodged to her left and circled back around, drawing the mindless construct into another chase. She drew the bird back over Julius and Danielle, allowing them to attack with their cold-based attacks.

Now that Julius knew Danielle was alongside him, he moved further away to hit the bird's other side. Danielle fired the extinguisher and Julius slashed as the bird passed over, freezing and hardening the bird's left leg and right talon. With a burst of speed, Dawn pulled away and turned back on the bird. She loosed a light ray from the shield's center, striking the frozen right talon and severing it from the body. The bird charged at her, a move Dawn dodged by diving underneath the bird. She performed a maneuver in the air to change directions in a climb, putting her behind the bird and allowing her to break the frozen leg with a charged shield slam.

The bird shrunk down as it tried to reform the broken body parts. The bird was now merely the size of a horse and shrinking fast. As it circled back around to chase after Dawn, Julius ran towards the opposite side of the bridge and left Danielle standing in the middle. Dawn continued the attack pattern she was using, keeping the bird on the chase as she flew back over Danielle.

Julius charged from his new position and leapt into the air. Julius had a strong vertical leap, strong enough to allow him to bring the Reaver's Claw through the center of the creature's body. A strip about three inches wide of solid stone formed as the blade sliced through the incorporeal creature. Danielle blasted it again with the extinguisher, freezing the creature's re-formed leg. The bird's flight was now slower and sluggish with the solid parts of its body. Dawn turned and noticed the stone strip through the bird's body. She blasted it with a ray of damaging light, breaking the bird into two halves.

The defenders on the ground, further away from the combat, started to celebrate the victory.

"We're not done yet." Dawn said as she watched the remains of the bird. "Look."

The two halves of the bird reformed into two smaller birds. Now, the birds were merely the size of people, but there were two now. Julius turned to Danielle, who still held her extinguisher at the ready.

"Danielle!" he shouted. "Go back and cover the others! Stand on the rim of the crater and keep that thing ready!"

Danielle took off across the bridge and stood near the rim of the volcano crater, keeping the fire extinguisher between the Light's Bulwark forces and the birds. One bird stayed on Dawn, charging her and being stopped by the Aegis. The other flew over Danielle and tried to splash the army beyond. Danielle discharged the last of the carbon dioxide in the extinguisher onto the bird, freezing its entire body as it passed over. Completely solidified, the bird lost its lift and crashed to the ground in a cloud of rock and dust. The defenders dove to the ground and covered their heads to protect against the flying debris.

Meanwhile, Dawn landed alongside Julius on the bridge. The bird hovered overhead, clawing at the pair with its talons and pecking with its beak. Dawn kept her shield raised to deflect the talon attacks. Julius countered the peck with the Reaver's Claw, freezing the bird's beak and part of its face back to stone. It continued to attack Dawn with its talons while she ducked under it to flank it with Julius. With the bird's backside exposed, Julius slashed wildly at it and froze parts of the body to stone. Dawn swiped at it with Spell-Drinker while backing off on the ground. Her feint didn't keep the bird's attention, and it turned to strike at Julius.

With the solidified back of the bird towards Dawn, she blessed her shield and struck hard with it. The stone portions of the bird broke off, fragmenting the bird's body. With every strike Julius made, he froze another fragmented section, which Dawn crushed with the power of the shield. Finally, as the last stone fragment was blown to bits, the creature was defeated.

"I think that's the end of it." Julius said as he scanned the sky. "No more enemies out here."

"Let's go then." Dawn replied as she walked up alongside Julius. The Light's Bulwark forces fell in line behind their leaders as they walked back across the bridge towards the enemy fortress. The bottom portion of an iron portcullis hung from above the entrance. Dawn and Julius walked through the gate side by side. As soon as they set foot on the floor beyond the gate, a mechanical rumbling could be heard. Everyone came to a stop to look for the source of the noise, and immediately the portcullis dropped, trapping Dawn and Julius inside the enemy fortress away from their allies.

Julius turned around and shook the bars. "We're trapped!" he shouted. "Rick, do something!"

"Nothing I can do," Rick replied. "I don't have a plasma torch."

"Julius, come on," said Dawn. "Let's worry about Aaron and Stacie first. Then we can deal with the gate."

"Okay, good idea. Being stuck here's bad enough, being stuck here with them alive's worse."

With that, Dawn and Julius turned their backs on their troops and entered the enemy compound.

Chapter 34

The Battle of Flame Point Apex

Flame Point Apex
Minutes after

Dawn and Julius threw the doors to the highest level of Flame Point open. Aaron and Stacie stood at the far end of the room awaiting them.

"So, angel, you have finally made it here." Aaron said tauntingly. "I don't suppose you came all this way to lay down your shield before me and surrender."

"Never." Dawn spat back. "I am here to end your reign."

"Nuh huh." Stacie taunted, waving her staff. Demonic energy bound Dawn and Julius around the ankles and wrists, pinning both to the wall under the display. "Now that we have you where we want you, I say we should deal with your friends outside," she said as she projected an image of the fortress's flesh works. "Armored zombies. The pathetic blades your forces brought won't even scratch them. We held these ones back, you see, for when the world ran out of ammo. Once primitive combat returned, these monsters would be our trump card, eliminating whatever remained of humanity. Watch as they decimate your precious defenders."

"While you're here, you might as well listen." Aaron started. "You two will make a fine first meal for our lord when we summon him to this plane. Tyadrig the Empty, the lord of darkness, is our god. It is he who granted us this power, and it is he that we claim this world for. With the elimination of humanity, Tyadrig will shape this world into his own creation. We will bring Jehovah to the defense of his world, and we will subdue him. Tyadrig and his brothers will take great delight in torturing him for all eternity. And we will make you watch... for a little bit anyway. Part of his torture will be watching the dismemberment of his pitiful angel and her love."

Aaron walked close to Dawn and brushed his hand against her cheek. "But first, I'm gonna have some fun with you."

"Apollo, grant me the strength," Dawn whispered, "to shatter these bonds."

The Solari Aegis glowed brilliantly. In a flash of light, the demonic energy bonds were shattered. Dawn and Julius planted their feet on the ground. Julius gripped his crescent blade with both hands, ready for battle. Aaron sprang back and drew Ondesverd and Damupanga. Stacie raised her staff in firing position.

Dawn charged at Aaron, keeping her Aegis raised in front of her. Aaron dodged left, bringing Ondesverd and Damupanga down into the back of Dawn's breastplate. Though the strikes failed to pierce it, they changed her momentum and caused her to stumble. Aaron pressed the attack, bringing both blades overhead into a downward strike. Dawn raised the Aegis to block both strikes, stabbing with Spell-Drinker towards Aaron's midsection. Aaron's armor blocked the strike, and the blade failed to drain any magic.

Stacie fired a ball of darkness at Dawn from behind. She was completely oblivious to the attack. Julius intervened, swinging his crescent blade into the path of the bolt and sending it harmlessly towards the domed ceiling. He moved quickly, closing the gap between himself and Stacie, and brought his blade across towards her midsection. She formed a magic shield to deflect the attack. Julius pressed the advantage, turning every momentum reversal into a strike in the opposite direction. Stacie struggled to keep the energy shields coming as fast as his strikes.

Aaron brought Ondesverd down in an overhead blow, to which Dawn raised Spell-Drinker to parry. The blades glanced off each other as any ordinary blades, with Spell-Drinker not consuming any magic from Ondesverd. Dawn struggled to hold Ondesverd back as Aaron slashed low with Damupanga. Her Aegis easily blocked the second blade. Aaron pressed the attack, stepping back into a double strike. Dawn raised her shield and blocked the attack. It was then that Dawn remembered what she had done to prepare for the battle.

From the position Aaron had forced her into, Dawn could see the sigil of Hephaestus on the back of her shield. Hephaestus was commonly regarded as a god of fire, but in reality, he was the god of iron working and the forge. When Dawn channeled the light of the Solari through the sigil, a strange barrier covered the Solari Aegis. All the damage that had been dealt to the bronze shield over the course of the war was repaired, and the metal that made up the shield was hardened and reinforced.

Aaron's next strike with Damupanga hit the reinforced shield. His blow destroyed the barrier that covered her shield, but the magic instead enveloped Damupanga. The African craftsmen who built the blade had little knowledge of ironworking. The only thing that made this blade special was its magic. The barrier of Hephaestus and its magic infiltrated every imperfection in the blade as the battle raged on. With every clash of metal, the blade was weakened.

Julius, meanwhile, had Stacie on the defensive. His speed, which had been increased through the magic they had imbued into the Reaver's Claw, gave him the advantage. He had her trapped in a corner, throwing up energy shields as fast as she could to block his attacks. Though he hadn't landed a blow yet, he was exhausting Stacie's magic at an incredible rate. Bursts of cold wind and moonlight intermingled with every strike Julius made against Stacie's energy shield.

Aaron brought Ondesverd high over his head in an arcing strike. Dawn slashed with Spell-Drinker at his midsection as she raised the Aegis overhead to block Ondesverd. The strike was ineffectual, simply glancing off Aaron's metal armor. Aaron attacked with Damupanga, attempting to dislodge Dawn's shield block. Dawn was forced to retreat to the edge of the room. Aaron bore down on her, his blades slashing diagonally parallel to each other like opposite colored bishops on a chessboard.

Julius broke from his attack and charged the distance across the room. It took Stacie a couple seconds to drop the energy shield before conjuring a fireball. With Julius no longer pressing the attack, she had a clear shot on his back.

Julius slashed wildly at Aaron, forcing the king of darkness to turn and parry with both blades.

Stacie loosed her fireball at Julius's back.

Julius slashed again, striking both blades Aaron moved to block with. A shower of cold and moonlight burst from the impact points.

The fireball landed against the back of Julius's coat and exploded on contact, but the flame was unable to harm him. The unique shape of his coat, thinner at his narrower waist and wider at his larger torso, built a perfect defense against such an attack. Julius had expected the fireball to be harmless. Before the war, he had tested his coat with a homemade flamethrower, using body spray and a lighter to turn flame on his coat. Comprised of layers of Kevlar and Marlan, his coat would neither ignite nor allow weapon penetration.

Dawn took full advantage of Aaron's tactical predicament. She charged him with the Aegis, slamming him forwards and knocking him prone. Stacie, now knowing that fireballs were useless, powered up a shadow bolt instead. Julius charged back towards Stacie, knocking the shadow bolt aside with the Reaver's Claw, as Dawn tried to finish Aaron while he lay prone.

Aaron sat up and deflected Dawn's strike with Ondesverd, using Damupanga as a crutch to aid his rise from the floor. He returned to the offensive, slashing with both blades against Dawn's raised Aegis. The shield deflected both blows, but once again, Dawn found herself unable to return the favor. Aaron pressed the attack, but the stresses in Damupanga were starting to take their toll. The combined effects of Hephaestus's magic and the poor craftsmanship of the blade weakened the weapon, to the point that now all that held it together was the magic of the blade.

Dawn noticed the frailty of Aaron's left hand blade. As Aaron slashed with Ondesverd, she parried it with her own blade, leaving Damupanga to strike against her shield. On contact with the shield, she loosed a blast of light. The blast hit Damupanga point blank, sundering the blade in half. Magic rushed from the broken blade into the air.

Aaron, outraged at the destruction of his blade, put both hands on the grip of Ondesverd and struck at Dawn with a brutal two-handed slash. Dawn raised her Aegis to block it, and though the blade never touched her body, the force of the blow pushed her backwards. Aaron pressed the attack, swinging Ondesverd downward at Dawn. She sidestepped his attack and slashed at his midsection with Spell-Drinker. Aaron managed to flip Ondesverd up to block the attack, but the magic from the ancient Norse blade started to spill out on contact with Dawn's blade.

Now on the defensive, Aaron used his free hand to try to grab Dawn's shield. He got a hand on its rim, using his full strength to pull it and her towards him. She tried to resist, but his strength and weight were too great. She stabbed at him with Spell-Drinker, but he pushed her attack away with Ondesverd. With a great pull, he snapped the pin that held the arm strap on the shield as she loosed a blast from its center. The light blast knocked Aaron back, but the damage had already been done. Without the arm strap, the mighty Aegis was only useful for its magic.

Dawn secured the shield to her back as Aaron stood again, gripping Spell-Drinker with both hands. She now fought her armored foe without a shield as she charged him. Aaron parried her attack with Ondesverd, but the anti-magic blade Dawn wielded drank more of the divine magic from Aaron's sword. With every clash of blades between the paladin and lich knight, more of Aaron's blade magic left his blade and entered Dawn's. After a few strikes, no more magic would flow from Ondesverd. Its divine power had been exhausted, drained into Dawn's sword.

The blade still held, and with it Aaron could still kill. He slashed horizontally with a two-handed strike. Dawn ducked down and raised Spell-Drinker upward to knock the blade off course. Aaron's powerful strike carried him over Dawn's head and back around, leaving her just enough time to strike. She slammed Spell-Drinker against Aaron's armor, draining a portion of the magic within him. She circled around him to dodge his attack, backing off as he tried to strike again. Without his full amount of animation magic, Aaron moved slower and struck with less power. He felt sluggish as he tried to charge Dawn and bring Ondesverd down on her.

Instead of continuing the dance that now Dawn could win, she turned the magic of Ondesverd back on Aaron. She held Spell-Drinker in front of her, point towards Aaron, and loosed all the magic it had drank. The demonic magic poured from the blade, striking Aaron and throwing him against the wall. As he struggled to regain his footing, Dawn charged with Spell-Drinker held overhead. She slashed at him with two hands, striking the armored hand he raised to block her attack. Spell-Drinker absorbed his animation magic with vigor now, having been recently drained. The blade thirsted for more as it hungrily consumed the dark magic Aaron had imbued himself with. He collapsed to the ground as more magic left his body, finally falling immobile as the last of it was sucked into Dawn's blade. Dawn finished Aaron with a sword blow to the back of his neck, severing his head from his body and ensuring he would never rise again.

Chapter 35

The Stone Sentinel

Flame Point Apex
Just after

"Enough." Stacie said as Dawn's blade severed Aaron's neck. "I surrender. It's over."

Julius raised the Reaver's Claw as to continue fighting. "Why shouldn't I just kill you anyway?"

Dawn held up her arm in front of him. "Let her finish. If we still need to kill her, we can then."

Stacie began. "If you slay me, all the remaining undead still on earth will cause you great difficulties. Though the intelligent generals have nobody to answer to, they still hold dominion over our massive armies. The generals would still lead the undead into battle. They would still attack you as you attempted to rebuild this world. But if you listen to what I have to say, they will not. I can destroy them, once and for all, and ensure that the dead stay dead and never come to life again."

"And why should I even believe you?" Julius asked. "You just tried to kill us!"

"I still have my honor," she replied as she looked down at Aaron's body. "Without Aaron and myself, our lord cannot be summoned to Earth. You won. You fought us, with all our magic, and you won. That victory should mean safety for you and yours. It is only right."

"My fate is sealed," she continued as she walked over to Aaron's throne. "This will be my last spell. It will absorb all the dark magic

231

I spread across the world. All the creation magic that I used to raise undead will return to this place. That includes the magic used to animate me. For I gave up my life that first day at the temple of Supay, side by side with Aaron. When my spell finishes, my body will harden and turn to stone, forming a silent and eternal guardian. So long as I remain in my petrified form, no animated dead will ever be able to exist on Earth again."

Stacie reached into her pouch and withdrew a white candle, just like the one she used for the first spell, and set light to its wick. "Air. I apologize for what I did to you. I poisoned you, I corrupted you, and I turned you against the natural order of the world. Now, I wish to make it right. Return the dark magic of your realm to me." She placed the candle to the east of the throne. Dark energy swirled around the room, forming into a purple-black ball above the candle.

She pulled a red candle from the pouch and lit it too. "Fire, I apologize for what I did to you. I turned you against the light's warriors. I turned you against the world's protectors, and I used you to further the ends of a dark god. Now, I wish to make it right. Return the dark magic of your realm to me." Stacie placed this candle to the west of the throne. Dark energy seeped through the bottom of the fortress, forming into a ball above the candle with the same void purple color.

Dawn and Julius watched, both with their weapons raised. Both were distrustful of the enemy warlock, expecting some great demon to emerge from the circle once it was completed. Neither had experience with this sort of magic, and so neither truly knew what to expect.

Stacie pulled another candle from her pouch and lit it, this one blue. "Water, I apologize for what I did to you. I poisoned you, both magically and physically, to destroy my enemies. I used you in a way you were never meant to be used, to further the ends of a tyrant. Now, I wish to make it right. Return the dark magic of your realm to me." She laid the candle at the south end of the throne, nearest Dawn and Julius. Dark energy once again formed into a ball above the candle.

She pulled and lit a fourth candle, this one green. "Earth, I apologize for what I did to you. I forged abominations and let them walk the world's land. I corrupted and poisoned you, merely to forge a void-spawned hell. Now, I wish to make it right. Return the dark magic of your realm to me." She laid the candle behind the throne to the north, pulling the magic from the ground and forming it into a ball above the candle.

Stacie sat down on Aaron's throne and placed a purple candle on the throne between her thighs. "Spirit, my deepest apologies go to you, for you were the alpha and the omega of our horrors. I warped and twisted you to breathe life into my abominations and demonic creations. With you, I became the most powerful warlock to ever exist, but the angels were able to defeat me still. Return the magic of my creations to me. Return the mindless to their natural states. Strip your blessing from my constructs and generals, and restore everything I manipulated to its previous states."

Stacie held her staff outward in her right hand and picked up the candle with her left. "To you, heroes."

Stacie's legs began to turn to stone.

"Tell your warriors... tell them that Aaron is dead. Tell them all is right with the world once again. But do not tell them what I did." The petrifaction reached past her hips now. "Tell them that when Aaron died, it destroyed the undead and returned them to eternal slumber." It climbed steadily, claiming her torso.

"Tell them that this place is not to be disturbed. Tell them--"

The petrifaction finally reached her face, cutting off her last words.

Dawn looked over at Julius. "It's over." she said. "It's finally over." She placed the Spell-Drinker in its sheath on her back, freeing both her hands. Julius affixed the Reaver's Claw across his back with its harness.

Dawn and Julius turned away from the now-petrified form of Stacie and walked back down the helix stairs into Stacie's spell laboratory. They had ignored all of this spell equipment as they climbed the stairs before. Dawn now noticed the three clear orbs with burning fires inside. With her new knowledge, the knowledge that Aaron had given her, she now knew what these were.

"Aaron said their god was Tyadrig the Empty. He said that Krovon the Fiery and Aarix the Toxic would be summoned elsewhere. I think these orbs are symbols of them. The purple flame of the abyss, the red flame of hell, and the green flame of the dark swamp."

"Let's smash them." Julius suggested. "That way, nobody can use them for evil. Undead can't walk the earth so long as the statue's here, but we don't know if these orbs can summon demons."

Dawn walked out into the lab and lifted the purple orb of Tyadrig, then placed it back down again. "I've got a better idea," she said as she raised Spell-Drinker. Dawn placed the tip of her blade against the orb, but nothing happened.

"That's odd. Spell-Drinker should absorb the magic from it," she commented.

"Let me just try breaking it." Julius suggested.

Julius lifted the orb of Tyadrig and flung it against the back wall, but it simply bounced and landed on the ground intact.

"Try another one?" Julius asked.

"Can't hurt." Dawn replied as she touched Spell-Drinker to the orb of Krovon. Again, it did nothing. Just like the other orb, it bounced when Julius threw it.

"We can't risk these falling into the wrong hands." Dawn mentioned. "Let's take them with us, at least until we find a way of destroying them."

"My guess is there's a special way to destroy them. A spell, or an artifact, or maybe a weapon we can craft, like Spell-Drinker was crafted by--"

Dawn cut him off. "Don't say his name. Don't ruin the moment."

"Anyway, I think that's how they'll be destroyed, is through some special weapon."

"Remember, we didn't actually kill Tyadrig." Dawn reminded Julius. "He wasn't summoned. We stopped the summon by killing Aaron. Maybe we have to kill the demons to break the orbs."

"That's a possibility too." Julius replied. "Anyway, let's take those orbs and get out of here."

Julius lifted the orbs of Krovon and Aarix, carrying one in each hand. Dawn picked up the remaining orb of Tyadrig. "Now we need to get out of here." Julius stated.

"One problem. That portcullis slammed shut behind us when we went in. That's why our friends didn't help us fight Aaron."

"Can you blast through it?"

"Maybe. I'll try. Otherwise we'll have to get someone Navy up here to cut it with a plasma torch."

Julius and Dawn walked down to the staging area on the first floor. From inside the fortress, they could see Rick at the back, ordering the rest of Light's Bulwark's defenders to hold their shield wall. Beyond them, across the bridge, was a field of slain undead.

"Get away from the door!" Dawn yelled at the refugees. "I'm going to blast it!

The defenders nearest the door moved away from it, giving Dawn a clear path. She raised the Solari Aegis in front of her by the metal handle, its strap still broken. She threw a shield punch, empowered by light, to attempt to knock down the door. The attack failed to break the iron portcullis, but the light released through the iron fence. It flowed like electricity through every bar in the gate, causing the gate to glow but not felling it.

"No good?" Julius asked her.

"Hold on, I've got another idea."

Dawn pushed the shield against the portcullis, allowing light to pour from the shield into the fence. She continued to add energy, intensifying the metal's glow. The metal gave off heat as it warmed up. The Light's Bulwark forces started moving away from the door and down the bridge.

"Dawn, you're making the gate hot!" Rick shouted as he ushered the defenders across the bridge.

"I know, I'm gonna melt it!" Dawn shouted back.

Dawn's light continued to pour into the metal gate, getting it to glow red and then yellow before it started to drip. As Dawn added more power to the gate, the melting process sped up. After a few minutes, the gate melted almost fully, giving Dawn and Julius an opening to walk through. Julius ducked down and pulled his overcoat over his head to protect him from the still-dripping metal. He walked through, and though a couple drops of molten metal fell on his coat, he was unharmed. Dawn held the Solari Aegis over her head to block the molten metal as she passed through.

"Radio the Navy. Get us out of here." Dawn ordered. Rick pulled the radio given to him by the Navy to his side.

"*Eisenhower*, this is Rick Sylvan of the Light's Bulwark Forward Attachment. We've won. It's over. Get us out of here."

The radio operator left the radio mic active as he flipped on the intercom mic. "Eisenhower, we've won!" he announced to the ship. "The Light's Bulwark angel beat the enemy king! It's over! It's finally over!"

Every pilot, marine and sailor aboard Eisenhower erupted into applause at the news. Captain Carrie White stood at the helm looking out over the open sea when the call went out. Rick could still hear over the radio as the captain gave new orders to her crew. "Chinook pilots, go get our friends and congratulate them on their victory! Communications, radio the others! Tell them we won! Tell everyone that it's finally over!"

The radio operator aboard Eisenhower flipped his switch to broadcast over the entire radio spectrum, allowing him to reach everywhere on earth with the aid of the satellites in orbit. "Attention living humans, the zombie war is over! Open your gates, lower your walls and raise your glasses in victory! USS Roosevelt! USS Lincoln! HMS Queen Elizabeth! Geneva and Light's Bulwark too! Now, we celebrate!"

Epilogue

Refugees of Gorgolon

Aboard the starship Amath'navar, High Earth Orbit
That Same Time

The starship Amath'navar was a vast vessel, larger than some natural moons. It was the final refuge of the Wutner race from the planet Gorgolon. Aboard, it had everything a civilization would need to sustain life. It was constructed in orbit above Gorgolon hundreds of years ago, as the pinnacle of Wutner technology. Equipped with everything from life support systems and food production to medical centers to recreation and entertainment, Amath'navar truly was an engineering marvel. Until this point, it had managed to carry the surviving Wutners the hundreds of light-years from Gorgolon to Earth, and even allowed them to procreate and raise their children.

In a room aboard the starship that appeared to be a classroom, an adult Wutner taught ten children history. A holographic display showed the planet Gorgolon. The teacher spoke to the class, who followed along and took notes. The Wutner people were human-like, or rather, dwarf-like, with their muscled bodies and stout frames. The Wutners all had perfect blue-white skin, without any blemishes or wrinkles. The adult male teaching the class stood about the height of a human male, but carried about fifty pounds more muscle on his frame than a human male athlete. He wore a uniform that consisted of a black shirt and black pants, with an emblem of a blue serpentine creature over his left breast. He had snow white hair that shimmered in the light,

237

and watery-blue eyes with no black pupil. His fingers seemed dextrous like human fingers, but they had horn-like points covering their tips. The students too had white hair and blue eyes, but the young Wutners had black pupils. They stood a comparable height to human children, with frames similar to the children that play American football. There wasn't as much size variation in the Wutner children as in humans, nor much color variation. They had distinguishing enough facial features to tell the various students apart, and each had their hair cut to different lengths and styled differently, though few other differences existed.

"Gorgolon was our homeland until the demon worshipers appeared," the teacher lectured. "These demon worshipers sought to summon a great beast, Krovon, from the plane of fire. To do so, they had to exterminate all living Wutners on the planet. They unleashed a terrible blight on our people, killing nine out of every ten. Then, the necromancers came, raising the fallen into mindless undead and arming them to fight us. With our population cut by so much, and theirs growing every day, we didn't stand a chance. Many hid behind the walls of Yarzenn, the great fortress city. We fled to the one place we would be safe, this starship. Eventually, Yarzenn fell, when the monstrous constructs pulled down the gates and let the undead in. The Wutners who fled to space lived, and the ones who held Yarzenn died. Since then, the time of your grandparents and great-grandparents, we have wandered space, looking for another civilization."

The teacher flashed several images on the holographic display. One depicted Krovon, the brother of Tyadrig. Another depicted the Wutners who turned from the light and embraced evil, becoming his necromancers and elite lich soldiers. Another depicted the former capital city in ruins after the plague and the battle. Yet another depicted the world now, after the takeover of Krovon. He had warped their once icy paradise into a demon-spawned hell, where lich soldiers commanded legions of undead slaves to construct a great temple to Krovon.

"The great captain Tyrelein, the first captain of Amath'navar, had a vision." the teacher continued. "In it, he saw a goddess of light aboard this very ship. Light poured from her in a powerful laser strike, from the Tower of Yarzenn to the Temple of Krovon, obliterating the temple. A captain of Amath'navar went to the surface of Gorgolon with her, each of them with warriors. The warriors of the goddess in his vision had peach skin, with eye colors ranging from brown to green. The goddess wielded as a weapon an ornate long blade, and carried a heavy piece of hard gold from which she commanded the light. Krovon himself rose to fight her, and though her heart-mate perished in the battle, the captain and the goddess stood at the end of the night victorious as the red star of Gorgolon broke the horizon in its ascent."

Another adult male opened the sliding door into the classroom. "Ryveth, get to the bridge! Something major's going on and you need to see it!"

Ryveth and the other adult Wutner ran to the ship's bridge, where the fourth captain and the entire bridge crew watched a display of human warriors intently. The warriors were holding a shield wall on the bridge to the fortress, keeping their shields raised to block the attacks of heavily armored undead. They struck back at first, but stopped and simply held the line and blocked attacks. Occasionally one of the undead would be knocked back by a shield bash and thrown into the lava below.

"What's going on here?" Ryveth asked as he entered the room.

"There's a major battle going on here." the captain replied. "Looks like these "humans", as they call themselves, are involved in a battle against the undead here. The evil magic seems to be emanating from the compound nearby. I think it's their main base. The humans already killed a flying demon here, plus a division of mindless and a commander. They appear to be--"

"Captain, the magic readings are way off! Something major just happened inside!" one of the males at the front exclaimed, cutting the captain off.

"Off how? Explain!" he ordered.

"I think a being of great magical power was just slain inside. Don't know if it's a human or a demon since I can't see inside, but whoever it was, they were definitely magical."

"Qulein, stay on those gauges! Alviox, watch the telescopes! See what emerges from that compound!"

"Yes, sir!" the two operators answered.

The entire bridge crew, including the educator, stood by as the gauges reading magic on the surface fluctuated. Suddenly, the dark magic readings went off the scale, followed by a reset to zero a few seconds later.

"What was that? The readings spiked, but now they're zeroing out!"

"They wouldn't zero out if the demons won."

"So what would cause them to spike if the demons didn't win?"

"Maybe a convergence?" Ryveth chimed in.

"A convergence... like all the magic gathered on the temple? Then what would cause it to zero out?"

"Well, if it was destroyed, or sent to another plane, it would disappear off our scanners."

"If the dark magic was destroyed or sent to another plane, then that means the humans won, yes?"

"It would. Just keep watching."

A wave of darkness emanated from the temple. It passed harmlessly through the humans defending the gate, but the attacking undead simply dropped to the ground.

A few minutes later, the main telescope focused on Flame Point showed Dawn melting the bars of the portcullis and exiting through the main entrance alongside Julius.

"That's the one I saw go in!" a bridge technician pointed out. "She's the one I said was flying around fighting the fire demon!"

Now that Tyrzek and Ryveth were watching the display, both reacted to Dawn's presence.

"That looks like the images they showed me in education!" Ryveth exclaimed.

"Of the goddess Tyrelein saw in the prophecy? It does look like her! Do you think it's actually her?"

"I didn't believe in her all through education. I taught it, because that's what I'm supposed to teach, but I never believed it. But look at her weapon, her shield, everything. It's all the same as Tyrelein's images. The other human with her, he's even the same as the vision!"

"We have to go down there. Me and you, Ryveth. You're the one who speaks the language without the translators. You're the one who deciphered the language. And I'm our leader."

"Captain." Alviox interjected. "If we drop the zone pods now, she'll probably attack us. She won't realize we aren't hostile."

"That's right. She's in combat still. Wait for her to fly back to her own fortress. Once they're settled in, then we'll land. We don't want to be attacked before we can ask for her help. Hopefully she has as kind of a heart as the goddess from the visions does."

"We should land outside the compound, not in the courtyard. First, our zone pods aren't that accurate. We could kill someone by landing on top of them, or damage the building. Plus, we want them to know that we are peaceful. They're all veterans of the zombie war, and theirs was just as terrible as ours. They held Yarzenn successfully, while we fled instead. That's the only difference."

"All of you are right," Tyrzek answered. "That's our plan. There is hope for Gorgolon still, and she's waving for an aircraft planetside."

The aliens were able to pick up a broadcast from the USS Eisenhower.

"Attention living humans, the zombie war is over! Open your gates, lower your walls and raise your glasses in victory! USS Roosevelt! USS Lincoln! HMS Queen Elizabeth! Geneva and Nethergarde too! Now, we celebrate!"

The entire bridge crew, without their translating headsets on, simply heard gibberish come across the radio. Ryveth, however, was the leader of the translation effort. Through the entire war, he had intercepted human communications and deciphered them as a code. He understood perfectly what the radio operator had said.

"They have declared victory! Their sailors are giving the order to celebrate!"

"Then we celebrate!" the captain declared. "Syva, get the special reserve out from the vault! One world is already saved, and our own can be too!"

Printed in the United States
By Bookmasters

Printed in the United States
By Bookmasters